DEBBIE MACOMBER

One Night

AVON

An Imprint of HarperCollinsPublishers

AVON BOOKS
An Imprint of HarperCollins*Publishers*
10 East 53rd Street
New York, New York 10022-5299

Copyright © 1994, 2010 by Debbie Macomber
ISBN 978-0-06-108185-9
www.avonromance.com

First Avon Books paperback printing: July 2010
First Harper special paperback printing: June 1998
First Harper paperback printing: August 1994

Avon Trademark Reg. U.S. Pat. Off. and in Other Countries, Marca Registrada, Hecho en U.S.A.
HarperCollins® is a registered trademark of HarperCollins Publishers.

Printed in the U.S.A.

30 29 28 27 26 25 24 23

Summer 2010

Dear Friends,

I'm so very pleased to see *One Night* reissued. This is one of my all-time favorite romantic comedies featuring two radio personalities. In the years since I wrote this story, I've become good friends and neighbors with Delilah (yes, that Delilah!) and also with Rhett Palmer, the Mayor of the Airway in Vero Beach, Florida, where Wayne and I winter. Both are well known and loved radio personalities. Personally, I love being on the radio. I've never looked or sounded thinner!

When I learned this book was going to be reissued I asked to review the manuscript to update it as much as possible. The original story was penned before the common use of cell phones and other devices we now all take for granted. If while reading you pause and wonder, "why in heaven's name didn't they just use their cell phone," I have the answer. They were either out of coverage or both phones needed to be recharged. So keep that in mind!

Generally, an author is critical of her own work. I'd forgotten the story and picked up the manuscript, convinced I was in for a long, tiresome afternoon. To my delight, I found an enjoyable read. I actually laughed out loud. My hope is that you will, too.

So sit back with a tall glass of iced tea, put up your feet, and enjoy. A good story is timeless. Cell phones in use or not.

Debbie Macomber

By Debbie Macomber

ANGELS EVERYWHERE
CHRISTMAS ANGELS
MRS. MIRACLE
SOONER OR LATER
SOMEDAY SOON
THE TROUBLE WITH ANGELS
ONE NIGHT
A SEASON OF ANGELS
MORNING COMES SOFTLY

To the two radio personalities
who rock my world
Delilah
and
Rhett Palmer

1

"You're fired," Clyde Tarkington announced. Carrie Jamison looked up at the station manager for KUTE radio and blinked back her shock. She opened her mouth, but words refused to come. "I don't understand," she managed finally.

"Which word?" Clyde asked, shuffling his fat cigar to the other side of his mouth. *"You* are *canned*, out of a job, unemployed, terminated."

"But . . ." It took her a few more moments to collect herself. "Who'll take over the morning program?"

Clyde chewed on the end of the fat cigar. "I haven't decided that yet."

Carrie noticed he didn't seem overly concerned about finding a replacement. She focused her attention on the scarred wood desk and resisted the urge to argue, to list her accomplishments, the success of her ideas.

"May I ask why?" She already knew the answer: Kyle Harris. The newscaster had been a thorn in her side from the first. But it wasn't all her fault. Kyle didn't like her either.

"You can't seem to get along with Kyle."

Naturally the good-ol'-boy network would fire her instead of the man. Carrie was surprised at Clyde. She'd always thought of him as fair. Now she knew otherwise; men stick together.

"We rub each other the wrong way," was all Carrie was willing to say.

"It's gotten much worse lately," Clyde said.

Carrie agreed. The tension between her and Kyle Harris had grown so thick in the last few weeks it could have been sliced, toasted, and served with coffee. It had come to a head when she tricked him into shaving off his beard. He'd never forgiven her, and to be fair, her tactics *had* been slightly underhanded. But she never would have believed she'd lose her job over it.

Clyde sat down, crossed his stubby legs, and seemed to wait for her response.

Carrie was fond of Clyde. He was the fatherly type, with a receding hairline, deep blue eyes, and a head and a heart for radio that she'd long respected. He was her boss and her friend—or so she'd once believed.

"How long do I have?" she asked, in a weak, almost unintelligible voice. "Two weeks?"

"That sounds fair," Clyde said.

He took the cigar out of his mouth and stared at the end of it. As long as Carrie could remember, she'd never seen him light one.

"Unless . . ." He paused, and his gaze met hers with the force of something physical.

"Unless what?" Carrie asked, eager now. She scooted to the edge of her seat, hoping, praying he would offer her a reprieve.

"Never mind," he said, shaking his head. "It'd never work."

"What?"

"I was thinking you two might come to some sort of agreement. But"—he released an exaggerated sigh—"you've worked together for nearly a year and haven't been able to get along in all that time. Nothing's likely to change now."

"We started off on the wrong foot," Carrie said, remembering when they'd met. One glance had told her they were headed for trouble. Her morning show consisted of bells and whistles, jokes and pranks. The newscaster was a stuffed shirt; to him the news was a somber business. Carrie had suspected Kyle Harris wouldn't be amused by her brand of comedy. And she was right.

From the first day, Carrie felt Kyle's mild contempt. It might have been her imagination, but she doubted it. He thought of her as silly and artificial, and she viewed him as a curmudgeon. The fact that he shared the same political views as her father hadn't endeared him to her either.

"Is this all because of Kyle's beard?"

A shadow of a smile quivered at the edges of Clyde's mouth, but he suppressed it. "In part," he said. No amusement leaked into his voice.

"It was all in fun."

Carrie wanted to shake herself for the things she'd said. She hadn't meant to insult Kyle by suggesting he had a face made for radio. It was a joke. She should have known better.

"The ratings for my show doubled that week," she reminded him.

"Are you suggesting we give you an award?" Clyde's voice rose half an octave in irritation.

"He hasn't grown it back," Carrie said, wanting to make light of the event. She found Kyle's clean-shaven face to be surprisingly appealing. Her perception of him had changed. Without the beard, his jaw was lean and strongly defined, giving him a distinctly rugged appeal she would never have guessed was there. She hated to admit how curious she'd been to discover the man behind the mask.

Clyde couldn't seem to decide if he wanted to stand or sit. He got out of his chair as if he were suddenly uncomfortable, walked over to the window that overlooked downtown Kansas City, and gripped his hands behind his back.

"Have my ratings gone down?" she asked nervously.

"No," Clyde admitted. "Don't misunderstand me, Carrie, you've done a good job. That's not the problem. The reason I'm terminating you is because of what's going on between you and Kyle. The rest of us aren't blind. We all work together, and we can't be one big happy family with the two of you constantly at each other's throat."

"I'm not the only one to blame," she said, to defend herself. It wasn't as if she'd started a one-woman war against Kyle Harris. He'd tossed out his own fair share of innuendoes and insults.

"It's become an issue with the staff," Clyde said. "In the beginning it was like a game; everyone got a kick out of the way you taunted each other. It isn't amusing anymore. What started out as fun has become destructive to the entire station."

She had no defense. "But—"

"I don't have any choice," Clyde said, cutting her off. He shifted his feet as if struggling to find a comfortable stance. "I did what was necessary. I canned you both."

"You fired *both* of us?" Carrie bolted out of the chair before she could stop herself.

"Don't misunderstand me," Clyde said, fixing his

steady gaze on her. "This isn't something I wanted to do, but it'd be impossible to keep one of you and let the other go. Not unless I wanted a mutiny."

Carrie appreciated his predicament; she just didn't happen to like it. "But you're willing to reconsider if Kyle and I can reach some sort of agreement?" she asked, sinking back into the hard wooden chair. It would be easier to negotiate peace talks in the Middle East, but she'd try anything in order to keep her position at the station. This job meant the world to her.

"I don't expect you to be bosom buddies," Clyde said. "Getting along shouldn't be that difficult. If you didn't work so hard at disliking each other, you might discover you have several things in common."

"I doubt that." Frankly, Carrie couldn't see how it would be possible for them to agree about anything. She was twenty-seven, with limited radio experience. Finding another plum morning position, especially in the Kansas City metropolitan area, would be difficult. All right, it would be next to impossible.

"May I go now?" Carrie asked weakly. She stood, her shoulders slumped forward with the weight of her troubles.

"I've already spoken to Kyle," Clyde said as she moved toward the door.

"What did he say?"

Clyde rubbed his hand along the back of his neck. "His reaction was about the same as yours. He was shocked."

"I see."

"He wants to talk to you, OK?"

She blinked at him from the doorway. "What choice do I have?"

Clyde set his cigar in a crystal ashtray. "None. Really, it's a shame you can't get along," he muttered. "You're both hard-working, decent people."

Carrie hadn't gone more than ten feet down the long, narrow hallway that led to her tiny office when she came face to face with Kyle Harris. Neither spoke for several long moments.

Carrie tried to think of something witty, but her brain had deserted her. For someone known for her quick repartee, this was serious.

She looked up at Kyle, who towered a full eight inches above her, and tried to view him from a fresh perspective. His shoulders were broad and tapered down to lean hips and a flat stomach. From the office scuttlebutt she understood he kept trim with regular exercise. He often participated in ten-K fun runs, sometimes to benefit charity.

Carrie hated exercise. If ever she was tempted to join an aerobics class, she would lie down and take a nap until the notion passed.

Kyle's dark, intense eyes were studying her as thoroughly as she was him.

Carrie couldn't help wondering what he saw. She was small, a paltry five feet four inches tall, and slender, although she never understood why since her appetite was monstrous and she was often hungry as a bear. She wore her long dark hair piled on top of her head, because she felt she needed the height. Unfortunately, more often than not, her tottering hairdo resembled Bart Simpson's mother's.

No one was likely to suggest she model swimsuits for *Sports Illustrated*. When it came right down to it, her best features were her breasts, not that she'd been really generously endowed. They were normal size when everything else about her came in miniature.

"I take it Clyde's talked to you?" Kyle asked.

"Yes."

"Do you have any plans for the rest of the day?" he asked.

"Not really. What about you?"

"I have some free time."

She was about to say they would soon have nothing but free time unless they could come up with a plan to convince Clyde they were about to change their ways.

"Could we meet for lunch?"

"That sounds like a good idea." Were they capable of spending time together without trading insults?

"You think we can manage to get along that long?" he asked. Apparently he had the same doubts.

"I don't know," she said with a half smile, "but I'm willing to try if you are."

They set a time and place, which took another five

minutes. He suggested a restaurant with linen table-cloths and waiters in starched uniforms. Carrie preferred a well-known and beloved barbecue place with blue-painted picnic tables that sat outside around an open pit, but she decided against pushing it. Someone as fastidious as Kyle Harris wouldn't enjoy getting barbecue sauce under his fingernails.

Instead they compromised on a generic place not far from the radio station.

Carrie arrived first, fifteen minutes early, choosing to sit out on the sun-dappled patio under the shade of an umbrella. A breeze cooled the summer afternoon. She drank iced tea and waited. It went without saying that Kyle would be on time.

The afternoon was lovely, filled with bright sunshine. Thin wisps of clouds scooted across an expanse of bold blue sky. Carrie had moved to Kansas from Texas a year earlier and had come to love her adopted state. Kansas was like a rainbow with its wide spectrum of colors. Much of the state was filled with woods, rolling green hills, and amber meadows. The land was crisscrossed by clear streams and rushing rivers. Although she wasn't much for sports fishing, she'd heard that Kansas yielded some of the best in the United States. Kyle fished. At least she'd overheard him bragging about a recent trip. She might have misunderstood, but it seemed he had the use of a cabin on some lake that he liked to escape to on weekends. She pushed that information to the back of her mind, because it didn't fit her image of him. She couldn't imagine Kyle relaxing. She couldn't ever imagine Kyle without his three-button vest and silk tie.

Carrie's family hadn't been keen on her leaving Texas, but the farther away she was from her headstrong father the better. Carrie was certain she was a disappointment to Michael Jamison. He'd wanted her to major in education rather than communications. The two hadn't seen eye to eye since Carrie turned thirteen. If the truth be known, she saw a good deal of her father in Kyle. Michael Jamison was a pillar of the community, a deacon of the church, and as opinionated as they came.

Kyle arrived and squinted into the sun as he pulled out a padded chair and sat across the table from her.

"I don't suppose I could talk you into dining inside?" he asked, shading his eyes with his hand.

"Didn't you bring sunglasses?" she asked impatiently.

"Obviously not."

Already they had started, and he'd barely sat down. This didn't bode well. "Let's trade places," she said, willing to swallow her pride.

"Never mind," he muttered, squinting at her while he removed the napkin from the white enamel tabletop. "Forget I said anything."

Carrie stood. "Please," she said. "I'd be happy to swap seats with you."

They did this graciously, and once she was settled again she looked over at him and smiled. He returned the smile. Maybe they could work matters out with a little effort.

"There, now," he said, smoothing the napkin across his lap. "That wasn't so difficult, was it?"

"Not in the least," she admitted, looking at the top of the menu. It was going to be difficult to choose what she wanted for lunch. She was in the mood for a Cobb salad, but the French dip sandwich sounded good too.

It took Kyle all of three seconds to decide on roast beef with mustard and tomato. The waitress came for their order and Kyle asked that it be put on one check. "I'll buy," he said.

If he was treating, Carrie decided to order lobster, but she didn't find any on the menu.

"Carrie?" Kyle said, looking toward the waitress, who was waiting, pen and pad in hand, for her to decide.

"I'll have the Cobb salad." She wasn't keen on the way he'd rushed her. Under normal circumstances she wouldn't have let him intimidate her into making a snap decision, but in the interests of goodwill she let it pass.

"All right," Carrie said, relaxing against the back of the chair. "Clyde has fired us both."

"But I believe he'll hire us back if we're willing to put our differences aside and start over."

"That was the message I got too," Carrie said. "It shouldn't be that difficult, should it?" She was optimistic they could find a common ground, if for no other reason than in order to remain employed.

"I agree. This may be a first for us."

They both punctuated his statement with a smile.

"I'm willing to call a cease-fire if you are," Kyle said next.

Carrie nodded. So far so good.

"Maybe we should start by getting to know each other a little better. I don't know what I did that set you—"

"You didn't do anything," Carrie interrupted. She reached for her iced tea. "It was—oh, I don't know, the way you first met everyone in that three-piece suit like you were some dignitary."

"At least I choose to dress as a professional," he snapped.

They both paused as if simultaneously recognizing they'd stumbled upon dangerously thin ice.

"I believe we've established that our first impressions of each other were negative," she offered after a stilted moment.

The tops of Kyle's ears had turned bright pink. She'd seen it happen before, so she knew he was struggling not to show how much she irritated him.

"Perhaps you could tell me what it is about me that troubles you so much." Even as she spoke, Carrie was aware that she was placing her neck on the chopping block. It was a generous gesture aimed at proving her sincerity in working through their animosity.

"You're a good deejay." Kyle sounded a bit hesitant. "Your wit is quick, and you have a way of making even the most mundane things interesting. The segment 'The News That Shouldn't Have Made the News' is very clever."

"Thank you."

He grinned. "You're welcome."

"You're an excellent newscaster," she commented, returning the favor. "Even when the news is bleak and it seems that nothing is right in our world, I come away feeling optimistic and hopeful."

"Thank you." He seemed surprised to learn this. "It seems to me we can respect each other professionally."

"It's just that . . ."

"Yes?" he coaxed when she didn't immediately continue.

"I might be putting my foot in my mouth by saying this, but it seems to me it'd help if you could learn to relax."

"Relax?" He repeated the word as if he needed *Merriam Webster's Collegiate Dictionary* to decipher the meaning.

"You know," she murmured, sorry now that she'd brought up the subject. "Let your hair down once in a while and stop being so serious."

A whole lot more than the tips of his ears went red

this time, and Carrie realized she'd made a major mistake. The color circled both ears and spread like a flash flood down his neck.

"Perhaps you should look at yourself before throwing stones," he suggested.

"I shouldn't have said anything," she admitted and then, because she was curious, added, "What about me? Feel free to speak your mind."

"Then I will." Kyle appeared downright eager. "You don't think before you speak. You say whatever comes to your mind, without censoring the thought. And while we're on the subject—" He stopped abruptly.

"Go on," she urged, with a saccharine smile.

What he'd said about her talking before thinking was true, but she'd hang before she admitted it.

The waitress delivered their order, and Carrie dove into her salad as if she needed to kill it before she ate the first bite. She stabbed the lettuce with her fork with so much force that a black olive leaped off the plate and rolled across the tabletop.

"Don't eat that," she snapped, as if there were some threat that he would, without sterilizing it first.

"You're as immature and stubborn as a two-year-old," he continued, "and you haven't got a sensible thought in your head." He attacked his sandwich as if he expected to bite into shoe leather.

"You're so caught up in your own importance you don't even realize how arrogant you look to everyone else." She took another vicious bite of her salad.

"You wouldn't want to know how others see you," he returned between gritted teeth.

"This will never work," Carrie announced. Calmly she set her fork aside and reached for her purse. She pulled out several bills, set them on the table, and stood. "I prefer to buy my own lunch, thank you," she said, and without a backward glance walked away.

It took a full ten minutes for the churning anger to leave Kyle. He wished he knew what in particular annoyed him so much about Carrie Jamison. He'd seen her with other people and admired and envied their easy camaraderie.

No matter what she said, it was a lot more than his choice in suits that had set her off that first day. Some of what she'd suggested about him contained a grain of truth. A tiny grain of truth. Mustard-seed-sized truth. All her talk about his being a stuffed shirt rankled. It simply wasn't true.

As for him, Kyle had decided weeks earlier what he found so objectionable about her. Carrie reminded him of his own dear sweet mother. Lillian Harris had never left the sixties. He'd read once that anyone who remembered the sixties wasn't there. His mother was one of the original flower children, protesting the war in Vietnam, preaching the gospel of love and peace. She'd made her living selling love beads and daisies on the sidewalks of Haight-Ashbury until she'd gotten pregnant with him.

In Carrie he saw the "don't worry, be happy" philosophy his mother followed. Kyle loved his mother, although he didn't exactly view her as a parent. He had mostly raised himself, although Lillian would be shocked to hear him say it. Even now that he was thirty, she called him at least twice a week and faithfully read him his astrology chart while Kyle listened politely and gritted his teeth.

Lillian meant well, but he'd lived the majority of his life escaping her clutches. He certainly wasn't keen on working with someone who reminded him so much of dear ol' Mom.

The days that followed proved to be more strained than the whole previous year, despite their best efforts to prove otherwise. Although Kyle never actually saw Clyde watching him and Carrie, the station manager was there, big as life. He remained hidden in the background, probing into the fractured relationship like a schoolboy prying at road kill with a long stick.

It didn't come as any surprise when Clyde asked to see them both in the office at the end of the second week. Kyle would have liked to work something out with Carrie, but their lunch and subsequent encounters had proved how impossible that was.

Carrie's eyes met his, filled with accusation and dread. He made sure his own gaze echoed the sentiment. The way he saw it, they were both decent people who simply brought out the worst in each other. Kyle had never said to any other woman the things he'd said to Carrie. He was convinced the same was true for her.

Clyde motioned toward the two wooden chairs in his office.

"Have you two anything to say before I give you your last paychecks?" he asked, eyeing them as if he expected to read the small print of their warring personalities across their foreheads.

"Of course," Kyle lied. "This job means a good deal to us both."

"Kyle and I deeply respect each other," Carrie added quickly, with a smile so dazzling it might have blinded anyone else.

Clyde's hands went behind his back. "That's not the way I hear and see it."

Kyle opened his mouth to protest, and he noticed that Carrie did too, but Clyde stopped them both with an outstretched hand.

"I'd hoped you two would work toward becoming friends."

"We're friends, aren't we, Kyle?" Carrie asked him hurriedly.

The bright, phony smile was back, and if he could see through it, Clyde would as well.

"Of course we're friends," Kyle answered, making

an effort to be convincing. "Good friends. Why, we had lunch just the other day and talked everything out. We made a few basic decisions."

Clyde frowned and started pacing the narrow space between them and his desk. He didn't say anything, and Kyle grew more uncomfortable with every sweep he made past the chairs.

"You know we're both signed up for the broadcasters' convention in Dallas next weekend, don't you?" Kyle directed to Clyde.

"Yes. From what I understand it's a great place to pass out your résumés."

"As Kyle was saying, we had lunch together and came up with a few ideas of how to overcome our differences," Carrie said.

"What ideas?" Clyde asked pointedly.

Kyle looked to Carrie at a complete loss as to what to say. He hated to lose this job. It was exactly the experience he needed before moving into television as a news director. He was willing to start at the bottom and gain the necessary experience. He certainly hadn't anticipated being fired.

"We decided to drive to the convention together," Carrie said.

Drive to the convention together? Where did she get that idea? Kyle bit back a reply. She'd actually suggest they travel together after their disastrous lunch? The woman was nuts. Or desperate. Probably both.

"Really?" Clyde paused mid-step and stared at them for a moment.

"It's a sort of sink-or-swim project," Carrie said, warming to the subject. "Kyle suggested it, and I agreed. We want to do whatever we can to convince you to give us another chance. If you still want to fire us after the convention, then by all means go ahead. All we're asking is that you give us this one last opportunity."

Kyle noticed that the deejay was perched danger-ously close to the edge of her seat. Another inch and she'd land on her fanny.

"Working at KUTE means that much to you?" Clyde asked.

"Oh, yes," Carrie said.

Kyle thought she might find work in the theater. Surely the woman had a flare for the dramatic.

Clyde said nothing for several moments. Then he grinned.

Kyle could read the handwriting on the wall. He was going to be trapped for a thousand-mile round trip in a car with a woman he intensely disliked.

"I want you both to take a couple of extra days off before the conference," Clyde said. "Get to know each other. I'll give you the time off with pay," he added.

"You'd be willing to do that?" Carrie said in a low, stunned voice. She flashed Kyle a triumphant smile.

He was pleased she was so happy. Personally he thought the entire idea was crazy.

"The way I see it, you're either going to cure what ails the two of you," Clyde said, "or end up hating each other."

Kyle didn't need the station manager to tell him which it would be. They'd end up murdering each other before the end of the convention.

2

Kyle had mapped out the route he planned to take—I-35 all the way—and had it on the seat next to him when he pulled up in front of Carrie's house. The way he figured, they could drive the whole 550 miles in one day and get this farce over with as quickly as possible.

The conference wasn't officially open until Friday evening, with a cocktail party, but he hoped to arrive late Wednesday night or early Thursday morning. He didn't think Carrie would disagree; he thought she wanted to visit her sister, who lived somewhere near Dallas. The less time they spent in each other's company, the better off they'd be. Frankly, he didn't know how they were going to manage this trip together and keep their sanity.

Kyle couldn't be sure of Carrie's feelings, but he strongly suspected they matched his own. He was planning on using the conference to scout out another job. There was no way they were going to settle their differences. It was a lost cause, and had been from the moment they'd met.

When he pulled up and parked in front of the small rambler that Carrie rented in the Kansas City suburb of Olathe, he was pleased to see her suitcase sitting on the porch. At least she was punctual.

No sooner had he climbed out of his black BMW than she opened the front door and stepped outside. She wore her hair in cascading curls that reached halfway down the middle of her back. This was a switch. Kyle couldn't remember seeing Carrie without that wacky piled-up hairdo of hers. It surprised him to discover how little she actually was.

He glanced away quickly, not wanting to look at her. He thought of Carrie as an Amazon, if not in stature then in attitude, and didn't want to see her as anything else than the nuisance she was. He'd already made up his mind about this situation, and although he was willing to make an effort, there were limits to what he would do.

Without a word, he took the suitcase out of her hand. She released it grudgingly. He loaded it into the trunk and opened the passenger door for her. She smiled her thanks, but he had the impression she would have preferred to open her own door.

So that was the way it was to be. Fine. Just fine. It was what Kyle had been expecting. What he'd planned on. She intended to make this trip as miserable as possible, sort of a "going down in flames" approach, he guessed.

Carrie was studying the road map when he climbed in next to her. Bracing his hands against the steering wheel, he opened his mouth to announce the route he'd planned and the stops he'd scheduled.

"Before we get started," she said, cutting him off in mid-breath, "there's something we should discuss. I was hoping we could make the best of this." She spoke stiffly, without looking at him. "There's no need to make each other miserable."

"I was beginning to think that was unavoidable."

She sat so straight it was as if her spine had been dipped in starch. "It is if you take that attitude."

"All right," he said reluctantly. "What do you have in mind?"

"Well, I tend to get carsick if we don't make regular stops, and I'd enjoy seeing the sights along the way, if that's possible."

Kyle tightened his fingers around the steering wheel and held his tongue. So much for clocking the whole 550 miles their first day out. From the sound of it, Carrie was going to demand a pit stop every thirty miles.

"Car trips with my father were nightmares," she went on. "He hated to stop for anything other than the bare necessities. We'd pull into a rest stop, and he'd sit there and fume at all the cars that were getting ahead of him."

Kyle could identify with that, but he was wise enough not to say so. There was something about getting behind the wheel of a well-tuned precision automobile that brought out the competitor in him. He enjoyed long-distance driving and considered trips of more than a few hundred miles to be something of a test course. He didn't need Carrie to tell him it was a male thing; Kyle was well aware this obsession was some primal part of himself.

"We can make stops as needed," he said, still determined to keep them to a minimum.

"Thank you." She released a slow sigh, as if greatly relieved.

Kyle headed toward the highway ramp and Carrie read the map.

"Are you planning on staying on the interstate?"

"Of course." This wasn't exactly a pleasure trip. He couldn't think of a single reason for an excursion off the main road. There certainly weren't any sights he was interested in seeing. As far as he was concerned, the sooner they arrived in Dallas the better.

"It's awfully boring," Carrie murmured. She sounded like a disappointed five-year-old. Great. From the sound of it, she was looking for him to entertain her as well.

They'd only gone a few miles when Kyle asked her if she needed a potty break. It was a weak attempt at a joke, but when she assured him she did, he ground his teeth and pulled off the next exit.

He'd known this trip was going to be a disaster the minute she came up with the suggestion.

Carrie was really trying to get along with Kyle, but he was making it impossible. He sat next to her, sullen and uncommunicative. Having suggested a rest stop, he stewed because she took him up on it.

Carrie had decided to make one last-ditch effort to get along with Kyle, but she wasn't putting all her eggs in one basket. Her co-worker had made it as clear as rainwater that he didn't believe their taking this trip together was going to work. If the first few miles were any indication, they were doomed.

She was meeting Tom Atkins in Dallas. Tom was an old friend from college. They'd done their internships together, and he'd phoned the night before to ask if she was attending the Dallas conference. Before she knew it, Carrie was pouring out her tale of woe. Tom suggested several solutions, all of which involved her moving. It rankled to admit defeat, but given no other choice, she'd promised to connect with Tom and scout out other job possibilities while she was at the convention. She'd already made plans to visit her sister as well.

Carrie's stomach growled, and Kyle cast her an accusing glance. She hadn't eaten much breakfast. Surely he intended for them to eat sometime.

"I suppose you're hungry."

"I can wait," she answered, willing to endure a few twinges of hunger in order to keep the peace. But only to a point. He'd learn soon enough it was better to feed her than press on until she became overly hungry.

"If I remember correctly, there's a gas station at the next exit," Kyle said. "If we're lucky they'll sell sandwiches and we can grab those and eat in the car as we go."

"I'm not eating in the car," Carrie said. Peace, it seemed, wouldn't come cheap. "We've been on the road forever. I need a break."

"You just had one," he cried.

"That was miles ago."

"Fine," he said, but it sounded like the one word had severely strained his patience.

"Listen, Kyle," she said. "We're going to have a lot of problems if you insist on complaining every time I suggest we stop. I need a rest room, and it wouldn't hurt either of us to stretch our legs." His attitude had been rotten from the moment he'd picked her up, and she wasn't going to take much more of this.

"Okay, since it's so important to you we'll take a

break. Is fifteen minutes satisfactory?" Kyle glared
at her.

"Thirty minutes."

"Thirty?" He made it sound as if it were a life-
and-death matter for them to get back on the highway in record time.

"Thirty," she repeated firmly.

"All right, all right."

The exit he remembered appeared five minutes
later, and he took it without comment. Pulling over
to the pumps, he started to put gas in the car while
she went inside. As luck would have it, the station
sold sandwiches encased in hard plastic containers,
sliced in such a way to reveal their contents.

Carrie opened the refrigerator case and sorted
through the limited selections. She opted for beef for
Kyle and turkey breast for her, along with two cans
of cold soda and a large package of potato chips.

By the time she finished paying for the items, Kyle
had topped off the tank and parked the BMW alongside the station near the rest rooms. Apparently he
intended for them to stand next to the car and eat.

Actually it felt good to stand, so she didn't make a
fuss, not that she believed it would do any good. Kyle
was being stubborn. He finished first and fidgeted
impatiently while she took her time, refusing to be
intimidated into rushing.

When she found him staring at the interstate, it
was all she could do not to point her finger at him.

Her assessment had been right from the first. Kyle Harris was exactly like her father.

"What?" he said.

"You're looking at the traffic," she said, as if this alone were enough to prove her point, "and you're thinking about all those cars that have gotten ahead of us."

He was honest enough not to argue with her. Encouraged by his silence, Carrie took the map he'd brought along and spread it open across the trunk of his car. "I'd like you to consider taking a different route," she said, without looking at him. She held an anticipatory breath.

"Carrie, we've already been over this."

"This will save us at least fifty miles. Look." She pointed to the map and ran her finger along its surface, outlining the two-lane highway, wanting to convince him this was actually a much better plan. She hoped he'd believe this was an overlooked shortcut. If she had her way, they'd soon be off the interstate, which bored her to tears. The scenery was sure to be more thought-provoking than the same bleak stretch of highway looming ahead, mile after tedious mile. Carrie loved driving through small farming communities. At least the back roads had character.

Kyle studied the map as if he strongly suspected she'd distorted the facts, but he couldn't very well argue with what was directly in front of his nose.

"I suppose we could go the way you suggest," he

admitted without much enthusiasm. He made it sound as if he was conceding something important and she should appreciate the sacrifice he was making for her benefit.

"Come on, Kyle," she said cheerfully, feeling generous. "Let's make the best of this, shall we? You don't need to give me the silent treatment. I know you'd rather not be taking this trip with me. That was understood from the beginning. But we're stuck together, so let's do what we can to get along, all right?"

"I know this isn't exactly your idea of a vacation either," he conceded, with a hint of graciousness.

Sucking in her breath and her pride, Carrie held out her hand to him, prepared to make the first move toward a peace accord. "Friends?"

He stared at her outstretched arm as if he expected her to be hiding an electric buzzer in her palm. When he did shake hands, it was briefly and without much enthusiasm. Carrie didn't need a crystal ball to know he trusted her about as much as he would a snake charmer.

"Friends," he agreed, but the word seemed to have a difficult time making it past his lips.

She beamed at him, to show she was proud of him. It wouldn't be so bad. These next days would be their swan song. With effort they could get along. Holding her tongue for more than a few days would be impossible.

The first hour after they left the freeway was peaceful, although Kyle gave her a fright when he turned on his radar detector and all at once beeping sounds came from the dashboard.

Kyle explained what it was. "I don't want to take the chance of running into a radar trap."

She asked several questions about the fuzz buster, and once she involved him in conversation they got along fairly well, which wasn't all that surprising. Men were pretty much alike, as far as she could determine. They could talk up a streak as long as the subject revolved around either their cars or themselves.

They sailed along at an even pace. Rolling waves of wheat fields bordered the road and stretched out on each side as far as the eye could see. Against a backdrop of bright blue sky, the sight was worth every bit of effort it had taken her to convince Kyle to drive this route.

"We're making good time," she said, noting that he was traveling well above the speed limit.

"Yes," he said, tossing her an almost-friendly grin. "The best part is that there aren't as many places to stop. If you need a rest room, you're going to have to take your chances out in the fields."

She stretched her legs out in front of her, folded her hands behind her head, and was silently complimenting herself on how well everything was going.

She should have known it was too good to be true.

And far too good to last for long. When she least expected it, the car lurched unexpectedly. Except for the restraint of the seat belt, Carrie might have been hurled forward. Immediately the BMW started to make a loud, incredibly discordant sound.

"What was that?" she cried.

"I hit something," Kyle explained as he eased the vehicle over to the side of the road and came to a stop.

Carrie leaped out. Kyle followed, frowning as he walked around his car. As if he were soothing an injured child, he gently patted the hood.

"Is that your muffler?" she asked, pointing down the road. Actually she wasn't all that knowledgeable about car parts, but she'd replaced her own recently and had a general idea of what they looked like.

He turned to see. "Along with my exhaust pipe," he agreed.

"What happened?"

"There was something in the road," he said without emotion. "Obviously I hit it." "Something" turned out to be a rock the size of a small watermelon, small enough to slip under the car and large enough to do considerable damage. Kyle had lost both the muffler and exhaust pipe, and he must have put a hole in the gas tank as well. Gasoline squirted onto the road.

This wasn't a happy turn of events. It went without saying this small accident wouldn't have happened if they'd remained on the interstate.

"Are you angry?" she asked, granting him plenty of space in case he chose to vent his frustration with a small temper tantrum. Then she remembered this was Kyle Harris she was dealing with. Kyle was far too dignified to release his irritation the way most people did.

"Why should I be angry?" he asked, confirming her suspicions.

"I'm sorry, Kyle."

"It isn't your fault," he reassured her smoothly.

After pulling the car parts and the rock off to the side of the road, he stood in the middle of the highway, arms akimbo, staring off into the distance. Carrie couldn't remember the last time they'd seen another car, let alone a farmhouse. Wheat fields stretched as far as the naked eye could see.

The sun was beating down, and Kyle wiped his hand across his brow. "This doesn't look promising."

"Someone will come along." She forced herself to sound optimistic. She glanced at her watch, silently praying that they were at least on a school-bus route. Looking down the road, she would have given her eyeteeth to find a bright yellow bus.

"Someone could come along," Kyle agreed, "but it might take a while. Next week, if we're lucky." He leaned his back against the side of the car and slowly sank into a sitting position. He stared vacantly into open space and went still and quiet as if he were meditating. He was probably wishing he'd never laid eyes on her, Carrie guessed.

She couldn't help but admire his restraint.

Lowering herself onto the grass beside him, she gathered her knees under her chin and pressed her forehead there.

"I feel terrible about all this," she confessed, willing to accept full responsibility for the mishap. If she hadn't suggested they take this shortcut, this might never have happened.

"It's not your fault," he told her for the second time.

"But I was the one who—"

"I said it wasn't your fault!"

"You don't need to yell at me," she snapped back. Then she realized what he'd done. Kyle was losing his cool. Unemotional Kyle Harris. The same Kyle Harris who rarely raised his voice. Carrie was ecstatic.

"Do it!" she said excitedly, leaping back to her feet. She knotted one fist to encourage him and punched the still afternoon air. "Let loose, Kyle. You have every right in the world to be angry. Go ahead, yell." She threw back her head and let loose with a scream herself to help him release his inhibitions.

He stared up at her as if she'd taken leave of her senses. "What's wrong with you? Have you been sitting too long in the sun?"

"No." She reclaimed the place next to him on the grass when it was apparent he wasn't going to follow her lead. "For a moment there, I thought you might be human. I was wrong."

"You think I'm inhuman because I don't throw a temper tantrum? I prefer to think of myself as mature."

"But don't you ever get angry?"

"Of course I do."

"How do you express it then? Everyone does, in one way or another." He didn't seem the type to beat his dog. He was kind to old ladies and good with children, she'd seen that for herself. In their increasingly heavy schedule of public service appearances, Kyle had never been anything but wonderful. Except to her, of course.

"I run," he explained in a thin, tight voice. "I know you'd rather I did something a bit more dramatic, like shoot everyone in a McDonald's or my local post office, but I prefer to vent my frustration in a more appropriate manner."

This was at the crux of their dislike for one another, Carrie decided. Probably the most unheralded, wild act Kyle had ever committed was tearing the DO NOT REMOVE tag from his pillow. She sincerely doubted that he'd done the things normal kids do, like skip school or eat paste. He was probably the best debate team member his school had ever produced.

"How long do you think it'll take someone to happen upon us?" she asked after several long minutes. She couldn't tolerate the silence any longer.

"Your guess is as good as mine."

An edge sounded in his voice, but that was the extent of his irritation as far as she could tell.

Five more minutes passed. Kyle stood, reached inside the car, and got the map. He spread it open. "My best guess is that we're about here," he said, pointing to an obscure spot on the map. "There's a town here." He moved his finger an inch or so down the road. "Maybe ten miles."

"Looks more like fifteen to me."

"Fifteen, then," he said with the utmost patience. "I'll head that way and you can wait here."

"You're not leaving me." She wanted that understood right now. Apparently he didn't know her as well as she thought.

"Carrie, we don't have any choice."

"I'm not sitting out here in the hot sun while you traipse into town." As it happened the afternoon was a balmy seventy-five degrees and she was in no immediate danger. Physical danger, at any rate. Emotional was something else.

"I can make the trip in half the time without you," he insisted.

"Maybe you can, but . . . I don't know why I object so strongly, but I don't want to be left here by the side of a deserted road all by myself."

"It wouldn't be more than an hour or two," he insisted.

Carrie was convinced Kyle viewed her as a nuisance, and for once she agreed with him. "You're right, I'm being silly. The only logical thing is for me to do as you suggest and wait here," she said bravely.

He studied her a moment as if he wasn't sure he'd heard her correctly. As if he was afraid she was going to change her mind, he opened his suitcase, got out his running shoes, and took off his loafers.

He warmed up by running around the car a couple of times; at least that was the excuse he gave her when she asked.

"You're sure about this?" He eyed her speculatively.

"Of course," she said, flashing him a stouthearted smile. It'd take more than being abandoned in the blazing sun to get her to admit what a coward she was. It wasn't likely she'd meet up with a mass murderer on a lonely country road. This was what she got from religiously watching reruns of *America's Most Wanted*, which was her all-time crime-solving favorite. Carrie had seen every episode since the show had first aired. She believed one day she too might solve a crime.

Carrie went the first few feet with him but quickly became winded. "Be careful." She raised her hand to bid him farewell.

He jogged backward for several steps, studying

her, before he turned, increased his speed, and took off. Watching him, Carrie was reminded of a gazelle, his movements were so fluid and graceful. Within minutes he'd disappeared around the curve in the road.

Carrie remained where she was, her fingertips pressed to her lips as she battled back some unnamed emotion. It wasn't that she was especially worried about him—other than his inability to express emotion, that was. As for his safety, she was sure Kyle could take care of himself. Nor was she overly concerned about her own well-being, except that she seemed a little rocky emotionally.

All right, a whole lot rocky. She couldn't remember the last time she'd felt this close to tears. And for what reason? For the life of her, Carrie didn't know.

She returned to the car and sat down in the shade of the disabled vehicle. No sooner had she checked her watch than she caught sight of a movement out of the corner of her eye. Looking up, she saw Kyle rounding the corner. He was coming back.

Leaping to her feet, she stood waiting anxiously for an explanation.

"I can't do it," he muttered. He bent forward and braced his hands against his knees as he sucked in deep gulps of oxygen.

"You can't run fifteen miles?"

"No," he said, as if she'd insulted him. "I can't leave you."

"Why not?" She'd thought she'd done an adequate job of convincing him to go on without her.

"Your eyes," he muttered, sounding as if he was angry with himself. If that was the case, he was more angry with her, although heaven knew he'd never admit it.

He wasn't making any sense.

"You looked at me with those big brown eyes like a dog-pound puppy. You made me feel I was leaving you to an unknown fate. We're both in this. If you think you can make fifteen miles, we'll go together."

"I couldn't jog that far." If the truth be known, she wouldn't make it around the next curve in the road without requiring CPR.

"We'll walk," he said kindly.

If he were a different kind of man he might have made a derogatory comment about her not being physically fit. Perhaps there was more to appreciate about the newscaster than met the eye, Carrie decided.

"You might want to change your shoes," he said, staring pointedly down at her sandals.

"Ah." As best as she could remember, everything else she'd packed had heels.

She did a quick check of her suitcase and was just getting ready to close the lid when she heard a car, a very old and sick car that coughed and choked its way down the road. Within seconds a battered blue pickup came into view.

"Kyle," she screamed on the off chance he hadn't noticed. "Someone's coming!"

The farmer wore denim bib overalls and a straw hat. He pulled over to the side of the road and stuck his head out the window.

"You folks having trouble?" he asked, then climbed out of the cab. "Name's Billy Bob," he said, nodded once, and then decisively held out his hand for Kyle to shake. Kyle introduced himself and Carrie and explained what had happened. Carrie inserted a word or two every now and again, accepting the blame for their predicament.

"Is there a chance you could drive us into town?" Kyle asked after a couple of minutes. "I'd be more than willing to pay you for your trouble."

The farmer rubbed his hand along the side of his jaw as if their predicament took serious consideration. "I don't suspect it'd be much bother, but you just keep your money inside your wallet. Folks around these parts are glad to help one another. We take pride in being neighborly." He held the door of the rusted-out truck open for Carrie. "You two climb on board and I'll get your luggage for you."

It only took him a minute or two to load the suitcases in the back of the pickup, which he did with surprising dexterity. Now that she watched him,

Carrie noticed Billy Bob seemed to be in a hurry, which wasn't the impression he'd first given them.

Billy Bob joined them in the cab of the truck and revved up the engine.

"I can't begin to tell you how pleased we are you came along when you did," Carrie said. She was sandwiched between the two men, so pleased at being rescued that it was all she could do not to kiss the farmer's sun-leathered cheek.

Only he wasn't tan. He must have been ill, she decided, because he didn't look as if he'd spent a day in the sun in years. His skin was as pale as a newborn's.

Kyle struck up a conversation and the men talked sports. Carrie was content to let the two chatter, but she noticed the way Billy Bob kept glancing into his rearview mirror as if he expected someone to come up behind him.

Now that she got a good look at him, she realized she had the impression she'd seen him someplace before. "You live around these parts?" she asked when there was a lull in the conversation.

"Me and the missus have a farm on the other side of Wheatland," he said.

"I suppose you've got a family?"

"Sure do," he answered with a tinge of pride. "Five."

His hands! That was what was bothering her so much. They were smooth and uncalloused, and his nails were clean and cut square and even.

The two men continued chatting, seeming to find a variety of subjects to discuss at length.

For one wild second Carrie thought she was going to be ill. It was all beginning to add up in her fevered mind.

This wasn't any farmer.

If his pale face was any indication, he hadn't spent a single day toiling under the hot sun.

Each bit of information tallied with the next, and the fact he kept checking his rearview mirror troubled her as well. Then there was the certainty she'd seen him before. His profile was familiar. Carrie was convinced she'd seen him, and she racked her mind trying to think of where it might have been.

It came to her then, all at once, like a flash flood.

She *had* seen this man. Recently, too, if her memory served her right. He'd been featured on *America's Most Wanted*.

3

"*Kyle*." The name came out of Carrie's throat more like a toad's croak than anything a human would emit.

Her co-worker glanced fleetingly in her direction and waited a few seconds, but when she didn't immediately continue, he picked up the conversation.

Billy Bob was a felon, Carrie decided. He must be in order to be profiled on *America's Most Wanted*. Unsuspecting, Kyle didn't understand the danger they'd innocently gotten themselves into.

Given no other choice, Carrie carefully jabbed Kyle with her elbow. Her voice had completely deserted her. She was taking deep, even breaths, hoping to calm down enough to speak coherently, although she hadn't a clue about what to say. Announcing that she'd seen Billy Bob on *America's Most Wanted* was likely to get them killed. She grabbed hold of Kyle, tightly pinching the tender skin of his upper arm.

"Ouch," he blurted out.

Unfortunately, Carrie couldn't make her fingers quit.

"What's the matter?" Kyle demanded when she stared up at him, silently pleading for him to read the message in her wide eyes. If he had a lick of sense, he'd figure out something was terribly wrong.

A full minute later, Carrie decided Kyle hadn't a clue.

"You've gone pale," Kyle said. "Are you sick?"

Enthusiastically she nodded her head as if overtaken by a sudden bout of the chills. Goose bumps ran up and down her arms, but they had nothing to do with the outside temperature.

"You're trying to say something?" Kyle coaxed.

She nodded her head wildly.

"Something's wrong?"

The man was a genius. Once more Carrie nodded with enough enthusiasm for her chin to bounce against her collarbone.

"Just say it," Kyle said impatiently.

"Yes," the driver of their truck concurred. "Just say it."

"He's not a farmer," Carrie blurted out breathlessly. "He's an escaped convict." Her words came out in squeaks.

"Oh, come on, Carrie!" Kyle said with an embarrassed laugh. "That's ridiculous."

"No, it isn't." Billy Bob's country twang disappeared faster than chocolate eggs at an Easter egg hunt. "How'd you know?" He gave her an approving grin, as if he appreciated her discriminating skills. "Damn. I thought I had the hillbilly part down good."

"You mean you're not a farmer?" Kyle demanded in a shocked, tight voice.

"Sorry about this, folks, but I promise not to detain you for long." With one hand on the steering wheel, Billy Bob reached for his boot and withdrew a small handgun. He waved it in the air, being sure they both caught a glimpse of it. Then he proceeded to point the barrel in their direction.

Carrie gasped and her hands automatically shot into the air.

"How'd you figure it out?" Billy Bob demanded of Carrie a second time.

"You're not tan, and your fingernails are too clean."

"Damn, you're right," he said, and then, glancing in his rearview mirror, he added, "Double damn. It looks like the law's about to catch up with me. I thought I had more time on them than this."

This gladdened Carrie's heart until she realized

that Billy Bob was likely to use her and Kyle as hostages.

They were nearing the outskirts of Wheatland, with blue and red patrol lights flashing in the rearview mirror. Carrie twisted around to see how far the authorities were from catching up with them, but it was impossible to gauge. The sirens sounded as if they were almost upon them, but the whirling lights were far behind. If she hadn't been so frightened, she might have been able to do something to detain Billy Bob. The gun barrel aimed in their general direction was plenty of incentive to do exactly as he said, however.

Carrie studied the community that they were fast approaching. A huge water tower stood in the distance to the left of town and a handful of grain elevators to the right.

The truck pitched as Billy Bob took an unexpected turn, heading down the train tracks. Carrie was thrown against Billy Bob's hard shoulder, and Kyle slammed against her. The truck pitched and heaved as it traveled down the uneven tracks. Carrie felt like a popcorn seed in hot oil. The ride nearly jarred her senseless. Then, mercifully, they stopped.

"Get out," Billy Bob ordered, slamming on the brakes. The abrupt action pitched them forward. "Now. Move it, move it, move it." Billy Bob's accent was replaced with an authoritative voice that would have struck fear in the heart of a drill sergeant.

Carrie and Kyle scrambled to do as he demanded. Kyle flew out the side of the truck and Carrie was shoved fiercely after him. She would have hit the pavement head first if not for Kyle, who caught her in his arms.

Billy Bob didn't waste any time making sure they weren't harmed. With the passenger door still open, the truck shot off the train tracks and down a side street to a back alley. Two wheels lifted off the ground as he careened into the alley.

"He's got our suitcases," Carrie shouted, running after him. She didn't know where she got the strength to do anything so incredibly stupid. It wasn't as if she had a chance of catching him, or that she'd know what to do if by some wild fluke she did.

"Carrie," Kyle said, catching hold of her around the waist. "Let it go. It doesn't matter."

"But he's got all our clothes."

"We've got our lives." Kyle's few words put everything back into perspective.

Carrie didn't know if it was by accident or design, but she found herself wrapped in Kyle's arms. He was strong and solid and she clung to him. He held her tightly against him as if he were infinitely grateful to have her in his arms. Carrie knew this wasn't necessarily true, but she didn't care. In that moment they needed each other. Their differences meant nothing. Their pride was gone, wiped away by a narrow escape with fate and a felon on the run.

Kyle brushed the hair away from her temples and examined her face, checking to be sure she was un- scathed. Perhaps he was studying her to be sure he was holding the same woman who'd irritated him all these months. Neither of them spoke. Together they trembled, two people who recognized how close they'd come to disaster and how fortunate they were to escape.

Their reprieve, however, didn't last long. Within another minute they were surrounded by patrol cars. Doors flew open and officers leaped out, using their vehicles as protection and aiming their pistols in Carrie and Kyle's direction.

"He went that way," Carrie cried, pointing out the route of Billy Bob's escape. No one there seemed to care. At least no one hurried after him, although she was certain one car and possibly two were still in pursuit of Billy Bob.

"We're not armed," Kyle announced authorita- tively.

Two sheriff's deputies stood and, while the others continued to train their weapons on Carrie and Kyle, instructed the pair to lean against the patrol car and spread-eagle their arms and legs.

"We're not criminals," Carrie said, fighting down her indignation. They were being treated as though they'd done something wrong.

"They're clean," the first officer announced.

"You can relax," the second officer said.

"Who's the man you're after?" Kyle asked, the minute he turned around.

Before the deputy could respond, too plainclothes detectives stepped out of an unmarked car. The older man introduced himself and flashed his badge. "Sam Richards," he said. "This is Agent Bates."

Carrie only got a glimpse, just enough to realize his identification was unlike any other she'd seen. Sam Richards was a member of the Secret Service, although he looked more like a congenial television weatherman than a government agent.

"Billy Bob must have threatened the President," Carrie mumbled disappointedly. She was convinced she'd seen him on television, but she couldn't recall a single episode of *America's Most Wanted* that had profiled someone with his eye on assassination.

Richards exchanged glances with another one of the law enforcement officers. The agent's bright blue eyes were what Carrie called catalog eyes. Her sister Cathie referred to them as bedroom eyes, but Carrie was a tad more conservative than her younger sister.

"We'd like to talk to you both," Richards announced.

"Of course," Kyle said.

"What for?" Carrie countered, unwilling to be subjected to much more of this. It was going to take more than a smile from Mr. Catalog Eyes to make up for the way they'd been treated thus far.

"Let's go on over to the sheriff's office," Richards suggested. "Collins won't mind."

The agent had opted to ignore Carrie's weak protest. He didn't bother to answer her question either, she noted. Before she could press further, she was placed in the back seat of a patrol car and driven through the center of town.

It seemed Wheatland hadn't seen such activity since last year's Fourth of July parade. Curious townsfolk lined both sides of the streets. Mothers hid their babies' faces, and men glared at them with narrowed, suspicious eyes. The town's youth were braver; several leaned against the lampposts and stared openly as the four vehicles pulled into the angle parking outside the sheriff's office.

Sam Richards held open the door to the office for her, and she stepped inside. It was like walking onto a television set from one of the old Andy Griffith *Mayberry RFD* shows. Clearly, Carrie had been watching too many reruns. The jail consisted of four cells, which were lined against one wall across from the sheriff's desk. From what she could see, business was slack. The cells were empty.

Sheriff Collins's desk stood behind a waist-high railing. A table and chairs dominated the remaining space. Once the three of them were inside the sheriff's compact office, they sat around the table and Carrie and Kyle took turns relaying the story of how they'd run into Billy Bob.

Sheriff Collins returned alone and whispered to the Secret Service agent as if he feared what might happen if Kyle and Carrie overheard him. From the hushed exchange she guessed that once again Billy Bob had slipped through the net of justice.

"It was all my fault that we left the interstate," Carrie explained, once everyone had reconvened. "But I thought we'd save ourselves a few miles and take the scenic route."

"All we got is wheat fields," Sheriff Collins threw in, as if he found her explanation weak. He eyed her suspiciously, and Carrie eyed him right back.

"But they're pretty wheat fields, and the road's a whole lot more entertaining than the highway."

"That's when I ran over a rock," Kyle cut in to explain. "It struck the undercarriage of my car, and the muffler and the exhaust pipe fell off."

"Kyle was going to jog into town, but he didn't."

"Why not?" Again it was Sheriff Collins, who looked as if he wanted to throw them in jail now and ask questions later.

"Before I could leave—"

"You left," Carrie corrected him, "then came back, remember?" She felt it was important to get every detail down exactly right the first time, otherwise there could be problems. Horatio Caine on *CSI: Miami* had solved entire mysteries on less.

"Why'd you return?" Richards asked, smiling encouragingly, as if they were all good friends.

Carrie wasn't fooled, but she wasn't so sure about Kyle. "Kyle wasn't gone more than ten minutes."

"Why'd he come back?" The room went still as if anticipating a confession, although she still hadn't a clue as to what Billy Bob was said to have done.

"Carrie was worried about being left alone," Kyle explained. She hadn't looked at him in several minutes and feared he wasn't overly pleased with her dragging in every detail of their story.

"He decided it would be better if we walked into town together," Carrie supplied. "But before we started, Billy Bob stopped and offered us a ride."

"His name's Max Sanders."

"Max Sanders," Carrie repeated slowly, testing the name on her lips. It didn't sound familiar.

"What's he done?" Kyle asked.

"That's not important just now."

"It is if you plan to detain us," Kyle continued smoothly, boldly confronting the Secret Service agent.

"Right," Carrie said, quickly siding with Kyle. "We're law-abiding citizens. We know our rights. It might be a good idea if we contact an attorney. What do you think, Kyle?"

"So you've had plenty of experience in dealing with the law, have you?" Sam Richards twisted a hardback chair around and straddled it.

"A little," she said defiantly, wondering just how far *Boston Legal* episodes would take her. "I interviewed a police officer once. He was selling tickets to the annual charity ball."

"We're employed by KUTE radio in Kansas City," Kyle explained. "If you check our identification, you'll see we're telling the truth."

"What's Max Sanders done to warrant your attention?" Carrie asked again, eager for as many details as she could collect.

"Counterfeiting."

"You mean he's passing fake money?"

"You got it. I don't suppose you'd mind showing us any money *you're* carrying."

"No problem," Kyle said, reaching in his hip pocket for his wallet. He opened it and handed over several bills for their inspection.

Apparently Kyle's money was good because they returned it after only a brief inspection. Because Kyle had been so willing to have his cash inspected, Carrie didn't have any choice but to allow the police the same privilege with her.

"How much cash did you bring?" Kyle demanded when she handed over a small wad of bills.

"Enough," she said, disliking his tone, "but my traveler's checks are in my suitcases."

Kyle briefly closed his eyes. "Mine too."

So it was more than just their clothes Max had absconded with; he had their money as well.

"Can we go now?" Carrie asked, growing discouraged with the entire process. They'd cooperated to the best of their ability, but she was exhausted. They needed to decide what they were going to do without a car, money, or clothes.

"We can't allow you to leave just yet," Richards said apologetically.

"Why not?"

"We have a few questions left. It'd help us a great deal if you'd answer them."

Carrie exchanged looks with Kyle, who seemed perfectly content. From experience she knew his calm outward appearance was often deceptive. Kyle could be brimming with animosity, but he'd never allow it to show. Especially now, when any display of negative emotion was grounds for real trouble.

"We're having a slight problem believing your story," Richards said cautiously.

"I knew they were lying the minute I set eyes on them," Sheriff Collins threw in excitedly. He was the type of law enforcement officer who needed nothing more than a fast patrol car and his rifle to fix whatever was wrong with the world. Carrie bet people called him Smokey behind his back.

"You don't believe us?" Carrie asked and jumped to her feet. Kyle could remain as calm and cool as he wanted, but she'd had it! She was tired and cranky. She'd been kidnapped, chased, threatened with a gun, and treated like a convicted felon. It wouldn't take much more to send her straight over the edge.

"We can't understand why a man who's on the run

would stop to help complete strangers," Agent Bates explained. "Especially knowing the authorities are no more than ten minutes behind him."

"Perhaps Sanders didn't know that," Kyle offered.

"He knew." The "congenial weatherman" wasn't nearly as affable now. "It doesn't make sense that he'd choose to play the Good Samaritan when he's got nothing to gain and everything to lose."

"He's got the counterfeiting plates with him?" Kyle asked thoughtfully.

"You got it," Richards confirmed.

"He's got more than the plates," Carrie said heatedly. "He's got our luggage and our money." She still hadn't figured out what she was going to wear once they arrived in Dallas. If they made it that far. Their first day had shown precious little promise.

"Exactly what was it you had in those suitcases?"

"My party dress," Carrie said. It would be impossible to replace the red-sequined evening gown she cherished. She'd found it shortly after Christmas at a drastically reduced clearance sale and instantly fallen in love with it. She hadn't a clue when she'd have the opportunity to wear such an elaborate gown, but she couldn't resist.

The dress fit over her hips like a sleek glove. The scooped neckline highlighted her greatest asset, and the slits that ran up the sides reached halfway up her thighs. The best part was knowing Kyle would heartily disapprove of her wearing such a revealing gown. Her father would have, and she could trust her co-worker's reaction to be similar.

"I'm asking what Mr. Harris packed," Sam Richards explained. "It's more likely Sanders will opt for a change of clothing from your friend's suitcase than from yours."

Carrie could feel the heat inching its way up her face. "Of course. It's just that . . ." She let the rest fade and made an effort to smile as if she'd been in on the joke from the first.

"What do you think?" Richards asked Sheriff Collins.

The local law enforcement officer shrugged. "He has a lot more to worry about than a change of clothes. We were hot on his tail, and he knew it. What would make a man like that stop to help two strangers?"

The question was directed at Carrie and Kyle.

"You think I have the answer to that?" Kyle asked, finally showing his irritation. Carrie nearly cheered. As it was she tossed him a brilliant smile, letting him know she heartily approved.

"It seems to me you guys aren't thinking clearly," she said. "It's really rather simple when you reason it out. Max Sanders may have realized you were close behind him, but he also knew you were looking for one man. By stopping and volunteering to drive us into town, he hoped to throw you off. You'd probably have driven directly past a truck carrying three people. Or he might have wanted to use us as hostages. Who knows?"

The room went silent.

"I don't buy it," Richards said. The sheriff and his two deputies were whispering in the background, casting distrustful looks at Kyle and Carrie.

Bates rubbed a hand along the back of his neck. "I don't know. There's more to this than meets the eye."

"Their story about the broken-down car checks out," the sheriff announced. He braced his hands against his hips and rocked onto the heels of his polished black boots. "There's a BMW pulled off to the side of the road just where they claimed there was."

"Just because their car's broken down outside of town doesn't mean they're who they say they are," Sheriff Collins said as if he didn't expect them to hear.

"Don't be ridiculous," Carrie cried. "You can't honestly believe Kyle and I are criminals. Why that's so ludicrous it's laughable."

"And now, if you men will excuse us," Kyle announced, "we'll be on our way."

Carrie pushed herself away from the table and stood, eager to leave. She'd had a full day, considering everything that had happened.

"It might be a good idea if you stayed around town for a few days," the sheriff instructed, his hard eyes trained on them.

"Not a chance," Kyle said. "We have a schedule to maintain. Once I've got the car fixed, we're out of here."

"Right," Carrie said, nodding emphatically. "We're out of here."

"I believe we've answered your questions," Kyle said stiffly. "I can't say it's been a pleasure, gentlemen, but it has been an experience."

"You gonna let them go?" Sheriff Collins was studying the government agents. Apparently he was waiting for their word to lock Carrie and Kyle in jail and throw away the key.

"We don't have any reason to hold them," Bates muttered.

"I just wish we knew what was going on in Sanders's mind."

"If you knew that," Carrie said with a sassy smile, "you'd have *him* in custody now instead of two innocent bystanders." Kyle opened the door for her, and together they walked out into bright sunlight.

Carrie squinted, flattened her hands against her stomach, and inhaled a deep breath of fresh air. Unfortunately this reminded her how hungry she was. "I don't know about you, but I'm starved."

Kyle didn't say anything right away. "You're hungry?" He repeated it as if he wasn't sure he'd heard her correctly.

"This is the way I deal with stress." At the moment she could have eaten her way through a Las

Vegas buffet. The sandwich and chips weren't an adequate snack, and it was nearly dinnertime.

"You want something to eat *now?*"

It wasn't as if this should be any revelation to Kyle. They'd worked together long enough for him to know her idiosyncrasies.

"Fine," he muttered. "Find something to eat and I'll meet you later."

"What are you going to do?" she asked, hurrying to keep pace with him.

"I'll make arrangements to get back to my car."

How like a man to worry about his precious car over his stomach, Carrie thought. "Isn't it more important to find someone to tow it into town?"

"No."

"Why not?" It seemed to her that Kyle should be more concerned with finding out how long it would take to have the car repaired so they could go on their merry way. The second they left Wheatland, she was going to suggest they head back to the highway.

He didn't answer her right away. Instead, he rubbed his hand along his face and looked beaten and tired. Carrie understood why. They were causing something of a distraction in town. People were staring. She realized there wasn't any help for it. All they could do was see about the car and leave as soon as possible. From the looks coming their way, they were marked as troublemakers.

"I need to find out something before I call a tow

truck," Kyle said, under his breath. The way he acted, one would think he was afraid of being overheard.

"Find out what?" she asked in a heated whisper, following him. Her growling stomach was forgotten for the moment.

"What the agent said made sense," he continued in low tones. "Sanders had to have a reason to stop and help us the way he did, and I think I know what it was."

"What?" Carrie was practically trotting to keep pace with him. He was walking with purposeful strides toward the edge of town. She had yet to figure how he intended to get back to the car.

"It doesn't matter, Carrie. Go find yourself something to eat, and I'll catch up with you later."

"Not on your life! I'm in this too. If you've thought of something, tell me."

Impatiently, Kyle glanced her way and his mouth tightened. She hated it when his lips got thin and his eyes flashed with disdain. Heaven knew she'd seen him do it often enough.

"Besides, shouldn't you be telling this to the authorities?"

Kyle shook his head. "I don't dare. It might implicate us."

"How?" Carrie lifted the hair away from her face, took in a single deep breath, and held it. Who would have ever believed such a little thing would lead to this?

"If my theory's right, Sanders left the counterfeit plates with us."

Carrie stopped dead in the middle of the sidewalk. Kyle had gone a number of steps before he so much as noticed. "He did what?" she called, racing to catch up with him.

"Don't look so worried, it's just a theory." He stopped walking and turned to face her. His expression was as intense as she'd ever seen it. "I want you to stay here. Do whatever you need to do to kill time. I'll be back as soon as I can."

She shook her head, but before she could protest, Kyle gripped her by the upper arms and stared intently down at her. "It has to be this way."

"But how are you going to get back to the car?"

"I'll hitchhike, and if no one picks me up I'll run. It isn't nearly as far as we first thought. It's less than eight miles, probably closer to six."

Before she could argue with him, she saw a black BMW being towed into town. "I don't think you're going to have a problem checking out your theory," she assured him with a smug smile, "especially since your car's here now."

Kyle wasn't in the best of moods, and being detained by two Secret Service agents didn't improve his humor any. He'd figured from the moment they left Kansas City that this wasn't going to be any joy ride. But he'd anticipated his trouble would involve Carrie, not the Secret Service and some small-town sheriff intent on proving his worth. Least of all, he hadn't expected to run into a counterfeiter.

He left Carrie and walked across the street to see exactly how long it would take to have the muffler, exhaust, and gas tank repaired. As for his theory about Sanders storing the plates in his car, he'd check that out later, although if it proved true, he wasn't exactly sure what his options were.

He didn't trust the sheriff. The Secret Service agents had left town; he'd seen them drive away. The way he figured, they'd probably gotten some updated information about Max Sanders. By now, he suspected, they'd have had time to do a background check on both him and Carrie and know they were squeaky clean. He wasn't as convinced that the sheriff shared their view. Kyle wanted to get out of Wheatland, and the sooner they could be on their way the better.

After looking both ways, he jogged across the street. As soon as he was on the sidewalk on the other side, the sheriff stepped out from between two cars.

"Howdy," he said, touching the brim of his hat, as if it was important to retain protocol.

"Hello," Kyle answered cautiously.

"You just cross that street?" he asked.

Kyle looked over his shoulder. "Yeah."

"Don't suppose you saw the crosswalk?"

Kyle shook his head. "Can't say I noticed."

Sheriff Collins scratched the side of his head. "I'm sorry to do this to you, boy. You seem like a decent enough sort. I'm not so sure about your friend, though."

"Carrie?"

The sheriff stuck his thumbs in his belt and leaned back on the heels of his polished boots. "These things happen when you start mingling with the wrong crowd."

"What things?" Kyle demanded.

"I'm afraid I'm going to have to lock you up," he said, reaching for Kyle's elbow.

"What's the charge?"

The sheriff smiled as if he'd personally caught him red-handed in Wheatland's bank vault. "Jaywalking."

4

Kyle paced the confines of his jail cell until he heard the sheriff's door open. It was Carrie. Her red face and snapping eyes told him she was madder than hops.

Glaring at him, she ground her hands into her hips, stood with her feet apart, and demanded righteously, "What'd you do now?"

Kyle swore this woman had the power to irritate him beyond reason. Her attitude suggested he was a regular jailbird.

"I didn't do anything," he shot back.

"Oh, sure, they trumped up some charge and tossed

you in the clink for no good reason. 'Go get yourself something to eat,' you said, and the minute my back was turned you do something stupid and get yourself arrested. Just tell me what the charges are, and I'll see what I can do to get you out of this mess."

"All right. If you must know, I was arrested for jaywalking." Kyle knew the charge was merely an excuse to detain him. What he didn't know was why Sheriff Collins felt it was necessary.

"Jaywalking?" Carrie repeated incredulously, stunned enough to drop her arms at her side. She recovered, however, and grinned widely.

"It isn't nearly as amusing from this side of the bars," he told her. By then Carrie was laughing and trying to disguise the fact, which did little to improve his disposition.

"If you'll stop laughing long enough, I'll tell you what you need to do to get me out of here," he said stiffly.

"Sorry," she murmured and cupped her mouth with her hand, but her dark eyes fairly danced with mirth. She pulled out a chair, sat down, and casually crossed her legs. "I really am sorry, Kyle. This whole thing is so ridiculous that it's either laugh or cry."

He wasn't appeased, nor would he be until he could escape this godforsaken town.

"All right," she said, "what is it you need me to do?"

"Find out when the bail's set and do what you can

to post it. Call Kansas City if you have to. Clyde will give you the name of a good attorney, if it comes to that." He couldn't stand still, but pacing did little to alleviate his irritation, so he stalked from one end of the cell to the other. He wanted out of there as quickly as it could be arranged.

"Who sets the bail?" Carrie asked.

"The hell if I know. Probably some backwoods judge."

"Okay, I'll get right on it." She hurried out the door.

The minute she was gone, surprisingly, Kyle wished he could call her back. Sighing deeply, he walked into the shadows and sat down on the edge of the thin mattress that made up his cot. Rubbing his hands over his face, he sorted through his limited options.

Several matters didn't set right. He'd had time to think about his and Carrie's encounter with Max Sanders, and there were a number of unanswered questions.

It seemed to him that Sam Richards, the Secret Service agent, wasn't stupid either. Richards must have suspected Sanders had planted the counterfeit plates in his BMW long before the idea struck Kyle. While Carrie and he were detained, Kyle guessed that his car would have been gone over with a fine-tooth comb.

Carrie claimed she'd seen Sanders on *America's Most Wanted*, but no one seemed to know anything about that. Yet there was something vaguely familiar

about the felon, something Kyle couldn't put his finger on. Carrie had noticed it first. Kyle also thought
he'd seen the counterfeiter before, but he had yet to
figure out where or when. It'd come to him, he decided, in time.

What surprised him most was that he'd rather liked
Sanders. Sure, the guy had waved a gun at them, but it
was a bluff and Kyle had known it, somehow. When
he could, he'd do a background check on Sanders
himself—he had his sources—but his guess was the
guy wasn't the violent sort.

The door opened, and Sheriff Collins strolled into
the room. He tucked his thumbs inside his belt and
smiled smugly. "We don't want any trouble, son. You
have to understand I'm just doing my job."

Kyle wouldn't give the sheriff the satisfaction of
a reply.

"Your little woman is raising all kind of cain," the
sheriff commented in passing. "Why, she threatened
to contact the Attorney General of these United States
if Judge Hawkins didn't immediately set your bail."

If for nothing else, Kyle could appreciate Carrie
for her talent as a rabble-rouser. The woman had a
gift for irritating just about everyone. One thing he'd
say for her, she had spunk. The trait had driven him
to the brink of madness in past months, but now he
found himself deeply appreciating it. By all that was
fair he should inform the sheriff that Carrie wasn't

his woman, but he decided to let the lawman worry about what she might do in order to save her man.

The door to the sheriff's office flew open and Carrie, ignoring Sheriff Collins, hurried over to Kyle's cell. "How much money do you have on you?" she demanded without preamble.

Kyle reached into his rear pocket for his wallet, which he'd been allowed to keep. "A little less than a hundred dollars."

"That isn't enough."

"For what?"

She stared at him. "For your bail. Judge Hawkins set it at two hundred and fifty dollars, and between us we've got less than two hundred."

"Here." Kyle reached inside his wallet for his VISA card. "Use this."

"Do you honestly think I'd ask for your cash if they took VISA? I hoped to get a cash advance, but the bank's already closed."

Kyle checked his watch and was surprised to realize it was after four. When he looked up, he found Carrie sitting at the table where they'd spent a good portion of the afternoon being interrogated. She was carefully counting out the cash they had between them. It would greatly help matters if Sanders hadn't driven off with their traveler's checks.

"Did you find out about the damage to my car?"

She nodded and continued to count. "It's not as bad

as it looked. The mechanic said he could patch up the gas tank and weld the muffler and exhaust pipe back on without much of a problem, but he strongly suggested you have your mechanic in Kansas City look at it again, once you're home. By the way, he'll take VISA."

"Great. Now what about the bail money?"

"You're sure this is all the cash you have?"

"I'm sure." Apparently she assumed he kept a hundred-dollar bill stored in the bottom of his shoe.

"That's what I thought." Her face fell. He noticed she was twisting the opal ring on her right hand until it was all he could do not to ask her to stop. He didn't know why she insisted on wearing such a traditional-looking antique ring when she chose to dress like Britney Spears most of the time.

"There's got to be some way of coming up with some cash," he said, more to himself than to her. It seemed spending the night in this flea-ridden jail was unavoidable, but the thought of any more time than that was intolerable.

"I'll get it," Carrie said, and her eyes glowed with a determination he recognized as unbeatable. He'd butted heads with her often enough to know what she could be like when she set her mind on something.

"How?" he asked.

"Easy." She flashed him a lazy smile. "I'll sell— something." With that she placed her hand delicately upon her hip and tossed him a smoldering glance over her shoulder. "See you later, big boy."

Kyle's heart stopped. "Carrie," he yelled, wrapping his hands around the bars and squeezing them so tightly his knuckles went white. "Don't do anything stupid. You'll be thrown in jail yourself."

Kyle had never seen a woman who could move her hips quite the way Carrie did as she made her way to the door with a provocative gait that really focused his attention.

"Carrie, stop. Let's talk about this." He could feel his heart start to race, and it irritated him to realize she was up to something. He knew instinctively it was something he wouldn't like.

She paused at the door, smiled prettily, and then blew him a deliberate kiss. "Don't worry, darling, I'll be back in no time with all the money we'll need."

"Carrie. Don't you dare leave this office." She pretended not to hear him and walked calmly out the door. "Carrie! I demand that you stop, right this minute!" Furious, Kyle rattled the bars until he banged his head against the steel rail hard enough for a knot to form. He rubbed his forehead, kicked the wall, and darn near broke three of his toes.

He might have yelled out in pain if Sheriff Collins hadn't laughed. "That's quite some woman you've got there."

It was on the tip of his tongue to shout that Carrie wasn't his woman, that they disliked each other intensely, had found it impossible to get along, and decided they couldn't work together. All at once, he found he couldn't say it. Not because it wasn't true because, God help them both, it was cold, hard fact. Yet in the space of a single afternoon, they'd become allies. At the moment, Carrie Jamison was his only contact with the outside world. He needed her.

Still chuckling, Sheriff Collins left the office. Kyle guessed he was going to see if Carrie had made good on her word.

Carrie loved it. Kyle had actually believed she intended to sell her body for the cash needed to spring him from the slammer. Apparently the newscaster had an elevated opinion of her charms—and a low opinion of her morals. She wasn't sure if she should be elated or depressed.

Traipsing across the street, Carrie made certain she was in a designated crosswalk. The last thing they needed was for her to land in a jail cell alongside Kyle.

The pawnshop was getting ready to close when she walked reluctantly inside. She hated to part with her grandmother's opal ring even if it was only for a few days.

"Can I help you?" the shopkeeper greeted her, leaning against the glass counter. He was a small, bald man with beady eyes who studied her movements as if he expected her to pull a gun from her purse and demand his money. Given her introduction to Wheatland, she couldn't say she blamed him.

As it turned out, the transaction went fairly smoothly. Within a matter of ten minutes, Carrie had the cash she needed, and she'd extracted from Mr. Dillon a promise that he wouldn't sell the opal. The only stipulation was that she contact him sometime within a week. No problem. The ring was too precious to her to give up voluntarily.

Although she now possessed the necessary funds to bail Kyle out of jail, it would still be morning before they'd be free to leave Wheatland. Given no option, Carrie started searching for a hotel room for the night.

Every five minutes or less, Kyle found himself studying the face of his watch and wondering what was taking Carrie so long. He stood and started pacing the way he had when first placed inside the tiny cell. The office door opened and he whirled around to discover a blond young woman no more than twenty-three or twenty-four wearing a pink waitress uniform with a white ruffled apron. She carried a dinner tray covered with a pink linen napkin.

Smiling prettily at him, she advanced a couple of steps. "I've brought your dinner," she announced shyly. "I hope you like chicken-fried steak with real mashed potatoes, corn, and a homemade biscuit."

After all Kyle had endured that day, the thought of food sickened him. "Thanks, but no thanks."

The blonde blinked as if he'd insulted her. "I brought along a piece of Melba's blueberry pie. Melba won a blue ribbon last year at the state fair with this pie recipe. It's the best blueberry pie in three counties."

"I didn't mean to offend you, it's just that I'm not hungry," Kyle murmured.

"That's all right," she said and blushed prettily. "I'm Mary Lu."

Kyle shoved his hands in his pockets. "Nice to meet you," he said stiffly. Unfortunately Mary Lu didn't show any signs of leaving, and Kyle wasn't in the mood to make small talk. The waitress continued to stand on the other side of the bars and, although he didn't know much about such things, seemed to be making eyes at him.

"I don't suppose you've seen a short brunette with long hair wandering around town, have you?" If Mary Lu was intent on staying, he might as well pump what information he could out of her.

"You must be asking about your friend."

"Yeah," Kyle agreed.

"You're not married or anything, are you?"

He wasn't sure about the *or anything* part. At the present he wasn't involved with anyone, if that was what she meant. Then again, she might be coyly referring to his relationship with Carrie. If that was the case, he could in all honesty admit there was nothing between them.

"I'm not married," he murmured.

Mary Lu set the dinner tray on the table, pulled up a chair, and crossed her legs, making certain he was allowed a view of her shapely thigh.

"What's Carrie doing?" Kyle asked outright, too anxious to hide his interest.

"I can't rightly say. The last I heard she was over at Dillon's Pawnshop."

"Pawnshop? What for?" His abruptness flustered the waitress, and he lowered his voice. "That surprises me, is all. I didn't think she had anything of value to hock."

"Are you sure you don't want any dinner?" Mary Lu inquired again, her voice soft and pleading. He examined her closely, certain if he stared hard enough he'd see her lower lip quiver.

"No, thanks."

"Is there anything I can get you?"

"Not a thing," he assured her.

"I mean, I could come back and keep you company, if you want." She blushed again. If Kyle hadn't been stuck behind steel bars, he might have found her attractive. He might even have been tempted to take her up on her offer. Then again, he might not.

"I appreciate that, but no, thanks," Kyle said. He didn't want to be unkind, but all he was looking for was to get out of this cell and leave Wheatland as soon as possible.

The door opened and Carrie stepped inside, carrying a white paper bag. She paused when she saw Mary Lu. The waitress had stood, pressed her face close to the bars, and was gazing longingly at Kyle.

Although there wasn't a thing to feel guilty over, Kyle felt much as he had when his mother found a package of condoms hidden in his underwear drawer. He'd been thirteen, and Lillian, who believed in free love, had been thrilled. Kyle hadn't the heart to tell her he'd been using them for water balloons.

"You want me to come back later?" Carrie asked stiffly, slowing her steps. She did this thing with her eyes that made them incredibly round, as if to say she was impressed that he'd managed to pick up a woman while in a jail cell.

"Don't you dare leave," Kyle snapped, more to hide his guilt than from any real irritation. "Mary Lu was just about to go, isn't that right, Mary Lu?"

"You can give me a call over at Billy Bob's Café if you—"

"Billy Bob's!" Carrie cried, at the same time as Kyle did.

Mary Lu leaped back a step. "Did I say something wrong?"

"No," Kyle assured her gently. They'd frightened the girl out of five years of her life.

Carrie waited until Mary Lu had gone before she

walked over to the table. She lifted the linen napkin and viewed the contents of the meal the apparently love-starved waitress had delivered.

"What'd you find out?" Kyle asked.

"The bailiff won't accept the money until eight o'clock in the morning, so you're stuck here for the night." She pulled back the pink napkin and glanced his way. "Are you going to eat this?"

"Is your stomach the only thing you can think about?" The words came out like bits of chewed-off steel. He was incarcerated and would be for several more hours, and all Carrie was interested in was dinner. *His* dinner, he might add.

She ignored him and wolfed down the biscuit. "I have some other news, but I'm not going to tell you if all you can do is bite my head off. It wasn't me who chose to flagrantly disobey the law."

"I jaywalked." He regained his composure by degrees. For all her talk about him liberating his anger, one would think she'd appreciate the fact he had vented his frustration. Doing time tended to do that to a man, he decided.

By now Carrie had pulled her chair up to the table and had helped herself to his chicken-fried steak. Looking at her, one would think she hadn't eaten in days.

"I thought you had some news," he said, irritated and not bothering to hide it.

"Oh, yeah, I almost forgot," she managed between

bites. She wiped the corner of her mouth with the napkin and set the fork aside long enough to give him the news. "The car will be ready first thing in the morning, and it isn't going to be the least bit expensive. I had Matt put it on my VISA card."

"Matt?"

"Matt's the guy who's putting your car back together. He moved to Wheatland about three years ago and had a rough time of it in the beginning, but the townsfolk have mostly accepted him now."

So she was on a first-name basis with the mechanic. That didn't take long, he noticed. "I understand you came up with the necessary cash to post bail," he said, needing to change the subject. If he didn't know better he'd think he was jealous of this faceless mechanic.

Carrie patted her hip pocket, the very one she'd taken pains to entice him with earlier in the day. "It's right here. You don't have a thing to worry about."

The fear she might lose it or someone might steal it sent a shot of adrenaline rushing through him, but he knew better than to suggest she put it somewhere for safekeeping. The mere idea would insult her, and at the moment she was his only link to the outside world.

Several questions hovered in the back of his mind, but he feared asking them might alienate her. He knew that she'd pawned something, but he hadn't a clue what. Then he noticed her opal ring was missing.

"You pawned your ring," he said softly, astonished that she'd willingly part with something she clearly prized.

"I didn't have any other choice." She stopped eating long enough to answer him and then returned to the steak with gusto. Kyle hadn't a clue how she managed to maintain her small frame. He'd known women twice her size who ate less.

"Mr. Dillon, he's the pawnshop owner, promised on his mother's grave he wouldn't sell that ring. I explained the circumstances and—"

"You told him about me being in jail?" Kyle didn't know why that offended him, but it did. He didn't like the idea of Carrie reduced to pawning her valuables for anyone—including himself, he guessed.

"Oh, no." Carrie was quick to correct his assumption. "I told him about Grammy, and how the ring had been in our family for years and years and handed down to the oldest daughter on her twenty-first birthday."

"I see," Kyle murmured. "I feel bad about all this."

"Oh, don't worry," she said, waving her hand. Then, as if she'd forgotten something important, she added, "I got a hotel room for the night. In case you're interested, that's what took me so long. It seems everyone in town's heard about the two of us and assumes we're hardened criminals."

"Wouldn't you know it? All of a sudden every hotel in town is booked solid," he supplied. "But you found something?"

"Sort of." She paused and stared into space. "You have to understand this isn't the type of place I'd normally choose. It's outside of town."

For the life of him if she told him it was a chicken ranch, Kyle wouldn't be responsible for his actions. He'd always thought of himself as a calm and collected person. Over the years he'd carefully trained himself to conceal his emotions. In the span of a single day that had all changed.

At the moment he felt downright explosive. "How far outside of town?" he asked with forced calm.

Carrie paused, the fork lifted and poised in front of her mouth. "Less than a mile, I'd say. It's a weird-looking place."

"Weird-looking," Kyle echoed, uncertain how to translate that.

"Yes, the first time I saw it, I thought it was the original Bates Motel. It reassured me when I discovered the proprietors are a middle-aged couple whose children have grown and left home. It's a bed-and-breakfast place now."

"I see." Kyle relaxed somewhat. Was he going to get a minute's sleep, worrying about Carrie? Somehow he doubted rest was an option.

"I brought you some dinner," she informed him, standing and handing him the white sack. "I didn't know about sweet Mary Lu." She pressed her clenched hands to her breasts and her shoulders rose with a dramatic sigh.

Kyle chose to ignore her. "I'm not hungry," he announced.

"Trust me, you will be."

"What is it?"

"A club sandwich, potato salad, and two large oatmeal cookies. I had Mrs. Johnson from Bates Motel make it up for you."

Kyle peeked inside the sack and reached for the sandwich. Maybe he could eat something, after all.

"Where's Sheriff Collins?"

"Probably home watching television," Kyle muttered as he peeled the cellophane wrap away from the sandwich. It astonished him how loosely run the jail was. If he was intent on breaking out, he'd wager all he'd need do was ask Carrie to search through a few drawers for an extra set of keys.

"I suppose I'd better get back to the Johnsons' place," Carrie said.

Kyle wasn't keen on having her leave, but he couldn't think of an excuse for her to stay. He never thought he'd feel that way about Carrie Jamison. Usually a fifteen-minute dose of the deejay was enough to last him for weeks. All at once he was frantically searching for something that would keep her with him. Kyle would like to believe this was due to his incarceration, but he doubted it.

She was almost to the door when he stopped her. "Carrie."

Eagerly she whirled around, as if she too were reluctant to part. "Yes?"

"Thank you."

"For what?"

He wasn't sure where to start. His indebtedness was multiple. "For everything, but mostly for pawning your ring on my behalf."

"No problem."

"I'm sorry it came to that. I'll get you the money the instant we get our traveler's checks replaced."

A slow, easy smile spread across her features, lighting up her eyes in such a way that seemed to reach across the room and touch him.

"You owe me big-time for that, fella." She blew him a kiss and was gone before she could see him catch it in his right hand and hold on to this imaginary part of her with a tight fist for several moments.

A deputy arrived shortly afterward with an older man who'd obviously been arrested for being drunk in public. At least the man was a happy drunk, who insisted on singing something about Tom Dooley and hanging down his head.

The officer placed the guy in the cell next to Kyle. The drunk waved to Kyle and fell onto the bunk. "Howdy."

"Hello," Kyle responded cautiously.

"I'm drunk."

"I noticed."

"You be quiet and sleep it off, Carl," the deputy instructed.

"You be quiet," Carl shouted, and thinking himself inordinately clever, he laughed.

"What'd they get you for, buddy?" Carl asked, sitting up long enough to pose the question and then promptly falling back onto the cot.

"Jaywalking," Kyle admitted sheepishly.

Carl let loose with a loud screech and leaped off the bed. He hurried to the cell door and gripped the bars. "I ain't stayin' in a cell next to a jaywalker! What kind of place is Sheriff Collins running here?"

"Shut up and go to sleep, Carl," the deputy advised again, sounding bored.

"I ain't safe. You put me next to a . . . a jaywalker."

"You know what a jaywalker is, Carl?" the deputy asked with infinite patience.

"You think I'm dumb? Of course I know. He walked all over those pretty blue birds. You put me in jail next to a bird killer. I don't have to take this." He braced his hands against the bars and rattled them with the full force of his strength. "I want out of here."

Kyle lay down on the lumpy cot and tucked his hands beneath his head. "My sentiments exactly," he muttered.

5

"*We're asking that you* contact the Secret Service if you run into Max Sanders a second time," Richards instructed them as Sheriff Collins unlocked the jail door. With a dignified gait, Kyle stepped out of the cell.

Personally, Carrie would welcome the opportunity to tangle with that scoundrel Sanders just so she could tell him what she thought of him. The man had caused her and Kyle nothing but grief.

Kyle accepted a business card from Richards and studied the phone number as if he intended to memorize it then and there. "Is that what this is all about?" he asked quietly.

Carrie wasn't deceived by his docile manner. Kyle was furious, and doing a marvelous job of restraining his irritation. But just barely. She'd seen him in this mood before, and if Richards knew what was good for him, he'd tread lightly.

First thing that morning, Carrie had gone over to the mechanic's and picked up the BMW. She'd guessed correctly that Kyle would be eager to be on his way.

The minute Kyle tucked Richards's card in his wallet, he strode purposefully toward the door. Carrie noted that he made no promises one way or the other to contact the Secret Service. Nor did he wait for her. Instead he left her to traipse obediently after him.

She scurried toward the door, then paused and turned defiantly back to the sheriff and the government agent.

"I think you should know I intend to write my United States congressman over the way we've been treated."

"Yes, ma'am," Richards murmured, but he didn't reveal the least bit of concern over her threat.

"I will, you know." She waved her index finger at them as positive proof. "Mark my words, this is no idle threat."

Kyle was in his BMW and had started the engine by the time she slipped into the seat next to him.

"You want to head back to the interstate?" she

asked, clicking her seat belt into place, certain he cursed the day he'd followed her recommendation to travel off the main road.

"No," he answered shortly, not bothering to explain his reasons. In one word he made it clear he wasn't in the mood to talk.

So this was the way it was to be. Carrie realized that Kyle intended to give her the silent treatment. That was dandy with her. She'd spent a miserable night sleeping in Mrs. Johnson's cotton robe. The woman had insisted on washing Carrie's clothes so she had something clean to wear in the morning. She would have picked up a few things for herself if she hadn't been so involved in getting Kyle out of the slammer. Now it would have to wait.

They traveled for half an hour without a word passing between them, but it wasn't a companionable silence. Carrie wanted to talk, but it was plain Kyle didn't.

Sometime later, he finally spoke. "The delay in Wheatland shouldn't cause much of a problem. We can stay overnight in Paris and still be in Dallas early tomorrow."

"Perfect," she said agreeably. She wasn't planning to meet Tom Atkins until the evening cocktail party, and that was her only concern. How she would miss the beautiful red-sequined dress! But she'd have time to visit her sister, who lived near Dallas, and Cathie could lend her something.

"Perfect," he repeated after her. She noticed how he purposely relaxed his fingers. Until then he'd gripped the steering wheel as though he were driving the Indy Five Hundred.

"How was your night?" she asked, making polite conversation.

"Miserable. Do you mind if we don't talk about it?"

"All right."

"How about you?" he asked.

Carrie opened her mouth to speak, but before she could utter a word, Kyle's radar detector started beeping loudly.

Kyle immediately removed his foot from the gas pedal to decrease their speed, but it was too late. The blinking red-and-blue light of a state patrol car was flashing in the rearview mirror.

Kyle mumbled something unrepeatable under his breath, pulled over to the side of the road, and stopped the car. "I wonder if I can manage to stay out of jail this time," he muttered.

Carrie squeezed his arm reassuringly. Kyle was as stiff as a three-day-old corpse.

The patrolman climbed out of his car and stepped up to the BMW. With a casual air, Kyle rolled down his window.

"Hello, officer." His tone was cheerful, albeit strained.

"Hello. May I see your driver's license and the car

registration, please." The officer was brisk and businesslike.

"Was I speeding?" Kyle asked. Carrie knew full well that he had been.

The officer was intent on reading over Kyle's license and didn't respond to his question. "I see you folks are from Kansas City."

"That's right."

Again Carrie left the talking to Kyle. The less she opened her mouth, the better. At least that was the way Kyle would view it.

"You two been married long?"

Kyle exchanged glances with Carrie. "We're not married," he told the officer, whose name tag identified him as Andrew Lindsey.

"Take my advice and don't do it."

"Do it?" Kyle repeated.

"Get married."

"You don't need to worry," Carrie said, leaning toward Kyle to get a better look at the patrolman. "We don't even like each other. We just work together. For one reason or another, we've never quite hit it off."

"I don't think the officer is interested in listening to our differences," Kyle said pointedly.

"Oh-oh." Andrew Lindsey opened the door and slipped onto the back seat. He removed his hat and rubbed a hand over his eyes. "That's the way it started with Gayle and me too. She was a secretary at the station, and the two of us couldn't see eye to eye on anything. The next thing I know, we're married."

"Married." Kyle laughed. "Trust me, officer, I'd rather eat skunk meat than marry this woman."

Carrie shot him a hot look, her temper rising. He didn't have to be so insulting. "I'd rather leap off a tall building than spend the rest of my life with this man!" she retaliated heatedly.

"You don't need to worry, it isn't going to happen."

"You're darn right it isn't going to happen. I'd be crazy to marry anyone like you."

"No more crazy than I'd be to marry you!"

"She left me, you know," Patrolman Lindsey said, his shoulders sagging. Carrie guessed he hadn't heard a word of their heated exchange.

"I'm sorry," she offered sympathetically, twisting around in order to see the other man. "When did all this happen?"

Kyle muttered something under his breath that she couldn't hear. Apparently he wasn't keen on her feeding this conversation.

"Last week," Lindsey answered. "It was totally unexpected. I left for work and couldn't see that anything was wrong and returned to find a note. If she was going to leave me, you'd think she'd take the kids with her."

"You have children?"

"Five."

"Five!" Carrie and Kyle responded together.

"The two oldest are in school. It's a good thing her mother lives with us, or I wouldn't know what to do with the three younger ones."

Carrie's eyes locked with Kyle's. "Her mother lives with you?" Kyle asked.

"Yeah. Gayle left me with the kids and her mother and a letter that claimed she needed to find herself. All she had to do was look in the laundry room. Everything else is in there."

"Oh, my," Carrie murmured.

"I haven't heard a word from her since. For all I know, she's off praying with some guru who wears flip-flops and eats sushi."

"She'll be back," Carrie said, letting optimism flow through her words.

"That's what I thought at first too," he mumbled. "Now I'm not so sure."

"Do you miss her?" Carrie could feel Kyle's eyes boring into her. It went without saying that he wanted her to terminate the conversation, instead of encouraging the other man to talk about his problems.

This was the real difference between her and Kyle, Carrie decided. He held everything inside until the weight of hauling all his emotions around bogged him down. She, on the other hand, freely spoke her mind. Of the two, Carrie considered herself by far the healthier one, emotionally.

"The real problem is we got along in bed better than anyplace else," the patrolman continued. "We'd argue all day and make love all night. We never could seem to find a middle ground."

"That's unfortunate," Kyle said impatiently.

Apparently his tone was enough to snap Officer Lindsey out of his depressed reverie. He looked up and seemed surprised to find himself in the back seat of Kyle's vehicle. He reached for his pad and pen and climbed out of the car.

After making a couple of notations, he peeled off a sheet. When he spoke his voice was filled with authority. "According to the radar reading, you were traveling seventy-two miles an hour in a fifty-five-mile-an-hour zone."

"Seventy-two?" Kyle sounded appropriately shocked.

"I've written out a warning," he said, handing Kyle the pad to sign and then removing the sheet of paper. "I'd advise you to observe the speed limit."

"And not to marry," Carrie threw in for good measure. "I'll make sure that doesn't happen, officer."

He left them with a weak, embarrassed smile.

Kyle and Carrie sat motionless until Officer Lindsey had started his patrol car and driven away. Then, all at once, the tension was gone and Carrie started to laugh. Kyle glared at her disapprovingly.

"I'm sorry," she said, unable to stop. She swiped at her eyes. "His wife left him with five kids and her mother, and he thinks she should look to find herself in the laundry room!"

Kyle chuckled too. "Then he advises us not to marry."

"Us!" she repeated, and they both doubled over. The idea of the two of them exchanging vows was ludicrous. They didn't even like each other. They laughed, stopped and looked at each other, and started to laugh once more.

Carrie suddenly realized that she was leaning companionably against Kyle, and his arm had found its way around her shoulders. Embarrassed, she righted herself and made a show of looking at her watch. "My, my," she said. "Time sure does pass when you're having fun."

"Fun," he repeated, quickly retrieving his wayward arm.

"Yeah," she said brightly.

Seeming anxious to be on his way, Kyle started the car and pulled onto the highway. Neither spoke, and Carrie found herself nervously picking at the threads of her skirt. When she saw Kyle's gaze move to her hands, she stopped.

Pulling out the map, she studied the route and mentally calculated how much longer they'd be stuck together in the close confines of the car. The space seemed to be evaporating, closing in on her, growing narrower with each mile they traveled.

Carrie found herself becoming aware of Kyle in ways that were completely foreign to her. Until now she hadn't noticed how broad his shoulders were or how deep his chest was. His eyelashes were incredibly thick, the ends golden. He found her studying him, and she instantly returned to picking at her denim skirt.

"You need a break?" he asked, as they neared the outskirts of yet another small town.

"No, thanks," she said, in a voice tight enough to cause him to glance her way.

"Is everything all right?" he asked.

"It's fine. I guess I'm a little tired is all."

She was tired? Between the drunk singing all night in the cell next to his and the deputy who listened to talk radio, he hadn't gotten more than a couple of hours' rest himself.

Kyle had never been comfortable defining emotions. He'd often envied women their ability to translate feeling into words. He sure didn't know what to say now.

"Do you know anything about the town of Paris?" he asked, as the silence started to concern him. If Carrie wasn't talking she was thinking, and a thinking woman was dangerous.

"Just what it says on the map," she said, reaching for the folded sheet. "Population twenty-five thousand. Big enough for the folks who issue traveler's checks to

arrange for us to pick up new ones. We should be able
to do a bit of shopping there as well."

"Great." Kyle was more than ready for a fresh set
of clothes.

"What time do you think we'll arrive?"

"Another hour or two," he said, guessing.

Actually he wasn't that far off. They arrived in the
farming community of Paris at two-thirty that afternoon. The sign outside of town boasted that Paris
had the only stoplight in Lamar County, which gave
them both reason to smile.

The main street resembled that of many of the other
communities they'd passed through: angle parking
with a narrow island that ran the length of the street.
Kyle pulled into a slot in front of the bank.

It didn't take long for them to pick up their replacement traveler's checks.

"We'd better see about getting hotel rooms," he
suggested next.

"Rooms already?" Carrie asked, blinking back her
surprise.

"I suppose you're hungry."

"As a matter of fact, I am. In case you hadn't noticed, we haven't eaten today." It went without saying that there was a very good reason. They'd had no
cash and just enough gas to make it from Wheatland
to Paris.

Now that she mentioned it, Kyle realized he was

famished himself. "All right," he said. "Let's get something to eat first."

They found a café and were coaxed inside by the delicious smells coming from the kitchen. To his surprise, the place was empty. This was exactly the kind of spot where town folks gathered for chitchat and to exchange gossip about their neighbors.

"Where is everyone?" Carrie asked.

"You folks sit anyplace you like." A waitress wearing a badge that said TRIXIE greeted them, seated them, and brought them ice water and plastic-coated menus. She was near thirty, Kyle guessed, and not bad-looking.

"I take it you two aren't from around these parts?"

"Kansas City," Kyle explained.

"You ever heard of Bubba 'Oink' Corners?"

"Can't say I have," Kyle admitted.

"Well, he's in town and most everyone's out at the Grange listening to him."

Bubba must be some country-western singer, Kyle thought.

"I'd be there myself, but I couldn't find anyone to work my shift for me." Trixie reached for the pencil that was positioned behind her ear. "The special today is stuffed pork chops, pork chow mein—or piggies in a blanket if you're in the mood for breakfast. We serve it twenty-four hours a day."

"I'll have a chef's salad," Carrie said, handing the waitress the menu.

"That sounds good," Kyle said.

Trixie stepped away from the table, writing as she moved toward the kitchen. Kyle's gaze followed her, not because she was particularly sexy-looking. He didn't know why he was watching her except it was better than admitting how pretty Carrie was with her mussed-up hair and pouty lips. He wasn't even aware of what he was doing until his gaze returned to Carrie. She gave him a look that would have grilled cheese.

"What?" he asked innocently.

"Nothing," she snapped, and proceeded to shred her paper napkin into even strips. Kyle had the distinct feeling she wanted to rake her nails across his face.

"Obviously something's troubling you," he said, hoping to sound calm and reasonable, knowing he didn't. Two days with her and the talent for remaining calm and cool he'd developed over his thirty years was gone.

"I said it was nothing," she said stiffly.

"Fine." He stood and walked over to the cash register, where someone had left a newspaper. He picked it up and carried it back to their booth. The minute he buried his face behind it, Carrie stuck her arm out and lowered the paper just enough for their eyes to meet.

"Do you always look at women like that?"

"Like what?"

"Like . . . like you're picturing them without their clothes on."

"Don't be ridiculous." If his mind's eye was entertaining any such sight, it was of Carrie, not some waitress.

He folded the paper and set it next to the silverware. "Are you jealous?"

Carrie rolled her eyes. "Hardly. It's just that I'd never noticed what a . . ." Apparently she couldn't think of a word adequate to describe him. "I just never thought you were that kind of man."

"What kind of man?" he asked loudly.

Trixie, who was standing at the counter with her back to them, turned around and stared. Carrie pressed her hands against the edge of the table and whispered heatedly, "The kind of man who mentally undresses women!"

Kyle wasn't sure if he was angry or amused. He leaned forward and whispered too. "You know, I was just beginning to think you might not be so bad after all, that there was some hope of salvaging a working relationship, but now I see I was dead wrong. Nothing's changed."

Carrie was silent after that, but he was fairly certain it wasn't because she didn't have anything to say.

Trixie delivered their salads and Kyle gave his attention to eating and reading the newspaper, although he feared his retention level was almost zero.

A couple of times he glanced Carrie's way and found her with her elbow on the tabletop and her head leaning against her hand, as if she were having trouble staying awake. She resembled a lost kitten.

Kyle immediately felt guilty. He struggled with that for several moments and decided she probably hadn't gotten any more sleep than he had and was just as cranky.

He set the paper aside. "I shouldn't have snapped at you," he said.

She turned to look at him, as if she suspected she hadn't heard him correctly. "I shouldn't have suggested anything so stupid. Even if you were looking at the waitress *that way,* it was none of my business."

"I wasn't," he said, wanting to be honest. "If anything, I was trying to not look at you."

"Why?"

"Because . . ." He'd walked into that one with both feet, and now that he was knee deep in cement there was only one way out: the truth. "Because if I didn't look at her I would look at you, and I didn't want to own up to how attractive you are."

She blinked twice as if she were struck dumb.

Kyle felt he needed to qualify his response. "You see, we've been at odds for so long that I've only viewed you one way." In all the time they'd worked together he had missed what an attractive woman she was.

"I know what you mean," she said sheepishly.

"You were pretty much one-dimensional to me as well."

"Friends?" he asked.

She smiled. He'd never seen a woman's eyes light up the way hers did. "Friends," she agreed.

They finished their salads and shared the tab.

"You ready to scout out a hotel now?" he asked.

Once more she shook her head. "I'm so tired, the minute I lie down I'll never find the energy to get up again. I'd rather do what shopping I need to do and then find a hotel room."

That she made sense was something of a novelty. Furthermore he agreed with her. "Okay, let's meet back here in an hour," he suggested, studying his watch. He didn't plan on taking that long himself, but he assumed she'd require more time than he did. "Is that all right with you?"

"It's fine," she assured him.

"As soon as I'm finished, I'll find a hotel and book us two rooms."

"That's a wonderful idea," she said.

They separated. Carrie headed in one direction and Kyle in another. It took him all of fifteen minutes to purchase what he needed for the weekend. From the men's store, he promptly scouted out the hotels.

He was late meeting Carrie by ten minutes, but that couldn't be helped.

"Did you get the hotel rooms?" she asked.

Kyle wasn't sure what they were going to do. "I found out what the Oink in Bubba's name means," he said, ignoring the question.

"I beg your pardon?"

"Remember Trixie telling us everyone had gone to listen to Bubba?"

"Yes," she said impatiently.

"Bubba's a hog caller. We've walked into the world championship hog-calling contest."

Carrie stared back at him blankly. "Are you leading up to something?"

"Yes," he muttered. "And you aren't going to like it."

"Kyle, please, I didn't get a wink of sleep all last night, and frankly I'm too tired to play games. Just tell me what's wrong."

"Every hotel in town is booked solid."

"Every room?"

"No," he said. "There's one room left. If we decide to stay in Paris, we're going to have to share a room and a bed."

6

"*I swear if you breathe* a word of this to anyone back at the station, I'll make your life miserable," Carrie said as she ripped the bedspread off the corner of the bed with enough energy to send the pillow flying halfway across the room.

"You mean more miserable than you already do?" Kyle asked her calmly.

She braced her hands against her hips, a smile quivering on her lips, and leveled her gaze meaningfully in his direction. "Exactly."

He retrieved her pillow for her and set it back on

the mattress. "In case you were unaware of it, I don't like this arrangement any more than you do."

She glared at him.

"If it'll make you sleep easier, I give you my word as a gentleman that I won't touch you."

Carrie was convinced he was telling her the truth, but she wasn't taking any chances.

His sigh was filled with righteous patience. "If you're so worried about it, I'll sleep on the floor," he said without emotion, although it was clear her lack of response had offended him.

Bunking down on the carpet had been his first suggestion and Carrie had rejected it, claiming, in a moment of generosity, that they were both adults and didn't need to do anything so drastic.

"Do you or do you not want me to sleep on the floor?" he asked.

Carrie stared down at the worn beige carpet. It looked cold and hard. He'd spent the previous night in a jail cell and must be as bone weary as she was.

"No," she answered finally, on the tail end of a yawn, "but please stay on your side."

"Trust me, you don't have anything to worry about," he muttered. "Just you promise *me* one thing."

"Yes?"

"That you won't touch me." He chuckled, but Carrie found little humor in his attempt at sarcasm.

She reached for the sack that contained a pair of shortie pajamas and her heart sank as she thought about her other purchases. Her shopping expedition hadn't gone nearly as well as she would have liked.

"Would you mind if I use the bathroom first?" she asked.

"Go ahead."

After a long soak in a hot bath, Carrie felt worlds better. Regretting the way she had complained about the one room and the lone bed, she figured she owed Kyle an apology. But when she came back into the room, she discovered he was sound asleep, so close to the edge of the mattress that he was in danger of tumbling off.

Smiling softly to herself, Carrie turned off the lamp on the bed stand and peeled back the covers. The bed was king-size, big enough for a family of five. There really wasn't anything to worry about. She regretted having made such a fuss.

She slipped between the cool sheets, pounded the pillow a couple of times to mold it to her liking, and then slowly, gratefully, closed her eyes.

Carrie was sleeping so deeply that the sound of running water filtered into her subconscious. She found herself staring at the moving surface of a pond. Beams of moonlight radiated off the black water and small waves rippled from the middle, slowly making their way toward the sandy beach.

On closer inspection she realized someone was swimming. She strained to see into the dark night, and after a moment she recognized Kyle.

Suddenly, without warning, he turned and held one hand invitingly toward her. Her first reaction was to hide behind a flowering bush, but he laughed, the sound of his mirth coming on the misty arms of welcome.

He called to her then, his voice almost lyrical. Still Carrie resisted. The urge to join him grew stronger. He was bare-chested, and for the first time she realized what a powerful man he was. His torso was strong and hard without the heavy muscles of a body builder. A thatch of curly dark hairs covered his chest and narrowed to a sleek line down the center of his abdomen.

The reasons why Carrie should ignore his invitation grew weaker and more flimsy as she listened to his coaxing.

Without conscious decision, she stepped out from behind the bush and walked toward the pond. To her delight it was as warm as bathwater. As she moved boldly toward Kyle, he stepped toward her. They met waist deep in the water, neither speaking, neither touching.

She looked up at him and saw his eyes were dark and intense. She smiled.

He placed his arm around her waist and drew her closer, as if he had every right to claim her as his own. She looped her arms around his neck, threw back her head, and . . .

Carrie bolted upright in bed, breathing heavily,

clenching the sheet to her breasts. Only then did she realize it had all been a dream.

Kyle stood just inside the bathroom door, a towel wrapped around his waist. He would have looked mouthwateringly sexy if his face hadn't been covered with thick shaving cream. Even at that, she took a moment to appreciate what should have been apparent to her all these months. Kyle was one hell of a man.

"Sorry," he muttered. "I dropped the can. I didn't mean to wake you."

"No problem," she murmured. The sound of water, she realized, had been from the shower. She laid her head back down on the pillow, flooded with a deep sense of disappointment.

Several minutes later, Kyle finished whatever he was doing and turned off the bathroom light. He appeared to believe she'd gone back to sleep and made every effort to be as quiet as possible. He was having some trouble making his way in the dark and must have stubbed his toe, because she heard a dull noise followed by a muted curse.

Sitting up, she reached for the lamp switch. Soft light illuminated the room. "Are you all right?" she asked, rising up on one elbow.

"I'm fine," he muttered, hopping toward the bed. "I didn't need that toenail for anything important anyway."

"Turning on a light isn't a sign of weakness, you

know," she said, exasperated not so much by him but by men in general and their ever-present need to appear macho.

"I didn't want to wake you," he said tightly. "It didn't have anything to do with weakness. I was being considerate."

"You'd already awakened me."

"I thought you might have gone back to sleep."

"I hadn't."

"Obviously." He pulled back the sheets and climbed into the bed, making certain he remained as far away from her as humanly possible. A couple of seconds later, he rolled onto his side, then a minute later onto his back.

"You settled now?" she asked.

"Yes."

She turned off the lamp, and the room returned to instant night. Not so much as a glimmer of moonlight showed through the heavy drapes.

"How long have you been up?" she asked into the silence.

"An hour or so. I fell asleep waiting for you to get out of the bathroom, then woke and knew I'd never get back to sleep until I'd showered and shaved."

"I shouldn't have hogged the tub for so long." She did feel bad about that. She'd been thoughtless and inconsiderate.

"Don't worry about it. I was asleep in five minutes flat."

The scent of his aftershave drifted toward her, and she found herself drawing in deep breaths of the pungent scent of rum and spice. He smelled of a Caribbean island, of sunshine and sandy beaches. As he had in her dream. She could feel the heat of his body.

"In all the confusion about the room, I didn't tell you what happened when I went shopping," she said, forcing herself to think of something other than the man next to her.

"Something happened while you were shopping?"

"Sort of. In light of the fact that I technically don't have a job when we return, I didn't feel I should be running up my credit cards."

"I know what you mean."

"The saleslady was very helpful. They had several items marked down to a rock-bottom price. According to her, a convent outside of town closed last year. The nuns used to order their shoes and such through the store, so there were several items in my size at a good price, especially the shoes."

"What exactly did you buy?"

"Nun shoes and a long black skirt. No one will know that a rosary's supposed to be strung along the waist—at least that's what the sales clerk claimed."

"Nun shoes?"

"They're heavy black things, but don't worry; no one will be able to see them under my skirt. I really didn't need shoes, but I couldn't resist them at that price."

Kyle chuckled, but it was obvious he'd struggled to hold it and failed.

"The blouse isn't so bad, although it buttons all the way up to my nose." She was the one who laughed this time.

The sound of her mirth drifted into silence.

"I don't think it's a good idea for you to laugh," he whispered.

"Why?"

"Because I get this uncontrollable urge . . ."

He rolled onto his stomach and raised his head. Their eyes met and held.

"Carrie?" His voice was low and rough.

When she didn't answer, he tucked his finger beneath her chin and elevated her face until it was level with his own. Then slowly, as if waiting for her to stop him, he lowered his mouth to hers. Their lips met tentatively, experimentally. His were warm and moist as they settled over hers.

The kiss was gentle and sweet, and Carrie trembled in its aftermath. All at once she felt terribly confused. This couldn't be happening. Not between her and Kyle Harris.

Nor should her heart be reacting this strange way. She eased away from him and discovered how cold and lonely it was outside his embrace. She wanted back, and with sweet abandon she leaned into his strength.

When his mouth claimed hers a second time, all

gentleness was put aside. It was as though he were a starving man and she a Thanksgiving dinner. Carrie felt herself responding as if she'd been held and kissed by him countless times, as if they were longtime lovers, intimately aware of every nuance of each other.

Carrie knew she should put an end to this. Yet, even knowing this was a mistake, something that would later embarrass them both, she couldn't make herself stop.

Kyle's hands framed her face and he whispered something about heaven, but she had the distinct impression he wasn't praying. His mouth sought hers once more, his kiss incredibly tender. Their lips clung as Carrie reluctantly eased away.

She discovered she was breathless, with little wonder. She couldn't very well claim she hadn't been kissed before, but she'd never experienced the powerful impact she did when Kyle kissed her. Her forehead was against his, and she kept her eyes closed, fearing what she'd discover if she opened them.

Kyle's hold on her tightened briefly, as if he wasn't yet able to release her. She didn't want to leave him either, and she buried her face in his shoulder. Not until then did she notice how harsh his own breathing was. It helped to know he was experiencing some of the same feelings.

"Those aren't exactly nun pajamas," he murmured breathlessly, as if in excuse.

"No."

"How about we try to get some sleep?"

Kyle envied Carrie her ability to fall asleep. He was having trouble himself, and not because he wasn't tired. Carrie lay on her side, her back to him. She shifted her weight, and her body grazed his thigh. He meant to move away, yet he couldn't make himself break this contact with her.

Rolling onto his side, he scooted next to Carrie, fitting his knees behind hers and resting his hand on the gentle curve of her hip. They fit comfortably together. It was as if he'd arrived home after a long trouble-filled journey. Closing his eyes, he felt his body relax as he drifted off to sleep, a smile on his lips.

The following morning, the first thing Kyle realized gratefully was that he was back on his side of the mattress.

If everything went according to schedule, they should arrive in Dallas in plenty of time for the cocktail party that evening. Although Carrie had complained her new clothes came straight from a convent, Kyle had no objection to her dressing like a nun. He'd prefer it if other men assumed she was broadcasting for one of the religious networks. He was far more comfortable having her wear a habit to the party than those shortie pajamas of hers. Those things would tempt a monk.

"Good morning," Carrie whispered.

"Morning. You ready to hit the road?" He couldn't think of anything better to say.

The words were followed by a short silence. "Not quite. I just woke up."

"I'll get dressed and get us some coffee," he suggested. "Want some?"

"Please."

He waited until her head was turned before climbing out of bed and quickly dressing. By the time he returned with the coffee, she was dressed and moving around the room. He noticed that her eyes didn't quite meet his when he handed her the steaming cup.

"I should be ready to leave in just a few minutes," she told him softly.

"Take your time."

She shot him a look as if she wasn't sure she'd heard him correctly, which wasn't unreasonable since he'd been keen to be on the road as quickly as possible.

It took her less than ten minutes to collect her things. Kyle turned in their keys at the front office, and without another delay they were off.

Not until they'd left town did he think about breakfast. "You hungry?" he asked, hoping she wasn't.

"No, thanks."

"Okay, then our next stop is Dallas." That should get a rise out of her, and it did.

"You're joking, right?"

He glanced her way and grinned. "Destination Dallas, with a stop or two along the way."

"That's more like it," she said, smiling.

There should be a way to package that smile of hers, Kyle mused. Funny, he'd never realized how appealing it was before, but then he regretfully acknowledged there hadn't been much chance to get to see it. Not with them snapping at each other at every opportunity.

He glanced over at her and noticed she was picking at her nails. She only did that when she was uptight about something. He didn't need a crystal ball to figure out what it was.

"I guess we should probably talk about what happened last night." He wasn't getting any awards for diplomacy. He just wished he knew what she was thinking.

"Last night?"

"I don't think we need to make a federal case over a kiss," he commented, then glanced in her direction. "Do you?"

"No, of course we don't. As you said, it was just a kiss."

"Right." He seemed satisfied, but Carrie was unwilling to drop the subject.

"It's understandable, really."

"How's that?" Kyle wanted to know.

"You have to admit we've been through a good

deal of emotional trauma in the last forty-eight hours."

"Exactly." He appeared to be in full enthusiastic agreement.

"It isn't every day you meet up with an escaped felon and get held at gunpoint, kidnapped, and then subjected to an interrogation by the Secret Service."

"Or spend the night in jail," he added.

She sighed and gestured feebly with her hands. "So it all makes a crazy kind of sense that you and I . . . that the two of us, being thrown together this way, would . . . bond in ways we hadn't previously."

"You're absolutely right," he said, and nodded once for emphasis.

"So we should ignore something as trivial as a kiss?" She made it a question because despite every excuse she'd offered, Carrie wasn't sure what to think herself. Kyle's kiss had meant something, only she wasn't sure what.

"Ignoring it seems the best option," he said. "It isn't likely to happen again."

So she was right. Kyle wanted to dismiss it, pretend it didn't happen, disregard the sensual explosion. If that was the case, she could say nothing more.

Carrie swallowed her disappointment. "It'll never happen again," she assured him.

"Right."

Kyle blamed himself for this mess. He should have known they were headed for trouble the moment he learned there was only one hotel room available. His hands tightened around the steering wheel and he slowly released his breath, wondering what he was going to do.

"Kyle."

"Yes," he answered anxiously.

"I think we should have turned, back there."

"Back where?"

"That Y in the road. According to the map, we should have gone right."

He sighed. "I didn't see any Y in the road."

"You didn't?" She carefully read over the map, then shook her head. "I think we're going the wrong way." Her words cut into the strained silence.

"We're fine."

"Look at the map yourself if you don't believe me," she suggested calmly.

Kyle was rip-roaring mad and so uncomfortable with the emotion that it was all he could do to keep the tires on the road. "We're going the right way," he insisted.

"Time will tell, won't it?" she said, with the heavy sigh of a martyr.

Time, as it turned out, was on her side. An hour later, Kyle was forced to admit they were hopelessly lost.

7

"*Why don't we ask* someone for directions?" Carrie suggested.

"Forget it," Kyle said stiffly. "I know exactly where we are."

Carrie clenched her teeth to keep from commenting. This was another one of those macho he-man things like fumbling around in the dark and risking injury rather than admitting he needed the light to find his way back to bed.

"Haven't we seen that barn before?" she asked, hoping none of the sarcasm she was feeling showed. Not that Kyle was in any danger of losing his temper.

The man didn't allow himself the luxury of being angry—unless, of course, it could be directed at her.

"No," he said shortly. "That's a different barn from the one we saw before."

"No, it isn't." It was the very one they'd passed no less than five times in the last hour. Carrie would stake her life on it. They'd been circling the area for so long she was dizzy. Getting Kyle to admit the truth would be difficult, cursed as he was with male pride.

"At the risk of flirting with danger," she said with a saccharine smile, "I'd like to suggest that it just might possibly be the same barn. If you'll notice there's a tractor parked out front, suggesting a farmhouse nearby. I was thinking—"

"I know exactly where we are," Kyle insisted heatedly.

"So do I! We're lost somewhere in the great state of Texas, and precisely where we are will be placed on our tombstones once we're found and buried."

"Might I suggest you're overreacting?"

"No, you may not. Just this once appease me. Please, Kyle, just stop and ask directions."

"Carrie," he said with a long-suffering glance in her direction, "in case you hadn't noticed, there isn't exactly a streetful of people to ask."

"We've driven past a dozen farms."

"I'll look like an idiot," he muttered.

"Do you think you'll be less of a man if you don't figure this out on your own?" she inquired.

He didn't answer, but she nearly cheered when he turned down a long dirt road. Soon a two-story house, freshly painted and gleaming white against the sun, showed in the distance. Civilization at last. She felt as if she'd been wandering for forty years in the wilderness.

No sooner had they pulled into the yard than a young woman with two small children stepped onto the porch. She wore jeans and a thin cotton top and held a squirming toddler on her hip. A second towheaded youngster, who could be no more than five, stood at her side.

Kyle turned off the engine and climbed out of the car, standing inside the open door. Carrie did too, surprised at the wave of heat that hit her full force in the face.

"Hello," the woman said, shielding her eyes against the glare of the sun. "Is there something I can do for you?"

"Can you direct me toward Paris?" Kyle asked. He must have assumed he'd find the road if he could retrace his steps.

"Oh, sure, no problem," she said and set the toddler down next to his brother. "You take a left out of the driveway and go down the road a mile or so until you come to a red mailbox with the name Wilson written in large white letters."

"A red mailbox," Kyle repeated.

"That's right, but pay attention, because just a

little way past the mailbox is a road that goes off to the left."

"Is that north or south?" Kyle wanted to know.

"I can't rightly say."

"Go on," Carrie urged, "we'll find it."

"Don't worry, the road's clearly marked. You couldn't miss it if you tried."

"I wouldn't bet on that," Kyle whispered.

"It's the one that's barred and says ROAD CLOSED UNTIL FURTHER NOTICE. Take a left onto it and—"

"But the sign says the road's closed," Kyle objected.

The woman made a weak motion with her hand. "It's been that way all spring. The county'll get around to repairing it within the next couple of months. You really don't have anything to worry about other than one little hole."

"Hole?" Kyle asked, and Carrie noticed that he placed his hand on his car as if the action would protect his already battered and abused vehicle.

"The road was washed out several months ago, but it isn't really that bad. The bad spot's a mile or so down from the ROAD CLOSED sign. Just be careful driving around it and you won't have a problem. From there on, it's smooth sailing to Paris."

As she finished speaking, Carrie noticed a thick plume of dust racing toward one of the outbuildings.

"That'll be my husband, Joe," the woman said.

"He'll probably be able to guide you better than me. That is if you don't mind waiting."

"We don't mind," Kyle said, and looked to Carrie. "A woman doesn't know how to give directions," he murmured under his breath.

"What do you mean?" Carrie said, ready to defend womankind. "We give directions as good as any man."

"Let's not argue about it, all right?" Kyle said, his voice and words strained.

"Fine, we won't argue, just tell me what you mean."

"All right," he said shortly. "Women can't tell east from west, so you use these ridiculous ways of getting from one place to another."

"Ridiculous means? What exactly are you talking about?"

"If you must know, a woman gives instructions to take a right at the beauty parlor on Main Street, and a man will tell you to head east."

"It's the same thing, isn't it?"

"No, it isn't," Kyle argued. "Men don't notice things like beauty parlors or red mailboxes."

"Sure, every man is a regular Meriwether Lewis, right? Unfortunately, we need to be in Dallas by nightfall. We don't have time to wait for you to direct us by the stars."

A muscle jerked in Kyle's jaw and his eyes narrowed as he studied her. "You're impossible."

"Me?" She moved away from the car and slammed the door shut. Kyle slammed his door too, and the pair glared at each other until another car door closed in the distance.

Kyle waited until the farmer was walking toward them before he broke eye contact. The man was middle-aged, Carrie guessed. He wore jeans, a shirt, and a hat to shield his eyes from the bright glare of the sun.

"I'm Kyle Harris," Kyle said, extending his hand, "and this is Carrie Jamison. We're in need of a few directions."

"Joe Brighton." The farmer removed his gloves to shake hands with Kyle. He touched the brim of his hat and nodded in Carrie's direction. "Come inside, out of the sun," he suggested.

Kyle hesitated. "We don't want to impose."

"No problem," Joe said, taking the porch steps two at a time. "This here's Adam," he said, reaching for his younger son. "And the beautiful woman's my wife, Kate." He kissed his wife on the cheek. The older boy let out a cry of protest, and his father grabbed him by the waist and tucked him against his side. "Seth's the one who's kicking and laughing." With that Joe led them into a large family kitchen.

"Glad to meet you, Kate," Carrie said, smiling at Joe's antics with his two young sons. The irritation she'd experienced moments earlier with Kyle was gone and she sent him an apologetic look. He too seemed to regret the exchange.

"You must be parched," Kate said, opening the refrigerator and taking out a tall pitcher of iced tea.

Joe invited them to sit down at the table. The two boys followed their father to wash up while Kate filled glasses with tea and ice and brought them to the table.

"We don't mean to put you out," Carrie felt obliged to say.

"It's no problem. We don't get many visitors out this way. I'm hoping you can stay for lunch. We have plenty."

"We appreciate the offer, but we can't," Kyle said. "We need to get back on the road. We want to be in Dallas by this afternoon."

Kate lifted the lid to a simmering pot of home-made soup, and the aroma nearly lifted Carrie out of her chair.

"There's more than enough," Kate insisted. "I put on a big pot of beef with barley this morning and baked Joe's favorite applesauce cake."

"On second thought," Carrie said, silently pleading with Kyle to reconsider, "we're already later than we wanted to be. A while longer shouldn't matter, should it?" She batted her long lashes, appealing to Kyle, hoping he remembered that they'd left that morning without breakfast. Personally she was famished, and it might be hours before they found someplace to eat.

"We insist," Joe said, coming into the kitchen. He slipped his arms around his wife's waist and nuzzled her neck. "How you feeling?" he asked, studying her.

"I'm fine, Joe. Honestly, you'd think I was the only woman in the world who ever got pregnant. As you might have guessed, we have another one on the way. It's barely three months and already he's worried."

Joe broke away from his wife, downed a full glass of iced tea, and poured himself another. "I don't know what I'm going to do with this woman. She just produces me boys. I told her she was going to have to keep at it until she gives me the daughter she promised."

Hands braced against her hips, her eyes full of happiness, Kate turned to her husband. "I made no such promise, Joseph Brighton."

"Please let me do something," Carrie offered, bringing her iced tea glass with her.

"You can help me with the sandwiches, if you want."

"While the women are fussing with lunch," Joe said to Kyle, "why don't I find a piece of paper and draw you a map. That's probably the easiest way of getting you back to the main road."

"Great."

The two men disappeared into the other room.

Carrie liked Kate immediately, and within minutes they were laughing and chatting. They worked well together, too.

"I was surprised to learn you and Kyle aren't married," Kate said conversationally, slicing tomatoes into impossibly thin sections. "I saw the way you two looked at each other. It reminded me of the way Joe looks at me when the boys are down for the night and he wants to sit on the porch for a spell."

"Kyle and I work together," Carrie said, hoping that would be explanation enough.

Kate stopped slicing. "You mean you aren't romantically involved?"

Carrie wasn't sure how to answer. She focused her attention on spreading mayonnaise across the slices of homemade bread. "Not . . . exactly."

"I can tell you'd rather not talk about it. I hope I didn't embarrass you."

"Not in the least." But Kate had told her what she feared the most. She was falling for Kyle.

And it showed.

Carrie could hear Adam and Seth laughing hysterically in the other room. Kate grinned knowingly. "Joe's crazy about his boys. Some afternoons he gets them so riled up, it's a real challenge to put them down for their naps."

The phony sound of two horses whinnying caused Carrie to laugh outright. She walked around the corner to discover both Kyle and Joe down on all fours. Kyle had Seth on his back and Joe had the younger boy. The two were charging at each other, enjoying the horseplay as much as the youngsters.

Mesmerized, Carrie watched Kyle with the children, thinking how natural he looked. Her heart started to pound loudly in her ears, and for no reason she could decipher she felt tears sting the back of her eyes. Blinking wildly, she managed to keep them at bay but wondered at their cause.

If she'd thought about it, she would have guessed that Kyle would be stiff and uneasy around children. That wasn't the case at all. Never had she seen him more animated. Nor had she witnessed him enjoying himself more. It was as if the mold in which she'd placed him had been broken. The pieces had fallen away and she was left to discover the attractive, exciting man behind the rigid wall.

A portion of her thoughts must have transmitted themselves to Kyle, because he turned abruptly and his gaze met and held hers.

He froze, the sudden movement unseating Seth. Kyle caught the youngster and reluctantly returned to their game, but twice more he looked at her, before they all sat down for lunch.

Somehow Carrie got through the meal. She joked and laughed and teased and practically did handstands in an effort to ignore Kyle; otherwise he might guess what she'd been feeling, which was something she had yet to understand herself.

Afterward, all four Brightons walked Carrie and Kyle to the car. Kyle and Joe exchanged handshakes and Carrie and Kate hugged. Both boys cried when they left, which was sweet but more an indication that they were ready for their naps than anything else.

Once they were on their way again, Kyle handed Carrie the sketch Joe had drawn for them. "Believe it or not, that closed road is the simplest means of getting back to the main road," he said.

"Isn't that what Kate said?"

"Yes," he admitted.

"Are you worried about the washout?" she asked.

"I'll be careful."

Carrie crossed her arms and heaved a giant sigh. "Given our penchant for bad luck, your confidence doesn't do much to reassure me."

"We'll be fine." He reached for her hand and kissed her knuckles. All at once, he seemed to realize what he was doing and abruptly dropped her hand.

Afterward they were both silent. Carrie pointed to the red mailbox Kate had mentioned, and no more than ten seconds later Kyle eased the BMW past the barrier and its sign.

After an awkward moment, Kyle cleared his throat. "I want to know what happened at the Brightons when you were watching me and Seth horse around."

Flustered and confused, Carrie lowered her head.

When she looked up, she saw Kyle was driving straight toward the sawhorse barrier in front of the washed-out space in the road.

She screamed and raised her hands to her face.

Kyle jerked the wheel sharply to the right. They swerved suddenly and came to an abrupt halt. Carrie was flung forward, but the seat belt locked, preventing her head from slamming into the windshield.

"Carrie!"

Before she could inhale, Kyle was holding her, his eyes searching her face.

"Are you all right?"

"I'm fine. I'm fine."

He wrapped his arms around her and held her tightly. A shudder went through him, and it was several moments before he relaxed.

"What about you?" she asked, shocked by how weak her voice came out.

"I'm okay." He stroked her back. "You've got me so tied up in knots I can't even keep my car on the road anymore."

"So it's all my fault?" Funny how Kyle could turn things around, she noted, but she was more amused than angry. It was too difficult to be angry for any length of time when she was in Kyle's arms.

"No," he whispered into her hair. "The fault is entirely mine."

They broke apart reluctantly, as if the near wreck had offered them a convenient excuse for what they'd been wanting to do all morning: to cling to each other. To hold each other and test the uncharted waters of the powerful attraction they shared.

Kyle climbed out of the car to see what damage had been done. Carrie followed. She sighed gratefully when she realized they'd narrowly missed the barrier. By driving off to the right, Kyle had avoided disaster. Unfortunately he'd driven into a marsh.

"Are we going to have trouble getting the car back onto the road?" Carrie asked. Already her shoes had filled with water and her feet made squishy noises when she walked. The smells weren't all that pleasant either.

"I won't know until I try." He climbed back into the car while Carrie made her way to the side of the road to watch. She wasn't sure Kyle would appreciate her advice just then, and held her tongue.

In the beginning it looked as if Kyle wasn't going to have a problem. His faithful car fired back to life and he slipped it into gear, cautiously inching forward. He was a few feet from the road when he got stuck. He tried once more, then climbed out.

"It looks like we're going to have to push it the rest of the way," he said, after checking the tires. "I'll bury the back end if I spin the wheels any longer."

"You think we can push it out?" Carrie wasn't nearly as confident.

"We don't have any choice, do we?"

She wished he hadn't said that. According to Joe

Brighton they could make Dallas in time for the party without a problem. Carrie would have sold her birthright for a store that sold real women's clothes.

Kyle opened the car door. With one hand guiding the steering wheel, he pushed with all his might against the door post.

"I'll help," Carrie called out, hurrying to the back end of the car. With her hands braced against the bumper, she heaved for all she was worth, which at the moment was a lot. If getting this car out of the marsh was all that stood between her and civilization, she was moving that BMW!

Slowly the vehicle edged forward and a surge of triumph shot through her, but the sense of success was short-lived; the car rolled back.

"Once more!" Kyle shouted.

Carrie's sandals sank deep into the mud, but she ignored it as much as she could and pushed, using every ounce of strength she possessed.

With a mighty shout, Kyle too strained in an effort to get his BMW back onto the road. The car inched forward, then seemed to slip. Kyle yelled once more and the vehicle unexpectedly lurched forward. Unfortunately, Carrie's feet were so deeply embedded in the thick mud that she lost her balance and fell down face first.

For a moment she was too shocked to move.

"Carrie?"

She was on her hands and knees by the time Kyle

reached her. He lifted her by the waist and hauled her out of the mire, then carried her in that position to the road, setting her feet down on the concrete.

She stood there, her hands caked with mud and the bottom half of her face covered with slime.

"Hold still," Kyle instructed and raced around to the back of his car to grab a blanket. Gently, he wiped the mud off her face.

When he finished, she spit and coughed. He cleaned off her arms next, while she struggled for composure.

"If you laugh, I swear I'll never forgive you," she muttered.

"I'm not going to laugh," he assured her and as a show of support he kissed her forehead.

"But you want to," she guessed, holding her arms away from her body, even though they were mostly clean now.

"No, Carrie, I don't have the faintest desire to laugh at you." Having said this, he proved otherwise by bursting into deep peals of laughter.

"I suggest you stop," she demanded.

"You're right," he said, barely managing to control himself. "This isn't a laughing matter." He stepped back to examine her, then slowly shook his head. "You're going to need to change clothes."

"Change into what?" she cried. "I only bought the one new outfit, and I was saving that for this evening's party. I haven't talked to Cathie since we left. She doesn't know I need clothes. The way my luck's going, she's probably working double shifts."

"Oh." He frowned. "Don't look so worried. By the time we arrive the mud will have dried and fallen off."

For the first time she looked down at herself and realized that she was covered from shoulders to ankles.

"I look like the bride of Frankenstein," she wailed. She was going to arrive at this all-important broadcasters convention looking as if she'd walked out of the Black Lagoon.

Kyle must have realized she'd reached her limit. "Sweetheart, I'm sorry," he said contritely, stepping toward her. "It's all my fault." Then, disregarding his own relatively clean clothes, he gathered her into his arms and comforted her. Carrie went willingly. Wrapping her arms around his waist, she buried her face against his clean shirt.

"I'll buy you another outfit before we reach Dallas," he promised.

"I need a bath."

"We'll find one," he promised.

"Where?"

"I don't know. Trust me. All right?"

She nodded, feeling infinitely better. "You called me sweetheart."

"I did?"

She nodded.

"I meant it," he told her and removed a long piece of limp grass from around her ear. "You may not believe this, but I don't think I've ever seen you look more beautiful than you do right this moment."

"I don't believe you."

He tucked his thumb beneath her chin and raised her face toward his. Gently he pressed his mouth to hers for a tender kiss. Then he grimaced. "Unfortunately, you taste like a lizard."

They both started laughing then, until they were forced to sit down to recover. A full fifteen minutes passed before they were back on the road.

They arrived in Dallas thirty minutes before the cocktail party was scheduled to begin. Kyle had held true to his word. They stopped in a small town on the outskirts of the city where Carrie bought a Mexican-style dress with an elastic top and new leather sandals.

A bath proved to be more of a challenge, and they ended up paying for one at a campground. Carrie didn't care if they had to go to a laundromat, she wasn't arriving at some fancy Dallas hotel looking like a street person.

The man at the front desk checked them in and handed them their room keys. "I'll ring for the bellboy," he said, with a smile thick with southern hospitality.

"That won't be necessary," Kyle said, accepting both keys.

"Our luggage was stolen," Carrie added.

"Oh, my. Have you contacted the police?"

"They were already there. You see, we were kidnapped by this man I thought I'd seen on *America's Most Wanted*. Then Kyle got thrown in jail for jaywalking, which was ridiculous, of course, but they needed time to check out our story."

"Kidnapped? Jail?"

"Carrie," Kyle muttered under his breath. "I don't think this man is concerned about our troubles."

"I wanted to explain why we don't have any luggage," Carrie said. She'd made a fool of herself. It was just that she was so grateful they'd finally arrived. She felt as if she'd won a survival course and was waiting for someone to step forward and give her the prize.

Kyle guided her across the crowded lobby and handed her a room key. Carrie studied everything around her, awed by the fact that they were safe and sound and her life could return to normal once more.

A cocktail lounge was to the far left, in a plush atrium alive with greenery. A coffee shop was situated to the right, reminding her it had been hours since they'd last eaten.

"What floor are you on?" Kyle asked, studying his key.

Carrie had to look at her own. "Ten. What about you?"

"Fifteen."

They stepped into the elevator, and he punched the appropriate numbers. The car went straight to the tenth floor, and the door yawned open for her. "I guess this is where I get off," she said, checking her key one last time to be sure there wasn't a mistake.

"I'll see you later," Kyle said, holding the door open.

"Later," she repeated, loath all at once for them to separate, which was silly. Reluctantly she took a couple of steps forward. "You're going to the party, aren't you?"

"Yeah, what about you?"

"I'll be there," she said hurriedly. Although it was a crazy notion, she would have given a month's wages if the hotel had announced they were full, except for one room with a king-size bed.

"See you at the party, then," Kyle said, releasing the elevator door.

The door started to close and Carrie hurried to block it. "You won't have any problem locating me," she said. "I'll be the one dressed like Sister Maria in *The Sound of Music*."

Kyle chuckled and she stepped off and allowed the door to close.

Carrie found her room. Although she'd taken a shower just two hours previously, she took another, letting the hot water spray over her for several minutes.

Feeling relaxed, she wrapped herself in a thick

terry-cloth bathrobe she found hanging in the closet and took a small bottle of wine from the tiny refrigerator in the base of the nightstand. It'd probably cost a fortune. A minute container of peanuts was nearly eight bucks. She didn't look at the price list, knowing she probably wouldn't drink it if she knew how much it cost.

Having been raised in a God-fearing, churchgoing family, Carrie rarely sampled spirits. This evening, however, she made an exception.

The wine was surprisingly good, and exactly what she needed to relax. Checking the time, she moved into the bathroom, dressed, and applied her makeup. When she finished, she carefully examined herself in the mirror, wondering what Kyle saw when he looked at her. Did he still view her as a nuisance, or did he see her as enticing and beautiful? Closing her eyes, she fervently prayed it was the latter.

The cocktail party was in full swing when Carrie arrived. After registering for the conference and pinning on her badge, she stood in the doorway, peering in, searching a sea of faces for Kyle. When she didn't immediately locate him, she sighed with regret and walked into the crowded ballroom.

Not knowing anyone, Carrie bought herself a second glass of white wine. She was eager to find Kyle. They'd spent the last three days together, hoping to find a common ground, and in that short amount of time Carrie had bonded so completely with her co-worker that she felt as if a part of herself was missing without him at her side.

Carrying the glass of wine with her, she strolled around the room, observing others. She recognized a few of the names on the badges, legends in the industry, deejays she'd listened to, studied, and admired for years.

"Carrie!"

She turned around to find Tom Atkins coming toward her. A smile lit up his face.

"Tom," she said, brightening as well. "You're a sight for sore eyes."

He laughed and hugged her. "It's good to see you. Now tell me about that newscaster who's got you so uptight."

"Oh, Kyle isn't so bad," she said, trying to remember exactly what she'd told Tom about him.

"That's not the way I heard it. You claimed he was impossible to work with and had made your life miserable. According to what you told me, he was out to have you replaced at the station. The guy sounds like a real troublemaker."

Just then Carrie caught sight of Kyle. She was so pleased it was all she could do not to walk into his arms. "Kyle," she said, raising her hand to attract his attention.

His eyes went from her to Tom and then back again as he joined them.

"Tom Atkins, this is Kyle Harris," she said, slipping her arm through Kyle's.

Now it was Tom's turn to look confused. "This is the jerk you were telling me about?"

8

Kyle was furious. He'd made an idiot of himself over Carrie. He was so crazy about her he'd driven clean off the road. Yet the minute they arrived in Dallas, she was warming up to another man.

As soon as he could, Kyle made his excuses and left Carrie alone with her cowboy friend. From that point on the evening deteriorated. It might have helped if he could stop thinking about her. But he couldn't. Three days with her, and whatever sense he'd possessed had deserted him completely.

What he should be doing was networking, making contacts with other radio stations, keeping his ear to the ground for a job. Heaven knew there wouldn't be one waiting for him at KUTE.

He'd forgotten how fickle women could be. Walking over to the bar, Kyle ordered a double scotch. He carried the drink around with him until the ice melted, then took his first sip. It burned its way down the back of his throat and he grimaced, wondering what had possessed him to order a drink he hated.

The answer to that was simple: Carrie.

He caught sight of her then, huddled over a table, her head close to Atkins's. She didn't resemble any nun he'd ever seen, he mused darkly. True, her skirt was long and black, but it clung to her hips like plastic wrap, outlining every womanly curve.

He had it bad, and it wasn't going to get any better with him standing there ogling her like a lovesick puppy.

A lone saxophone played in the distance, the low, deep notes calling out the blues. Appropriate music for a man who felt as if he'd been hit with a brick alongside the head.

He downed the rest of his scotch, walked over to the bar, and set the glass down. The bartender was about to pour him another when Kyle's hand stopped him.

"You don't want another drink?" the man asked, looking surprised.

"Just give me what's left of the bottle."

"The bottle?" The guy's eyebrows shot halfway to his hairline. "My guess is there's a woman involved in this."

"Isn't there always?" Kyle answered with a half-hearted chuckle. He signed his name to the tab, charging it to his room number, and left the party.

Kyle had never been much of a drinker, but there were times when the only solace he could find was at the bottom of a bottle. He'd pay dearly for his weakness in the morning, but at the moment he didn't care. It wasn't every night Kyle, who thought of himself as sane and sensible, was forced to admit he'd been a fool.

The couple on the elevator gave him an odd look, but Kyle ignored them. Let 'em think what they wanted. He lifted the bottle to his lips and downed a generous sip of the scotch, then bared his front teeth and shook his head several times. If he was going to take up drinking, he'd best learn to like it.

His hotel room was dark and lonely. He flipped on the one dim lamp. Shadows moved against the opposite wall as he sank into the chair and set the bottle on the table.

He loosened his tie by wiggling it back and forth several times and freed the top button of his starched shirt. It was time to get good and drunk.

He was about to search for a glass when a knock sounded against his door.

Kyle wasn't in the mood for company and ignored the summons. There wasn't anyone he was interested in talking to. The knock came again, louder this time, more determined.

"Come on, Kyle, I know you're in there."

Carrie.

Kyle exhaled sharply, marched to the door, and jerked it open. His eyes slammed into hers and for a moment neither one of them spoke.

"What do you want?" he demanded.

"To talk to you."

"Another time," he said gruffly, and started to close the door.

Carrie's foot blocked it. Damn those eyes of hers, he thought. They looked up at him wide, dark, and appealing. It was like mistreating Bambi.

"Please," she said softly.

He shrugged and stepped aside. She walked into the room, sat down in the chair, and propped her feet against the bed, exposing her heavy black shoes.

Her gaze followed his. "Do you mind if I take these off? They're killing my feet."

"Feel free."

She slipped off the shoes and flexed her nylon-covered toes.

Kyle went into the bathroom and returned with a glass.

"Bring two," she instructed.

"Do you drink hard liquor?" he asked, surprised.

"Not generally, but it's what the house is offering."

Kyle grudgingly did as she asked. When he set the glasses down on the table, Carrie reached for the bottle and poured them each a generous portion.

She sampled hers first, and Kyle watched her, curious as to how well she handled her liquor. He had to give her credit. The only outward sign that the scotch had affected her was that her eyes started to water. She blinked furiously for a couple of seconds, then gasped as if she'd been holding her breath.

Kyle sat down next to her. "You wanted to talk?"

"Yeah," she said. It sounded as if her voice came from the bottom of a tin drum. She took a second drink and then coughed so hard he had to pound her on the back.

"You all right?"

She nodded. "I . . . think so. What is this stuff, toxic waste?"

"Scotch."

"Oh." She studied the contents of the glass as if she were expecting it to spell out the future. Kyle guessed she was looking for courage. "I wanted to explain about this evening. You see, I've known Tom Atkins since college, and before the conference I asked him to—"

"Do you mind if we don't discuss your college sweetheart?" he snapped, in no mood for whatever confession she intended to make.

"Kyle," she said softly. Her eyes fairly glowed. "You're jealous."

His first instinct was to deny it, but she'd see through that soon enough. "Think what you want." He took a liberal sip of liquor.

"We're old college friends. The emphasis is on the word *friends*."

"Great." He looked at his watch, hoping to give the impression he had people to see, things to do, and her unexpected arrival was detaining him.

The room went silent. He wondered how long she intended to play her little game.

"I'd be jealous too," she said, in a voice so low he had to strain to hear. "If I arrived at a party and saw you with another woman, that is."

Kyle was sifting through her words, attempting to derive some meaning, when Carrie feverishly waved a hand against her face. "Is it hot in here, or is it just me?"

"It's hot." He stood to check the air-conditioning, and when he turned around he found Carrie standing and unfastening the buttons of her white cotton blouse.

"What are you doing?" he demanded.

She glanced up at him and blinked. "Cooling down. Don't look so shocked, you've seen me wearing far less."

He opened his mouth to argue with her and realized she was right. As far as he was concerned, those baby doll pajamas of hers were designed for *Playboy* covers.

"How much have you had to drink?" he asked. That might explain a good deal.

She paused as if she needed to think about the answer. "A couple of glasses of wine—maybe three, all told—and now the scotch. Not *that* much. I'm not drunk, if that's what you're thinking. At least I don't think I am." She hesitated and ran her hand over her face. "Then again, I might be just a little bit tipsy; otherwise I'd never have had the courage to come up to your room."

Tugging the blouse free of her waistband, she looked up at him once more. "Would you mind very much if I removed my pantyhose? I'd forgotten how much I hate these things. Generally I wear thigh-highs, but they didn't sell them in Paris." Not waiting for a reply, she hiked up the skirt and gathered it around her waist, exposing her thighs and long, shapely legs.

Carrie was a petite thing and he'd never thought of her as long-legged, but just then they seemed to zoom all the way to her neck. Kyle swallowed uncomfortably, unable to take his eyes away.

Hooking her thumbs over the top of the nylons, Carrie was just about to shimmy out of the pantyhose when she lost her balance.

Kyle sprang into action. With her pantyhose halfway

down her thighs, Carrie would have fallen head first onto the floor if he hadn't leaped to his feet and grabbed her.

Unfortunately his own balance was precarious at best, and before he knew it they both toppled. Kyle attempted to twist around so that he took the brunt of the fall, but as it happened they landed on top of the bed.

Both were breathing deeply, unevenly. The side of her face was pressed against the mattress, scant inches from his own. They stared at each other for several silent seconds.

"I've made such a mess of everything," she whispered, her eyes wide, her look crestfallen and miserable.

"No, you haven't," he countered, his own voice barely audible.

Her eyes drifted shut and it seemed words weren't going to convince her, so he did what he'd been wanting to do from the moment she walked into the door. He kissed her.

Big mistake.

The moment his mouth met hers, Kyle knew there was no stopping. With a deep-seated groan, he gathered her into his arms. She came willingly, eagerly, wrapping her arms around his neck, and with a sigh she kissed him back.

She felt so good in his arms, Kyle couldn't make himself stop.

"Kyle?" she said, between kisses.

"Hmm?" His tongue outlined the shape of her lips before he kissed her again.

"Never mind." She sighed. "It isn't important."

Kyle smiled down on her before lowering his mouth to hers once more. She tasted of scotch and woman, both equally potent, equally stimulating. His intention that night had been to get good and drunk, but he'd rather get intoxicated with Carrie.

They continued to kiss and undress each other at the same time. Kyle shucked off his shirt but had something of a problem ridding himself of his tie. Carrie tried to help him, but the silly thing got caught on his ear. It was hell to break away from her, even for those few seconds, in order to discard it himself. While he was up, he turned off the lamp.

The room went dark and still, and the intimacy of the night wrapped itself around them. Kyle's breathing was labored. If there was ever a time for them to reclaim their sanity, it was now.

"I want to make love to you," he whispered, lying down next to her. His arms felt empty without her, but he didn't want his touch to influence her. If she decided she wanted out, the time to go was now, but he'd be hard-pressed to let her leave. He'd never wanted a woman this way before. His whole body seemed to throb.

"I know what you want," she whispered. "I want you too."

Kyle heard the desire in her voice and knew this was the reason she'd come to his room, but whether she was willing to admit it or not was another matter entirely.

"Who would have believed . . ." she murmured.

"Believed?" He kissed her, wondering how much longer he could hold off.

"You and me? This is the craziest, most wonderful moment of my life."

"Carrie."

"Hmm?"

"Be quiet."

They slept. Kyle didn't know how long. He woke in the middle of the night. The alarm clock on the nightstand said it was just after two. Carrie had tossed off the sheet and slept on her back. Her arms were positioned above her head and her foot was braced against the side of her knee.

For a long moment Kyle studied her. A man could grow accustomed to sleeping with a woman like this, he thought contentedly. Grow accustomed to loving a woman like this.

Unable to resist touching her, he ran his finger down the silky, fragile skin of her abdomen.

Her eyes drifted open and, yawning softly, she smiled up at him. "Is it morning yet?"

"Not quite."

She lowered her lashes until they brushed against the high arch of her cheekbones. "I should go back to my room."

"No," he said heatedly, then immediately lowered his voice. "Stay."

Her smile widened. "If I do, is it sleeping you have on your mind?"

"No."

She laughed softly. Kyle had never heard anything more musical in his life. Lifting her arms, she tucked them around his neck and kissed him, amused still when their lips met.

"What's so funny?"

"You." Exerting pressure, she rolled him onto his back and braced her hands against his shoulders. "Who would have ever believed it would be like this for us? Not me!"

Kyle chuckled too.

Afterward, sated, exhausted, they fell into a deep sleep.

When Carrie opened her eyes she felt as contented as a cat napping in the sun. Kyle was asleep at her side, and for a few moments she did nothing but study him, reveling in the way his chest moved in the slow, easy rhythm of slumber.

Her head throbbed with the beginnings of a pounding headache. She'd definitely had too much to drink the night before. Then again, she'd drunk exactly enough.

The wine had given her the courage to confront Kyle, and the few sips of scotch had sent her inhibitions flying out the window.

If this trip had accomplished anything, it had helped her revise her opinion of Kyle Harris. He was definitely more man than met the eye. She didn't know what he ate for breakfast, but there was definitely a tiger in his tank.

It seemed they slept in fits and starts, waking after brief interludes to reach for each other once again. A dam of longing and need had burst wide open between them, and they'd done their level best to make up for lost time.

Carrie shifted onto her back and realized she was sore. With little wonder. Nibbling on Kyle's ear, she whispered, "I'm going to take a bath."

His arm inched around her waist, pinning her against him. "Now?" he asked, his eyes closed. "What time is it?"

"Eight." The first session of the conference was scheduled for nine. If they wanted to attend the early workshops, they needed to get going.

"You want me to order breakfast?"

"Please." She kissed the tip of his nose and moved off the bed.

Humming to herself, she ran the bathwater and sank into the steaming comfort of the tub. Settling into the bubbles, she braced her head against the back of the porcelain base and closed her eyes. A couple of minutes later, Kyle knocked and padded barefoot into the room.

"I just came in to see if you needed anything," he said.

"I'm fine, thanks," she replied, smiling up at him. He'd put on his pants but left his shirt unbuttoned.

Now that he was with her, Kyle didn't seem anxious to leave. Sitting on the edge of the bathtub, he reached for the washcloth. "Need any help?"

She eyed him speculatively. "I can manage, thank you."

His shoulders sagged. "You're sure?"

"Kyle, the first workshops start in less than an hour."

"You want to go?" He sounded shocked.

"We paid for them, didn't we?" she asked instead.

"Yes, but . . ." He paused, stood, and stuffed his hands inside his pants pockets. A slow, steady smile began to form and his dark eyes gleamed. "It's been my experience that the first workshops aren't of much interest."

"They usually aren't very well attended, are they?" Carrie asked.

"From what I can tell, the subject matter is downright boring."

"Boring," she repeated, and then sighed and eased herself down into the warm, muscle-soothing waters.

"You're sure you don't need me to wash your back?"

Carrie closed her eyes and handed him the wash-cloth.

A knock sounded at the door. Kyle closed his eyes and groaned.

"Who's that?" Carrie asked.

"Room service," he muttered.

He left her and closed the door. While Kyle paid the waiter, Carrie climbed out of the tub, dried off, and wrapped herself in the thick terry-cloth robe the hotel provided.

She came into the room just as Kyle was pouring the coffee. "I'm starved," she announced, lifting the silver dome and sniffing appreciatively. He'd ordered her a low-cholesterol meal, but she didn't object.

"I'm hungry myself."

Carrie giggled. "No wonder." She reached for a half slice of toast and munched on it while Kyle set their plates on a small circular table next to the window. Then she sat down and took a second piece of toast. "Feed me, Seymour."

Kyle grinned. "My plan exactly." He reached for the miniature jar of ketchup. "All I can say is thank God for the Pill."

Carrie froze. "What makes you think I take birth control pills? And what makes you assume birth control is a woman's responsibility?"

Her questions gave Kyle some pause. "You came

to my room, remember? It makes sense that if you wanted to make love you'd take care to prevent a pregnancy."

"I came to *you?*"

"Yes," he said. "Our making love was what you intended, wasn't it?"

For one wild second, Carrie was afraid she was going to slap him. "No, it wasn't. I wanted to apologize for what happened with Tom and explain that we're only friends."

Kyle set his toast aside and took a deep breath. "I can see our discussion is upsetting you. I apologize, Carrie. You're right. Birth control is something we should have discussed before we became . . . involved. We didn't, so we'll just have to live with it."

Slowly Carrie stood and started moving about the room, collecting her clothes. It wasn't what he'd said that upset her so much as what he'd implied. Apparently Kyle assumed she had an active sex life, so active it was necessary for her to be on the Pill.

His implied opinion of her cut deep. With one careless statement, he'd left her feeling unclean. He took what had been a beautiful, special night and made it into something sordid and cheap.

"Carrie," Kyle said, taking hold of her arms, stopping her. "What are you doing?"

She pressed the hard ball of her clothes against her abdomen. "I'm going back to my room."

"But why?"

"We're here for a conference, remember? And as I said earlier, we paid good money to attend these workshops. I think we should go to them, don't you?"

"No," he said emphatically. "Let's talk this out."

She looked up at him and bit her lower lip. "Not now. I need to think."

Carrie was grateful that she didn't meet anyone in the stairwell. The last thing she needed was to be seen wandering through the hotel, wearing a robe and carrying her clothes.

Once in her room, she sat on the end of the bed, attempting to sort through her feelings. Kyle was right. She had gone to his room for all the wrong reasons. Her sole purpose hadn't been to entice him into bed, but to be fair the possibility had been in the back of her mind. It had started when they shared a bed in Paris, maybe even before then; Carrie didn't know anymore.

She reached for the phone and dialed her sister's number. If she was lucky, Carrie might reach Cathie before she left for work.

Cathie answered on the fourth ring, sounding breathless and impatient.

"It's Carrie," she said, and immediately burst into tears. "I've been such a terrible fool, and now I don't know what I'm going to do."

* * *

Kyle looked for Carrie most of the morning. He made a point of stopping in a number of workshops. One would think, after the fuss she'd made, she'd at least show up for one or two.

But he hadn't so much as caught a glimpse of her all morning. He wasn't entirely sure what he'd said that was so terrible. All right, maybe what he said about the Pill had been out of line, but they'd need to discuss it sooner or later.

As for her comment about responsibility being shared, he didn't have an argument there. She was right. The minute he realized what was going to happen, he should have made a quick trip downstairs.

Okay, so he'd made a mistake, but it wasn't the end of the world. It was just one night.

Knowing Carrie, all she needed was a little bit of time and space and she'd work matters out for herself. He'd be patient and wait for her to contact him, although it was going to be difficult. He wanted this settled as quickly as possible.

Whether they could resolve their differences would be the true test of how strongly they'd bonded in the last few days.

It worried him a little. All right, it worried him a lot. He was willing to do whatever it took to make matters right between them.

When Kyle hadn't heard from her by early afternoon, he couldn't make himself wait any longer.

Against his better judgment, he went to a house phone.

"Carrie Jamison's room, please," he told the operator.

"One moment," came back the tinny voice. "I'm sorry, sir, our records show she checked out of the hotel this morning."

9

"*What do you mean* she disappeared?" Clyde Tarkington bellowed.

"Carrie's checked out of the hotel. I thought you might have some idea of where she might be." Kyle was fast growing desperate, desperate enough to call KUTE, hoping Clyde might have heard something. That woman would be the death of him yet.

"You two still egging each other on?" Clyde asked.

"No," Kyle said, and impatiently jerked his fingers through his hair. "We had a minor misunderstanding."

"It doesn't sound so minor to me," Clyde said. It

sounded as though the station manager was enjoying this.

"She's got a sister living somewhere in the Dallas area," Kyle continued. "Have you got any information about her?"

"Give me a minute. There might be something in the file."

Kyle had never been more impatient in his life. Leave it to Carrie to drive him to this. He found himself clenching and unclenching his fist, needing to do something, anything, to alleviate this terrible tension.

"It doesn't say anything about a sister in her employment file," Clyde said, coming back on the line.

"She mentioned her casually, but for the life of me I can't remember her name."

"I've heard Carrie mention her myself. Seems to me her name's Cathie," Clyde supplied.

"That should be enough information," Kyle murmured. "I'll take it from there. But Clyde, listen, if you hear from Carrie, I'd appreciate it if you'd let me know right away."

"No problem."

"I'll be in touch."

"See you bright and early Monday morning."

Kyle relaxed. All wasn't lost. At least he still had a job.

For the next hour, he sorted through telephone directories until he located a Cathie Jamison in

Euless, Texas. Not wanting to risk Carrie's knowing he was coming, Kyle left Dallas, drove to Euless, and, with only minor difficulties, located Carrie's sister's apartment. If his luck held, Carrie would be there and they could sort out whatever was wrong.

The woman who came to the door might have been Carrie's twin. Cathie Jamison possessed the same deep brown eyes and upturned nose, but her soft, dark hair was cut short, flattering her face.

"May I help you?" Cathie asked.

"My name's Kyle Harris," he said quickly. "I'm looking for Carrie."

"You're Kyle Harris?" Cathie said, and leveled her gaze on him. "I'd rather burn in hell than give you any information about my sister." With that she slammed the door.

Apparently Carrie and her sister shared more in common than a strong family resemblance.

Kyle rang the doorbell a second time. Cathie must have been waiting for him to do exactly that, because his finger had no sooner left the buzzer when the door flew open.

Before Cathie could issue any dire threats, Kyle spoke. "In case you're interested, I really care about your sister."

Cathie's shoulders sank as she released a long, deep breath. "In that case you'd better come inside." She held the screen door open.

Kyle glanced around the compact apartment,

hoping Carrie might be there, but if so she was hiding in the bedroom.

"I take it you've talked to your sister."

"This morning." Cathie motioned for him to sit down. "Would you like something to drink?"

"Nothing, thank you. Was Carrie upset?"

"You might say that. She babbled on about a number of things. To be honest, she wasn't making a whole lot of sense."

Kyle sat closer to the edge of the sofa cushion. "What was she saying?"

"Something about wearing nun's clothes, and hocking Grandma's opal ring because you'd gotten yourself thrown in jail. There was more about wishing she'd left you in the slammer, but I don't think she was serious."

Don't be so sure, Kyle thought.

"The part that completely baffles me is this felon she thought she saw on *America's Most Wanted* who took your traveler's checks. Does any of this make sense to you?"

Reluctantly Kyle nodded. "Every word of it."

"In between all this you two got involved?"

"Exactly." He steadily held her gaze. "Did Carrie tell you about last night?"

Cathie nodded. "Carrie likes to give the impression she's something of a free spirit, but beneath all the bold talk and the crazy way she does things, my sister has strong values. She isn't nearly as different as she wants everyone to believe. You'd need to meet our father to fully appreciate what I'm saying."

"What's your father got to do with this?"

Cathie folded her legs Indian style beneath her. "He's great, don't get me wrong, but he's got these old-fashioned ideas about women and what role they should play in society. Dad thought Carrie should be a nurse."

"Carrie?" For the life of him, he couldn't picture her in a white uniform. Kyle admired Carrie's talent as a deejay. She was bright and witty and fun. Her personality was ideally suited to radio.

"I know. Carrie goes weak in the knees at the sight of blood, but Dad was convinced she'd overcome that in time. It came as a real shock to him that his daughters had minds of their own."

"What about you?"

Cathie laughed softly. "He thought I should be a schoolteacher. I'm not as strong-willed as Carrie, and I didn't defy him quite as openly as she did. The thing is, Dad and Carrie might argue, but they're close. He's long since forgiven her for majoring in communication. And with Carrie blazing the trail for me, life was much easier."

"So you're a teacher, then?"

"Not exactly," Cathie said, shaking her head. "I'm a nurse."

The irony produced an involuntary smile. "Carrie told me once that I was a lot like her father."

"From what she said about you, I think that must be true," Cathie responded. "You're like Dad in more ways than even Carrie realizes. But you aren't here to listen to talk about our father. You want to know about Carrie."

"Yes, please. Where is she?"

Cathie looked at her watch. "If the flight landed on schedule, she's back in Kansas City. I dropped her off at the airport earlier this afternoon."

Kyle was on his feet. "She flew back?"

"Yup. I don't know what you said, Kyle, but I've never seen Carrie more upset."

Carrie let herself into her house, picked up the mail on the floor, and sorted through it as she made her way into the kitchen. The red light on her answering machine winked at her, and she absently pushed the switch. Four days of messages played back one by one, interspersed with a number of hang-ups.

Then Kyle's voice captured her attention. The mail slipped from her fingers and spilled onto the countertop.

"Carrie, it's Kyle. Listen, whatever it was I said, I apologize. I didn't mean to hurt you. I know an answering machine isn't exactly the way to be telling you this. I should have said it much sooner." He paused and she could almost picture him squaring his shoulders. "I think I love you, Carrie. I don't know when it happened, probably when you pawned your grandmother's ring to bail me out of jail. All I can tell you is that I've never spent a more miserable day in my life than this one.

"I drove out and met your sister. It took a little persuasion, but I finally convinced her I wasn't a monster and we had a nice long talk. I didn't get your note until I got back from Euless. It would have saved me a trip, but that's all right, because I was happy to get to know Cathie.

"If you'd like to talk to me, and I'm hoping you will, I won't be at the hotel. I'm checking out as soon as I'm finished here and will be driving directly to Kansas City. Maybe by then you'll have had a chance to think matters over and will be willing to sit down and talk things out."

Carrie slumped down into the kitchen chair and covered her face with both hands. She'd been impulsive most of her life, but it had been a mistake to leave Kyle like that. Her note had been brief and to the point. All she'd said was that she was flying home and hoped he enjoyed the rest of the conference.

The phone rang. Thinking it might be Kyle again, she leaped up to answer it.

"Hello."

There was a pause, followed by a click. Carrie stared at the receiver and then slowly replaced it. With an unlisted number, she didn't often receive crank calls. Yet there'd been a series of hang-ups on her answering machine. Odd.

Tired and emotionally spent, Carrie ran her bath-water and soaked for a long time in the scented tub. Then she climbed into bed, convinced she was exhausted enough to sleep for a week.

For the better part of the night, Kyle drove from Dallas to Kansas City, arriving early Sunday morning.

He started rehearsing what he intended to say to Carrie the minute he hit the Kansas state line. He didn't want to fight with her, not when they could be making love.

Instead of stopping off at his house, he drove directly to Carrie's. That might not be the wisest thing to do, but he couldn't bear to wait any longer.

When she didn't answer the front door, he walked around to the back of the house and found her squatting on the grass, sticking Martha Washington geraniums in a redwood planter on the patio. She was wearing cut-off jeans and a cotton shirt with the tails tied at her midriff. Her hair was held away from her face with a red bandanna. Kyle thought he'd never seen a more beautiful woman.

"Hello, Carrie."

She glanced over her shoulder and froze. "Kyle." She rubbed her forearm across the perspiration that moistened her brow. "I see you got back all right."

He nodded, his carefully prepared speech lost. "I just got in."

She nodded and stood, looking uncertain, unprepared. "Would you like to come inside for some iced tea?"

"Please." He followed her and removed his sunglasses, folded them, and stuck them in his shirt pocket. After driving for the last ten hours, he wasn't inclined to take a seat, so he stood while she took a glass pitcher from the refrigerator.

"I realize I can be obtuse at times," he said, smiling his thanks when she handed him the glass. He paused long enough to take a deep swallow. "That comment about birth control pills was stupid. You're right, Carrie. The responsibility should be shared."

"That wasn't what upset me." She inhaled deeply and raised her head so that their eyes met. "It was the implication that I'm routinely involved with men when you should know I'm not."

"Carrie, don't be insulted, but I honestly haven't paid any attention to your social calendar. For all I know, you could be going out with four or five different guys."

"Sleeping with them too, apparently," she muttered under her breath.

"I wouldn't know, that's the point," he argued. "What do you know about my love life? Nothing, right? I'm not holding that against you. Carrie," he said, taking a step toward her, "I don't care if you've had ten lovers—"

"You don't care?" She stared at him as if seeing him for the first time and finding plenty to fault.

"I'd *care*," he replied heatedly. "I only want you to have one lover. Me."

"What kind of woman do you think I am?" she asked softly.

He'd been deceived by that calm, reasonable tone before. It spelled danger. Frantically he struggled for a way of combating her anger. "You're warm, generous, loving—"

"Loose, immoral, unprincipled," she concluded.

"I said nothing of the kind," he said calmly. One of them needed to remain level-headed. "You're putting words in my mouth."

"You seem to believe I'd make love with you while involved with someone else." Each word was spoken distinctly as if she wasn't leaving room for misunderstanding. "Worse, you know how many hours I put in at the station. You've seen for yourself the hours upon hours that go into scheduling interviews, promos, and public service announcements, yet you think I can keep a handful of lovers happily satisfied on the side."

"What I was trying to say is that it doesn't matter to me how many lovers you've had—*in the past*."

Carrie briefly closed her eyes and gritted her teeth. "How generous of you. Your previous lovers don't concern me either."

"You're twisting everything I say into an insult. I didn't drive all this way to fight with you."

"This isn't what I want either," Carrie admitted.

"But I swear, every time you open your mouth you make it a thousand times worse."

Frustrated, Kyle stretched out his hands, palms up. "Tell me what you want."

"I think it'll probably be best if you left. We both need time to think this out."

"All right," he responded stiffly. He had his pride, and if she didn't want him around he could accept that. Forget the fact that he'd driven like a madman to get back to her. "Answer me one thing," he said.

"Okay."

"Is there a chance you could be pregnant?"

Carrie blinked as if she'd never considered the prospect of there being consequences to their one night together. "Heavens, I don't know." She counted days and stopped when she reached the night she'd spent with him.

"Well?" he asked, anxious to know.

"On a scale of one to ten?"

"However you want to put it," he said.

"One being no chance of my getting pregnant, and ten being the day I was at the peak of the fertility cycle."

"All right, tell me on a scale of one to ten."

Long before she spoke, Kyle saw her reply working its way up her throat. The word seemed to have to fight its way past some restriction.

"Ten."

Kyle pulled out a chair and fell into it.

"That doesn't mean I *am* pregnant," she was quick to say, but he noticed that she promptly scooted out a chair and sat down herself. Bracing her elbows against the tabletop, she buried her face in her hands. "I wish you hadn't asked. Now it's going to worry me."

Kyle felt the same way. "How soon will we be able to tell?"

"How am I supposed to know? A couple of weeks, I guess. I've never been pregnant before, and this might come as a shock to you, Kyle Harris, but I've never been at risk either." She turned to him, her eyes wide and appealing. "What will I do if I'm pregnant?"

"You? We're in this together. As I recall, I was there as well."

"True, but as you so eloquently pointed out, I was the one who came to *your* room, and you were under the impression I'd accepted full responsibility for birth control."

"Why don't we wait until we know what we're dealing with before we start fighting about whose responsibility a pregnancy is?" He stood and rubbed a hand over his face. "I'll see you Monday morning."

"Okay," she murmured and walked him to the door.

He hesitated. Neither of them had felt comfortable enough to convey how they felt about the possibility of Carrie's being pregnant. It was still too new, too shocking. Like Carrie, he'd never been in this situation before. Frankly, he didn't know what he was feeling, other than wanting to kick himself for being so stupid.

"May I kiss you?" Kyle didn't know where the question came from, but all at once it was there. It wasn't as if he'd forgotten the taste of her. It had haunted him for over five hundred miles. He was curious, he guessed, to discover if their time together had been a joke fate had played on him. He needed to know if what they'd shared was real.

"Kiss me?"

"Just once," he coaxed.

"But I've been working in the yard. Good grief, I'm all sweaty and—"

"I've kissed you when you were dripping mud," he reminded her.

A soft smile turned up the edges of her mouth. "I suppose one kiss would be all right."

"Nothing more," he promised and gathered her in his arms. She stood on her tiptoes and raised her arms to him. Her breath felt moist and warm against his throat. The mere act of touching her produced a deluge of achingly familiar feelings.

He'd meant the kiss as an experiment, but his need for her far outweighed his curiosity. She opened her lips to him and Kyle instantly deepened the contact, seeking her as a political prisoner yearns for freedom, as someone freezing reaches for a blanket.

Leaving her arms was impossible. Kyle stepped away from her and exhaled sharply. "That pretty much answers that," he murmured.

"You had a question?"

"Yeah, but I don't anymore." Blindly he turned away from her and stumbled out the front door.

"I'll see you Monday?" she called after him.

He reached his car, raised his arm, and nodded. Monday. A whole day away. Only heaven knew how he was going to last that long without being with her.

10

Carrie was trying to rest, but that was impossible. The fact was, she might very well be pregnant. In the last few days she'd attempted to convince herself otherwise, but it was time for her to face the truth.

The first person Carrie thought who might help her was Cathie. Her sister worked rotating shifts at the hospital, so keeping track of Cathie's schedule was next to impossible. If luck was with Carrie, which it hadn't been up to this point, she just might catch her sister at home. Carrie sat down on the sofa, tucked her feet beneath her, and dialed Texas.

After four rings the answering machine automatically came on. Carrie listened to her sister's short recorded message, drew in a deep breath, prayed she sounded cheerful, and said, "Cath, it's me. I thought I'd check in and let you know everything's hunky dory on my end. I do have one itty bitty medical question for you to answer, though. Nothing important, mind you, just some information I need . . . for a good friend of mine who might be in a family way. My question is, How soon after conception is it possible to tell if a woman's pregnant? I'lltalktoyousoon." The last words were spoken so fast they jumbled together, and Carrie wondered if her sister would be able to make sense of them. Or the phone call itself.

Replacing the receiver, Carrie wandered back to the bedroom and lay down. When she woke, it was mid-afternoon. To her surprise and delight, her first thought was food. Her appetite had been absent these last few days, and all at once she felt as if she could eat her way through every fast food restaurant in town.

Her phone rang while she was layering cheese on bread for a toasted cheese sandwich.

"Hello," she mumbled distractedly, thinking it might be Kyle. She'd been avoiding him. She wasn't sure how to deal with the newscaster just yet. That decision would need to be faced soon but not now, when her head was muddled with other matters.

Whoever was on the other line hung up. Glaring at

the phone, Carrie replaced it in its cradle and went back to assembling her sandwich.

Within a minute the phone rang a second time. Sighing, Carrie looked over to the wall and decided to let her answering machine pick up the call. She wasn't interested in playing silly hang-up games with some weirdo.

The machine clicked in with her sister's frantic voice. "Carrie, I just got home and heard your message. You're pregnant, aren't you? You didn't honestly expect me to believe that business about needing information for a good friend, did you? That's the oldest trick in the book."

"Cathie." Carrie spoke into the telephone receiver. "Hold on a minute." She walked over and turned off the answering machine. "Hello," she said, making sure she sounded downright chipper.

Now that Carrie was on the line, Cathie stopped speaking.

"I'm here," Carrie said, wondering what had gone wrong with the connection.

"Yes, I know," Cathie said, sounding nothing like her usual cheerful self. "You're pregnant?"

There wasn't any need to hide it, Carrie decided. The truth would come out soon enough. "I don't know yet, but I think I might be."

"You think you might be!" Cathie echoed, aghast.

"It's too soon to be sure. That's why I asked you."

Once more Cathie was uncharacteristically quiet.

"Are you all right?" Carrie asked, growing concerned.

"Of course," Cathie snapped, sounding oddly hysterical. "But then I'm not the one who's pregnant. You apparently have had some time to get used to the idea. I haven't. How far along are you?" The last question came out breathless as if her sister were badly in need of oxygen.

"It'll be two weeks on Friday. You didn't honestly think Kyle and I were up playing pinochle all night in his hotel room, did you?"

"No, but I figured if you spent the night together, one of you was smart enough to use some form of birth control."

"We didn't."

"Obviously. Now let me think about this."

"I should tell you what's been happening to me," Carrie said, and went about describing the symptoms she'd experienced since her return from Dallas.

"What's Kyle got to say?"

"He hasn't said anything yet."

"But you must have seen him?"

Cathie knew they worked together. "Of course."

"Does he know?"

"I think he suspects."

"What are you two going to do if you're pregnant?" Cathie asked, sounding very much as if she was at her wits' end.

"I don't know." Carrie hadn't wanted to think about her continuing relationship with Kyle just yet. As sure as the sun shines in August she knew what his reaction to a pregnancy would be. He'd grit his teeth and suggest they marry. Carrie would prefer to raise the child herself than have a martyred husband.

"It could be all this worry's for nothing," Cathie murmured on an optimistic note.

"True," Carrie concurred, but all of a sudden she knew with a certainty she didn't question that she was carrying Kyle's baby.

"You can have a blood test done at your doctor's office," Cathie said, "or you can buy a home pregnancy test at the local drugstore."

"Okay," Carrie murmured, disheartened.

"What are you going to tell Mom and Dad?"

This was another aspect of the situation Carrie wasn't prepared to face just yet. "Eventually there won't be any way to hide it from them, but I'm not going to mention it until I'm absolutely certain."

"Don't tell Dad who—"

Carrie knew what her sister almost said. Their father would raise Cain. One thing was certain: Michael Jamison must never learn Kyle was the father of her baby. When and if he discovered the truth, Michael would make all their lives miserable.

* * *

Rarely had Kyle been more eager to leave the radio station. He was tired of waiting to hear from Carrie. It was time for a confrontation.

He stopped off at a grocery store on his way, picking up several items he felt she would need and probably hadn't bought for herself. First he'd cook dinner for her, he decided, and then they'd talk. Seriously talk.

First and foremost he intended to clear up what it was he'd said that had set her off in the first place. He'd tried once to make amends and utterly failed. This time would be different. He promised himself he'd listen more carefully. He'd try harder. Once they had that out of the way, they could face the second major crisis of their relationship: whether Carrie was or wasn't pregnant.

Carrie answered the door, her eyes widened as if she were surprised to see him. She looked a bit uncertain, which wasn't like her.

"I know you said you needed time, but I can't wait any longer," he said.

It could have been his imagination, but she seemed reluctant to let him inside the house.

"I brought us dinner," he said, moving into her kitchen and setting two grocery bags on the countertop.

"I ate just a little bit ago."

"That's fine," he said. "I'm not hungry yet myself." He took the milk and other items that needed to be refrigerated out of the sacks and left the rest on the counter.

When he'd finished he turned to find Carrie standing as far away from him as was possible and still be in the same room. She was wearing cut-off jeans, and the tips of her fingers were inserted into the front pockets. Her hair was up in a high ponytail and she was barefooted. She watched him wearily.

"First off," he said, "I thought we should talk."

"What about?"

"Us." Kyle pulled out an oak chair but didn't sit. Carrie didn't seem inclined to do so either. He braced his hands against the back of the chair.

"If you want to discuss us as a team employed by KUTE, I think you should know—"

"No." Kyle cut her off. She was avoiding the issue, but he wasn't going to let her. "We're going to settle whatever it is that's wrong between the two of us."

She folded her arms over her chest. "That's pretty autocratic of you to decide the subject of our discussion without first . . . Kyle, are you even listening to me?"

Kyle had trouble answering her. Not because he didn't know what he wanted to say; the words clogged his throat, unable to squeeze past a deep and sudden awareness of her.

"Kyle?"

"Sorry."

"What's wrong?"

His fingers bit into the wood chair with enough strength to cause his hand to ache. "You aren't wearing anything under your blouse," he said impatiently.

"What in the name of heaven has that got to do with anything?"

"I can't carry on a serious conversation if you're dressed like that." He motioned with his hand. "For heaven's sake, go put something on."

"I most certainly will not. In case you hadn't noticed, it's miserably hot and I'm not going to put on a bunch of extra clothes because you think I should."

She didn't understand it wasn't women in general who plagued him but one particular feisty one. Her. Otherwise he agreed with what she was saying.

"All right," he said slowly, drawing in a deep breath. "We'll forget that."

"Good." She waited an impatient moment and then continued. "Go on, I'm listening."

Kyle looked her way, but try as he might he couldn't make his gaze reach any higher than her breasts. This wasn't like him. Kyle was a man who liked being in charge, a man in control of his own emotions. There'd been other women in his life, but none who had affected him physically as deeply or profoundly as Carrie.

All at once, he needed to sit down; otherwise she'd witness the powerful influence she had on him, and he wasn't keen on having her learn how weak he was when it came to her.

"Sit down," he said, "and we'll talk all this out logically."

"All right." She made it sound as though it were a major concession. "I imagine you want to discuss what happened in Dallas, and at this point you're probably terrified of the consequences."

"That's not it at all," he returned heatedly, surprised with the vehemence of his reply. With just about anyone else, he could disguise his irritation; not with her. Carrie had the power to reduce him to a babbling idiot within minutes. "I want to know what I said that you found so insulting."

Her face tightened. "I believe we've already gone over that. Trust me, rehashing your opinion of my morals isn't going to solve anything."

Kyle momentarily closed his eyes as the frustration ate at him. "This isn't going to work."

"That's what I said," she said in heated tones. "Not when we have far more important subjects to discuss."

"Like what?"

She eyed him as if trying to decide if she should have his IQ tested. "In case you'd forgotten, I could very well be pregnant."

"We don't know that yet." The subject had been keenly on his mind every day since they got back from Dallas, but he wasn't about to tell her.

"True, I haven't been tested yet, but—"

"Let's cross that bridge when we get to it, all right?"

"No," she said, and he noticed how pale she'd gone. "You don't want to discuss it because you're worried sick it might be true."

"We aren't going to discuss this subject until we know for sure what we're dealing with. Why get ourselves all upset over nothing?"

"Upset! Who said I was upset?" she cried.

"I know I'm not!" he shouted back.

Carrie blinked at him several times as if he'd taken her by surprise, and after a moment the hint of a smile caused the corners of her mouth to quiver.

"What's so all-fired funny?" he demanded, then deeply regretted his lack of patience. She was worried sick and all he could do was berate her, shout at her, when he should have been looking for ways to comfort her.

The humor drained from her eyes, and she stood. "Nothing. It's just that . . . oh, Kyle, it was sweet of you to bring dinner, but really I won't be hungry for ages."

Her words were a dismissal, but Kyle wasn't going to leave. He moved out of the chair, walked over to where she was standing by the kitchen counter, and took her in his arms. She came without resisting, as if she too had been waiting for this moment, dreading it yet desperately needing him to hold her.

Kyle kissed her lightly, making sure the contact between them was warm and gentle. She didn't open her lips to him, but then he hadn't expected that she would.

Not at first.

So he kissed her again and again, lightly, tenderly, on her temple and cheek.

Between kisses he whispered how beautiful she was and with some finagling managed to free her hair so the glorious weight of it spilled into his waiting hands.

After a few moments he felt the tension ease out of her body and she relaxed against him. Taking her by the hand, he walked into the living room, sat on the sofa, and brought her down into his lap.

Kyle wasn't sure what he intended. One moment they were arguing and the next she was in his arms. It seemed the most appropriate place for her to be. They certainly didn't have any trouble communicating on the physical level; anything else was a disaster. Kyle figured they could work on the verbal aspects of their relationship later. Just now he had more pressing interests.

"I don't think this is a good idea," she said, slowly.

"Please, let me hold you a few minutes," he whispered.

She didn't seem eager to slip out of his arms either, and that encouraged him.

Neither of them spoke for several moments.

"You know what I was just thinking?" Carrie whispered.

"No."

"Do you remember that state patrol officer who stopped us just outside of Paris?"

"The one whose wife had left him?"

"Yes. Do you remember what he said about their relationship?"

"Not really." Kyle wasn't thinking all that clearly and marveled that Carrie could.

"He claimed the only place the two of them could get along was in bed. That's the way we are too," Carrie said. "We can barely exchange a civil word, but the minute you kiss me, I'm putty in your hands."

She had this all wrong. It was the other way around. She was the one who wielded the power over him. When he held and kissed Carrie, she had absolute control over him. For a man who prided himself on his restraint and discipline, this was an admission he'd rather not make, especially to her.

"The answer to that is simple enough," he said, being facetious. "It's to keep you in bed. I promise you we'll both be happy."

"You'd like to keep me barefoot and pregnant, wouldn't you?"

She sounded angry when he'd only been kidding her. "I was teasing," he said gruffly, disgruntled that she couldn't have figured that out on her own. "Lots of couples communicate best in bed," Kyle went on. "It's not so bad, is it?"

"No," she agreed reluctantly. "As long as neither one of us has anything to say, we're in fine shape."

"What have I said that's so offensive?" he asked, genuinely wanting to know. "I'd do anything to make matters right between us."

"Why?" she asked. "So you can get me back in your bed?"

Kyle needed to think about the answer. He didn't want to be anything less than completely honest. Apparently she found his lack of response insulting. She climbed off his lap so fast, she nearly fell onto the carpet. Laughing was not the appropriate response.

"Don't you dare laugh," she ordered. "In fact, it'd probably be best if you left."

"You don't mean that." He gestured weakly with his hands, wondering how all his good intentions had backfired once more.

To prove her point, Carrie walked over to the door and opened it.

Kyle stood and glared at her. He should never have tried to reason with her. This woman was driven strictly by her emotions.

Next time he'd know better. She'd dented his pride once too often. He was through with coming to her house with his tail between his legs. He was through begging her forgiveness for imaginary crimes he was supposed to have committed.

It was only fair that she know of his decision. He

paused, his hand against her screen door. "I won't be back until you invite me."

She laughed softly. "That's the best news I've heard all day."

Kyle looked at her and felt a sinking sensation. He didn't know what he'd done that was so terrible. For that matter, he wasn't convinced Carrie did either. Fighting with him was a convenient excuse to hide the uncontrollable physical pull they felt toward each other. If that was the way she wanted it, fine. He was in no position to argue, not if he intended on maintaining his pride.

Carrie managed to make it through the next couple of days without another confrontation with Kyle. At the station he was stiff and polite toward her, doing his best to ignore her as much as possible, to act completely indifferent.

At least that was what he wanted her to think. Carrie knew otherwise. A couple of times she felt his gaze on her, but when she looked toward him, he'd focused elsewhere.

He'd meant what he said about the next move coming from her. He didn't speak to her unnecessarily, didn't phone her, and, other than professionally, kept almost entirely to himself.

None of this behavior was any different from before they'd taken their trip together. She'd been perfectly happy then. Now, however, she was miserable. Pride could be a burdensome thing.

Friday morning didn't start out well. The check Carrie had sent almost two weeks ago to retrieve her grandmother's opal ring from Dillon's Pawnshop had been returned with a note. She tore open the envelope to learn that Dillon was sorry, but his assistant had sold the ring by mistake, and there was no record of the buyer's name.

Carrie was crushed. The opal had been in her family for three generations.

The fact that she and Kyle had a public appearance to make that afternoon didn't help matters any. Mr. Tidy was opening a tenth laundromat in the city and had asked KUTE's morning personalities to come for the grand opening.

As usual there would be free hot dogs, popcorn, and balloons to contend with, in addition to the ribbon-cutting ceremony. Under other circumstances Carrie would have enjoyed the outing. Not so this afternoon.

Since they both would have to return to the station when the opening was over, Kyle suggested they take his rented car.

"Yours isn't back from the shop yet?" she asked, once they were outside.

"Not yet. They told me it'll probably be ready this evening."

"I hope everything works out all right," she mumbled, feeling incredibly sad. She looked out the side window and waited for him to start the motor. When he didn't, she turned back and found him studying her. "Is something wrong?" she asked defensively. "Is there lipstick on my teeth?"

"No," he said, quickly starting the engine. "I was just thinking. . . ."

"About what?" she pressed, when he didn't immediately answer.

"Nothing," he said, after a moment.

A heaviness weighted down his voice that gave her cause to wonder. Could it be that Kyle was as frustrated as she was? She strongly suspected he found the strain of maintaining his pride as cumbersome as she did.

"I'm sorry," she murmured when he was out on the roadway.

"Sorry? For what?"

She exhaled slowly. "For raising such a fuss the other evening. You were . . . I don't know what you were doing, but I overreacted. I . . . we need to put all this nonsense behind us."

"I couldn't agree with you more." Kyle grinned and Carrie felt as if the sun had come out from behind a black cloud. He reached for her hand, his fingers curling around hers.

"It doesn't make any sense," she said.

"What doesn't?"

Carrie shook her head. "We're barely able to be civil to each other and yet I'm miserable without you."

"I'm miserable too."

A crowd had gathered by the time Carrie and Kyle arrived. The broadcasting booth was set up and Carrie interviewed David Bond, the owner of Mr. Tidy's, who was one of the station's most prominent advertisers. Afterward she handed out balloons and spoke with several people who had come for the grand opening. Kyle was busy as well.

They stood on the platform for the ribbon-cutting ceremony, and after the owner had said a few words Carrie was handed a giant pair of scissors.

Smiling, she glanced out over the crowd. Suddenly her gaze came to rest on one man who was studying her intently.

She gasped, and the platform started to buckle beneath her feet.

"Kyle . . . Kyle." Blindly she reached out for him. Within the space of a heartbeat he was there at her side, his arm protectively around her waist.

"What's wrong?" he asked, and she heard the unfamiliar sound of panic in his voice.

She blinked up at him. "Billy Bob's here. I saw him in the crowd."

"Billy Bob?"

"The man who kidnapped us."

11

"*Where?*" Kyle searched the crowd, but he didn't see anyone who so much as remotely resembled Max Sanders. It seemed that every eye was on them, so he urged Carrie to use the huge scissors and cut the ribbon.

A cheer rose from the crowd and David Bond stepped toward the mike, promising free fabric softener to the first five hundred customers. The group charged the doors as if fabric softener was all that stood between them and ruin.

"Do you see him?" Carrie asked, clinging to Kyle. It felt incredibly good to Kyle to have her in his arms again. It didn't matter that what she was saying made no sense. A man like Max Sanders wasn't interested in free fabric softener.

"You don't mean Max Sanders, do you?"

"Who else could I possibly mean?" Carrie cried.

"I don't see him."

"But he was there." She grabbed hold of his lapels with both hands. "I swear to you I saw him."

"Carrie," Kyle said with a good deal of patience, "I'm sure you *thought* you saw him."

"I should have known you wouldn't listen," she said, breaking away from him, using her elbows as if she were suddenly in need of breathing room. "He was there, I swear to you, Kyle. The man who kidnapped us was here no more than a minute ago."

"Couldn't it have been someone who strongly resembles Sanders? It doesn't make sense that he'd be at the opening of a laundromat. The man's on the run."

The anger and hurt that flashed into Carrie's beautiful eyes were nearly his undoing. In that instant Kyle would have done anything to have seen Max Sanders himself.

"You're right, of course," she said stiffly. "I must have been mistaken."

"Was he wearing farm clothes?" Kyle asked, unwilling to drop the subject.

"No. He had on a suit."

"A suit?"

"A shirt and tie," she amended. "He looked like a businessman, an everyday kind of person."

"Are you sure it wasn't someone who looked a lot like Sanders?"

This gave her pause, but not for long. "I don't think so. The resemblance was far too striking to ignore."

"I see," Kyle said, although he didn't.

The trouble with Carrie, Kyle decided, was that she watched too much television. She was addicted to those crime shows.

"It went well, don't you think?" he asked, breaking into the silence. He had the sinking suspicion that he'd done something terribly wrong again and offended her without meaning to.

"Yes." Her voice was so low he wouldn't have known she'd spoken if he hadn't seen her lips move.

When he pulled into the KUTE parking lot, Carrie opened the door and all but leaped out of his car, heading for her own.

"Where are you going?" he asked, surprised by the urgency with which she moved.

"To talk to the Secret Service."

Kyle's fist tightly closed around his keys.

"You don't have to believe me," she said, her shoulders square, her words defensive. "But I know what I saw, and nothing you say can convince me otherwise. If Sanders is here, there's a reason, and personally I'd prefer to avoid a second meeting with that scoundrel."

"Carrie, be reasonable. Do you even know where there's an office for the Secret Service? I don't. It isn't likely they have one in Kansas City. If we're going to do anything, we should contact the agent we met in Wheatland."

She hesitated, as if she would have preferred him not to make sense just so she could defy him. "All right," she finally agreed.

"We don't have anything to worry about," he said with a decided lack of confidence. Until now, he hadn't considered that they could be in any real danger.

Not that any of this made sense. That was the reason he had so much trouble believing that Carrie had actually seen Sanders. To Kyle's way of thinking, bumping into the kidnapper a second time was too much of a coincidence to be plausible. Unless it was on purpose. "We'll talk to Agent Richards and go from there," he said, fishing the business card from his wallet. He studied the phone number, recounting the anger he'd felt when Sam Richards had handed it to him after releasing him from the Wheatland jail cell. It seemed a lifetime had passed since then.

"I think we should," Carrie agreed.

He followed her inside the radio station and into her compact office. Closing the door, he noted how terribly pale Carrie was. When she stood by her desk, he realized that her hands were trembling. It dawned on Kyle that she was frightened.

Perhaps he should have been more troubled than he was, but Kyle didn't fear Max Sanders. No matter what crime Sanders was alleged to have committed, the man had meant them no harm. Otherwise he wouldn't have risked being captured to set them free.

"Sweetheart, don't look so worried."

Carrie closed her eyes. "Please don't call me that," she whispered huskily.

"Why not?"

"It makes me uncomfortable."

He shrugged as if it didn't matter to him one way or the other, but it did. Her words stung. Kyle wanted to know when he'd gotten so sensitive. It didn't sit well with him.

Needing to touch her, he cupped her shoulders. "I'll make the call."

"No," she returned heatedly. "You weren't the one who saw him. I did. I'm not even sure you believe me."

His lack of faith hurt her, but he didn't want them to sound like fools either. Carrie had a way of exaggerating things. He wished he could make her understand that he was only trying to protect her. "I believe you saw someone you thought was Sanders," he said after a thoughtful moment. "Someone with a strong resemblance."

"I saw *him*," Carrie replied excitedly.

"Then that's what I'll tell Sam Richards." Before she could protest, he reached for the telephone receiver and punched the number on the business card.

Carrie fidgeted while Kyle was on hold.

"Don't you dare make light of this," she cautioned, her dark eyes boring holes into him.

Kyle placed his hand over the receiver to assure her. "I promise I won't."

A long minute passed before Kyle was patched through to Agent Richards. "Richards here."

"This is Kyle Harris," he said crisply, wishing now that he'd let Carrie do the talking.

"Sanders has contacted you?" Richards broke in expectantly.

"Not exactly. Carrie and I were doing a promotion this afternoon, and she strongly believes she saw Sanders in the crowd." He kept his voice as level and as unemotional as he could, not allowing his skepticism to bleed into his message. He was simply reporting what she had seen, or what she thought she'd seen. Unfortunately there could be a world of difference between the two.

Richards's enthusiastic reaction surprised Kyle. Within the next couple of minutes the agent had made an appointment to talk with Carrie and Kyle that evening. Kyle gave Richards his address and they agreed on a time.

"What did he say?" Carrie asked anxiously when Kyle had replaced the telephone receiver.

"He wants to talk to us. We're to meet him at my house this evening at seven."

Carrie nodded, her eyes wide and anxious, uncertain now for the first time. "There isn't much to tell."

As far as Kyle was concerned, there wasn't anything to tell. Carrie thought she'd seen Sanders. What Richards failed to understand was that a day didn't pass when she wasn't convinced she'd rubbed elbows with one of the FBI's ten most wanted.

"Does Richards believe me?" she asked.

"Of course," Kyle responded, sounding blasé. "Why shouldn't he?"

"Well, first off, you don't. Besides, I threatened to write my congressman the last time I saw Richards. I was upset about the way we . . . the way you'd been treated."

"You threatened Richards? When?"

Carrie shifted her gaze away as if she was embarrassed. "The morning you were released from jail. It made me mad how they forced you to spend the night behind bars, and I didn't want him to think he was going to get off scot free."

With some difficulty, Kyle hid a smile. Carrie's anger could be downright intimidating. He should know, after all the times he'd butted heads with her. It pleased him immensely to know she'd ruffled a few feathers on his behalf.

Such loyalty shouldn't go unrewarded. Without thinking, without considering her response, Kyle turned her into his arms and kissed her. What started as a simple kiss of appreciation quickly turned into something far more.

Carrie sighed and opened her lips to his, and Kyle took immediate and grateful advantage. Then she stiffened and flattened her palms against his chest and twisted her mouth free. He was relieved to note she was breathing as heavily as he. If they were going to be drawn together like this, then at least the feeling was mutual.

"I think you're wonderful," he whispered into her hair. He kept his hands loosely about her waist, reluctant to break the contact, however fragile. "It isn't every day someone threatens a Secret Service agent on my behalf."

"I may be wonderful," Carrie said, not sounding completely herself just yet, "but you seem to think I need bifocals."

"Carrie." He sighed her name, not knowing what else to say. He didn't understand why it was so important that he believe she'd seen Sanders. Frankly, he was far more comfortable believing she hadn't.

This was the first time Carrie had been inside Kyle's house. It was spotless. Even the magazines were neatly filed on the lower half of his mahogany coffee table. He subscribed to four newspapers, including *The Wall Street Journal,* she noted, flipping through the papers immaculately stacked next to the fireplace.

"Make yourself at home," Kyle had said, heading for the back bedroom. He paused in the hallway and turned back to her, jerking his tie back and forth in an effort to loosen it. "I'll only be a minute."

"What time did Richards say he'd meet us here?"

Kyle looked at his watch. "Another twenty minutes or so."

She nodded and strolled about the room, her hands behind her back. Everything was so orderly. It bothered her that one man could be so tidy. His entire life had been spent uncluttered and clean.

The phone rang just then. Kyle didn't answer on the second or third rings, and she wondered if she should or let the answering machine catch it. On impulse she reached for the receiver just as it pealed for the fourth time.

A pause followed her greeting. "Is Kyle there?" asked a distinctly feminine voice. The low sultry tone conjured up visions of a generous body and a long-standing intimate relationship.

Carrie stiffened. Kyle had never mentioned another woman. Not that he would, especially. The thought that he might be involved with someone else produced a curious ache in the area of her heart. She slowly lowered herself onto the leather recliner.

"He isn't available at the moment," Carrie said in her best business voice. "May I take a message?"

The woman hesitated, then asked, "I recognize your voice, don't I?"

This happened sometimes, but generally people didn't remember where they knew her voice from.

"To whom am I speaking?"

"Carrie Jamison," she admitted reluctantly. "Kyle and I work together."

"Carrie." The lilting voice lifted with enthusiasm. "Kyle's mentioned your name a number of times."

Carrie bet he had, and she strongly suspected it hadn't been in a complimentary manner.

Just then Kyle stepped into the living room. Carrie placed her hand over the mouthpiece and glared at him. "It's for you," she said sharply.

"Who is it?"

"I don't know . . . some female." She handed him the receiver as if she were afraid of contracting some fatal illness by holding on to it another minute.

Frowning, Kyle took it from her, but his gaze refused to leave hers, as if by staring at her long enough he could convince her she was the only woman in his life.

Carrie watched as Kyle's face tightened.

"Yes, Mother," he said.

Mother? Carrie mouthed. She wouldn't believe that if her life depended on it. If Kyle thought she was stupid enough to believe his mother was on the other end of the line, he didn't know her nearly as well as he assumed.

"Yes, Mother," Kyle said a second time, clearly impatient to be off the line. "You're right, I should

have phoned you earlier. The convention was great."
His gaze briefly connected with Carrie's. "Especially
the first night."

Tucking her arms around her middle, Carrie
moved away from him and stared out the window.

"We're seeing each other," Kyle continued. "Yes,
we're serious. No. . . . No, I believe that's my
business. . . ."

Whatever else he meant to say, he didn't. Carrie
couldn't decide if she was relieved or not.

"I don't believe that's any of your business," he
repeated. This was followed by a series of "no's"
until he sighed heavily and held the receiver out to
Carrie. "Mother wants to speak with you."

Carrie hesitantly took the phone from his hand.
"Hello?" she said.

"My dear girl, I can't tell you how pleased I am
that you and Kyle are seeing one another."

"Thank you." Carrie wasn't sure what to say. The
woman's voice wasn't any less sensual, but now that
she listened objectively she could tell it was more
mature. This actually was Kyle's mother.

"If anyone can cure my son of his stuffy Republican ways, it's you. I love your morning show and
listen to it religiously."

Carrie didn't think it was fair to mention that she
probably would have listened anyway because of
Kyle.

"I'm Lillian Harris, Kyle's mother."

"I'm pleased to talk to you, Mrs. Harris."

"Call me Lillian, please. I feel as if I already know you." The words were raised and excited. "Kyle needs someone like you, my dear. Heaven knows why he's turned out the way he has. We're nothing alike."

"Neither are we," Carrie felt obliged to say.

"I know. I was about to give up on that son of mine. Knowing he's dating you has given me real hope. Kiss my Ringo for me, won't you?"

"Ringo?" Carrie repeated. Kyle groaned and sank into the recliner.

"That's his given name, only he had it legally changed to Kyle when he was eighteen. He never appreciated the Beatles, I fear. Unfortunately, there's a good deal about me my son doesn't understand or appreciate, but that's neither here nor there."

"It was nice talking to you, Mrs. Harris."

"Lillian, and it's Ms. Harris. I never married."

Once more Carrie's gaze flew to Kyle, who was giving her his full attention as she hung up. Her head was buzzing with this newfound information. Kyle's given name was Ringo? Her Kyle?

"All right, all right," Kyle demanded, coming to his feet. "What else did she say?"

"That really was your mother?"

"Of course. Did she introduce herself as Summerlove?" He shoved his hands in his pants pockets. "She does that from time to time to impress my friends."

"Your mother's name is Summerlove?"

"Of course not. She was born Lillian Harris, but for a brief time, one summer I believe, she was a flower child in California. That's where she met my father, who abandoned her the minute he learned I was on the way. If he even knew about me, that is; not that he would have cared one way or the other. Unfortunately those days were the best of my mother's life. In her mind, she's never left Haight-Ashbury. Never forgotten the one man she loved. In fact, she didn't even know his legal name. Moonrunner," he said, laughing sarcastically, "is all she was ever able to tell me about my father. Her precious Moonrunner. She's been chasing moonbeams ever since. She's got one foot in the seventies and another in the present. If you want to pity anyone, pity my mother."

Carrie sensed the pain in his voice more than she heard it. "Go ahead and laugh," Kyle said bitterly. "Ringo's a great name for a kid, isn't it?"

"I'm not laughing."

"But you wanted to," he challenged. "I read the amusement in your eyes. Go ahead. I don't blame you, it's downright hilarious."

For months Carrie would have sold her eyeteeth to have something on Kyle. His cool, unshakable composure had left her wanting to say or do something that would rattle him. Just once. She wasn't greedy, not by any means. One time was all she wanted.

Now the moment had come, Carrie found herself incapable of saying anything. Instead she felt a burning compassion for a little boy who'd been taunted and teased because of an unusual name.

The need to touch him was irresistible. Barely aware of what she was doing, she stepped onto the leather ottoman so that their gazes met at eye level.

"Come here," she instructed, urging him forward with her index finger.

He took two steps in her direction, just enough for her to reach for him and put her arms around his neck. She was surprised by the resistance she felt when she pressed her mouth to his.

Whatever hesitation Kyle had experienced earlier vanished completely. He groaned and wrapped his arms completely about her. Taking control of the kiss, he angled his mouth over hers, kissing her until a frightening kind of excitement took control.

"Now you've done it," he said, between kisses.

"Done what?" she asked on the tail end of a sigh.

"You don't kiss a man like this and expect it to end there."

"You don't?" It took several moments for her brain to assimilate what he was saying. Even then she found his words difficult to decipher.

"Not to worry, I'm prepared this time."

"Prepared?" Carrie was vaguely aware she was beginning to sound like a parrot.

"The drugstore," he murmured, his lips tenderly moving against hers. "I have everything we'll ever need."

"You got it at a drugstore?"

His hands were in her hair, splayed at the sides of her face. "Has anyone ever told you that you talk too much?"

"No," she said with a giggle.

Groaning, he lifted her from the recliner; her feet dangled six inches off the ground. He was kissing her as if this were the only way to convince her how badly he needed her in his bed.

The sound of the doorbell seemed to come from a long way away. The buzz had to battle its way through the fog of desire that had taken her by storm. Thank heaven Kyle was in control of his senses.

"That must be Richards," he murmured, his breathing heavy. His shoulders moved up and down with a hard sigh as he slowly lowered her feet to the floor. He pressed his forehead to hers, but when the doorbell sounded once more he abruptly broke away.

She reached out to him, pressing her hand against his forearm when he started to move away from her. "You bought . . . you went to the drugstore?"

He nodded. "We don't have a thing to worry about. I've got a ten-year supply, although the way I'm feeling right now we could exhaust all my resources tonight."

Where she found the strength to smile, Carrie didn't know.

By the time Kyle returned with two Secret Service agents, she'd managed to compose herself.

"Hello again," she said, exchanging brief handshakes with both Sam Richards and Agent Bates, whose first name turned out to be Charles.

"Sit down," Kyle said, motioning toward the sofa.

Once everyone was seated, Richards reached for a pad and pen. He directed his attention to Carrie.

She didn't like this man, but she trusted him. She had no choice. "I saw Max Sanders this afternoon," she announced.

The two government agents exchanged looks but gave no outward appearance that what she'd said surprised them in any way.

"Aren't you going to laugh and tell me it's implausible and that I only *think* I saw Sanders?" She said this for Kyle's benefit, certain the three men would get a real laugh over her allegedly finding Sanders in a crowd.

"We're not the least bit surprised," Agent Richards replied. "We've been waiting for something like this to happen. If anything, we're surprised it took this long."

Carrie tossed a triumphant look at Kyle and bit her lip to keep from saying she'd told him so.

"What do you mean you've been waiting?" Kyle demanded. He wasn't taking this information sitting down, she noted, but now that he was on his feet he looked ill at ease. "Next thing I know you're going to tell me you're having us followed."

Richards and Bates briefly lowered their eyes.

"You've been following us?" Carrie cried, leaping to her own feet, standing next to Kyle.

"You've tapped the phones as well, haven't you," Kyle said, and although it was in the form of a question, it wasn't one.

Not answering, Bates flipped through the pages of his small pad. "We figured something was about to break after all the hang-up calls you've been receiving."

"That was Sanders?" Carrie cried, wrapping her arm around Kyle's. "I've gotten several. What about you?" she asked him.

He nodded. She noticed that his jaw had gone rigid and his skin had paled beneath his tan. He tucked his arm protectively around Carrie's shoulders, as if having her close meant he was better able to guard her.

"What's he want?" Kyle asked, his voice level and hard.

"We believe he left something with you."

"What?" Carrie wanted to know.

"Your guess is as good as ours. We went over your car with a fine-tooth comb and found nothing. But we aren't the only ones looking for him. Sanders has double-crossed the wrong people. We know he had to get rid of what he had with him, and fast. Somehow he found a way of leaving it with you."

"You think he gave us the plates?" Carrie asked. "Surely we would have found them if that were true."

"You were his only chance."

Kyle wasn't buying that. "Did you ever stop to consider he might have used us as a decoy?"

The two agents briefly glanced at each other. It seemed to Carrie that they needed some unspoken mutual approval before one of them had permission to speak.

"That thought has crossed our minds," Richards said, "but if that were the case, Sanders wouldn't be paying you this much attention. One thing's for certain. You've got something he wants."

"How can you be so sure?" Carrie asked.

"He wouldn't be risking his neck hanging around Kansas City otherwise. Trust me, the men who want Sanders aren't going to slap his hand and tell him all is forgiven. Frankly, I thought Sanders was smarter than to double-cross his cronies. Apparently I was wrong."

"You think I've got something he wants?" Kyle asked.

"Or Ms. Jamison."

"Me?" Carrie whirled around and faced Kyle. "I think this is the perfect time for a vacation, don't you? I want you to meet my parents anyway. We could—"

"I'm sorry, but we can't allow you to leave town," Bates cut in.

"We can't leave town? In other words we're sitting ducks?" Her voice rose a full octave.

"It wouldn't do any good," Richards said calmly. "He'd just follow you, and where Sanders goes Nelson follows."

"Nelson?"

"Philip T. Nelson," Bates said, as if he fully expected them to recognize the name. "He's a topnotch counterfeiter with a record that goes back fifteen years. He'd done time for just about every crime, including murder."

"Murder?" The word had a difficult time escaping the trap in her throat.

"We don't mean to frighten you, Ms. Jamison, but it's better that you learn the truth from us instead of bumping heads with one of Nelson's boys."

"Sanders is getting desperate if he's taken the risk of being seen," Richards said, holding eye contact with Kyle. "Be on your guard."

Kyle nodded.

"Be on your guard," Carrie repeated. "What's that supposed to mean?"

"Just be careful," Bates advised. "We've got a twenty-four-hour watch on you both, so you don't have to worry. Maintain your usual routine and leave the rest to us."

"Pretend nothing's different," Richards added.

"That shouldn't be any problem," Carrie said sarcastically.

A half hour later, long before Carrie's questions could be fully answered, the two agents left. The instant the door snapped into place, Kyle took Carrie by the shoulders.

"I'm not letting you out of my sight. From here on, wherever you go, I go."

"Are you nuts?"

"Yes," he snapped. "You can move in with me . . . my place is bigger."

"Kyle, you're not making any sense."

He moved from her shoulders to her arms, his grip punishing. "Don't you understand?" he said, his eyes burning into hers. "This changes everything. There are men out there who think we've got something we don't. Your life is in danger. If they ever got hold of you, there's no telling what would happen."

"That's why you want me to move in with you?"

"Yes," he said with ill grace. "I need to keep an eye on you."

"Richards and Bates said we're being watched. We don't have anything to worry about."

"Yes, we do, Carrie." He wouldn't let her make light of their predicament.

"But why do I need to move here?" she wanted to know. "You could live with me just as easily."

Kyle's gaze narrowed. "This is my turf. Besides, I have two bedrooms."

Carrie couldn't help but laugh. "Do you honestly think we're going to need two bedrooms?"

12

Across the street from Harris's house, Sanders hid behind the bushes and waited until it was dark. The minute Richards and Bates arrived, he knew his ploy had worked. The woman had seen him at the grand opening just the way he'd planned. Good, that was exactly what he wanted.

Someone needed to warn those two innocents that they were in serious danger. An agent sitting in his car outside their respective houses was next to zero protection. At least now they were aware of what they were up against. The thought of Nelson getting his hands on either of them was enough to make his skin crawl.

Sanders could have saved himself a good deal of trouble if he'd been able to get to Kyle Harris's car. This business was frustrating the hell out of him. He'd broken into the young man's garage and found a car all right, but it wasn't the BMW. Sanders wished he knew what the kid had done with the car. His best guess was that Harris had taken it to a repair shop, but it wasn't the BMW dealer in town. He should know, he'd checked.

Damn fool kid didn't have a clue to the danger he was in. The woman either. There was nothing Sanders could do but bide his time. Once the car was back, he'd get what he needed and be on his way.

He was getting too old for this, Sanders decided. He was losing his touch, too. Not a good thing to do at this point in his career. The thought of retiring on some tropical island was beginning to hold substantial appeal.

If he lived that long.

With Nelson on his tail, the future wasn't nearly as bright as he would have liked. He hadn't wanted to involve those kids, but he didn't have any choice. Someone had ratted on him. That day he'd seen the state patrol car he wasn't immediately concerned. His disguise was adequate, and the truck was clean. But then he'd seen the interest he'd generated and the way the state patrolman had radioed his dispatcher.

That was when Sanders knew there was an APB out on him. What surprised him was that the authorities didn't immediately pursue him. Not long afterward, he noticed he was being followed. That was when he left the highway and tried to lose the tail. His luck didn't hold. From the looks of it, he was within a hair of being captured when he stumbled on those two kids.

Involving someone else, especially a nice young couple like Kyle Harris and Carrie Jamison, wasn't his style. Protecting them wasn't his job either, but he couldn't help it; he felt responsible.

That was the crux of his problem, feeling responsible. He hadn't been cut out for this line of work, but he'd never managed to convince McKinzie of that. Over the years, he'd given up trying.

One thing he had to do, though, before he made his move was prove to this couple exactly how vulnerable they were. Slipping through the bushes and across the street, he moved carefully toward the house and then disappeared into the night before anyone knew he'd been there.

Then he sat back and smiled.

Carrie peeked inside the brown paper bag. "You bought all this at a pharmacy?" she asked, withdrawing several interesting-looking products.

Kyle grabbed the sack out of her hand and stuffed the prophylactics back inside. "Never mind."

"What's in the box?" she asked, cranning her neck for a better view.

"What box?"

"The big one."

He looked decidedly uncomfortable as he removed a home pregnancy kit and set it on the kitchen table. "We're going to need it, aren't we?" he asked, studying her closely.

Carrie had the distinct impression that he was looking for her to tell him it had all been a false alarm. "I think we might," she said, disliking the way her voice dipped several decibels. She was far more comfortable ignoring the fact she was a tiny bit behind schedule.

"You're late?"

"A little," she said with a shrug, wanting to make light of it.

"How late?" His voice was clipped and anxious.

"Not much," she announced cheerfully. "Just a few days."

"Exactly how many is a few?"

"Three, four—but I'm usually as regular as a clock."

"Why didn't you say something earlier?"

"I don't know."

Kyle peeled open the home pregnancy kit as if all the answers to life's problems were packaged inside. He pulled out the container and the instruction booklet and set them on the tabletop.

Folding her arms, Carrie announced in serious tones, "I'm not taking a home pregnancy test."

Kyle flattened the instruction sheet against the table. "Why not?"

"I'd prefer to make an appointment with my gynecologist."

Kyle considered this for a moment, then asked, "How long will it take before you can get one?"

"Not long. A week or so."

His look told her he found that unacceptable. "According to what this package claims, a pregnancy can be accurately read within a few minutes. I say we go for it now."

Carrie bit into her trembling lower lip. "Now?"

"You have something better to do?"

Scrubbing out the bottom of her refrigerator came to mind. "Not really." She lowered herself onto the chair, feeling very much as if she were standing next to a hangman.

Kyle read the instructions aloud. It was a simple procedure, she decided. Painless—physically, at least. Emotionally was another story. Personally she'd rather not know this soon. If she was pregnant, heaven help her, she didn't want to have to deal with all it entailed quite yet. Nor was she prepared to deal with Kyle's reaction.

"Are you ready for step one?" Kyle asked when he'd finished reading.

"Trust me, Kyle, I think we're way past step one."

He looked up and grinned; then he sat down next to her and reached for her hand. Carrie's fingers curled tightly around his.

"What are we going to do if I'm pregnant?" she asked, and then shook her head, not wanting an answer. She already knew. "You're going to insist we get married, aren't you?"

"Of course," he returned.

Briefly, she closed her eyes. "I was afraid of that."

"You don't want to marry me?"

The indignation in his voice startled her. "It isn't a question of wanting," she said, trying hard not to trample his maddening pride.

"Apparently we need to clear the air right here and now," Kyle said, in dictatorial tones that raised her hackles. "If you're pregnant, there's no question of what we're going to do. We'll get a marriage license first thing Monday morning."

"For all you know, the child might not even be yours," she said, although if he even seemed to believe her she'd slap him.

Kyle closed his eyes and flattened his hands on the tabletop as if he meant to push himself upright. But he didn't. Apparently this was a technique he employed to control his temper.

"We're leaping to conclusions here without knowing the facts," he said. "Take the pregnancy test, and then we can argue to your heart's content."

Knowing it wouldn't do any good to debate further, she carried the test kit into the bathroom with her and followed the instructions. When she'd finished, she set it on the bathroom counter and set a timer.

Kyle was pacing in the kitchen when she returned.

"You didn't believe me," she murmured, unable to hide the hurt she'd felt earlier in the day.

"About what?"

"Seeing Sanders."

"You watch too many crime shows."

Carrie was stunned. "That's probably the most insulting thing you've ever said to me." She breathed deeply in an attempt to rein in her exasperation. "I'm a conscientious citizen, and you make me sound paranoid."

"I don't mean it like that," Kyle said, and she knew he was telling the truth. Unfortunately, it was too late. He'd gone way beyond irritation.

"We insult each other on a regular basis," Carrie said without rancor. "My goodness, is it any wonder our relationship is so rocky?" She pushed the hair out of her face and held it back with both hands. "Now you're insisting we get married. Frankly, I don't understand why."

"There's the small matter of a child—or the possibility of one, at any rate."

"True," she said smoothly, "but answer me this. If

I'm not pregnant, will you rush out for a marriage license Monday morning and demand we go through with a wedding?"

"Of course not," Kyle said, stalking to the far side of the room. All at once, he seemed to realize what he'd said. "I'd still want to marry you, just not next week."

Carrie sat down and mulled over his response. So much for any illusions she had. So much for thinking their relationship was more than a physical one. Kyle had set her straight in the space of a single heartbeat.

"That's answer enough," she whispered, through a throat that had gone dry and tight all at once. "It doesn't matter what the results of the pregnancy test are."

"Of course it matters."

"Not as far as I'm concerned. We're not getting married under any circumstances."

Kyle's dark eyes burned with frustration. The timer dinged in the other room.

She momentarily shut her eyes, and it seemed the oxygen froze in her lungs. Moving just then felt impossible.

"You ready?" Kyle asked.

Carrie wondered if she would ever be ready. "I guess," she said. Together they walked down the narrow hallway to the bathroom.

The test container rested on the counter.

"Blue is for positive," Kyle reminded her as they each took one step forward.

They studied the results.

"That doesn't look blue, does it?" Carrie asked, her voice strained and willowy.

"I'm afraid it does."

"It's only sort of blue, don't you think?"

"Sweetheart, if it got any bluer we could sell it as cleanser for toilet bowls. The sky doesn't get that blue. If color is any indication, you're carrying triplets."

Carrie placed her hand over her mouth. She wasn't sure why. Perhaps she was keeping herself from saying something she shouldn't, or holding in a deep well of tears. The last thing she expected was to start laughing. But that's what happened.

"Personally, I don't think this is a laughing matter," Kyle said sternly.

"I don't either," she insisted, between hoots. "But it's so typical of me. You have to admit, I'm not the type to ever plan a pregnancy."

"True," Kyle agreed, and then with a martyr's sigh said, "We'll apply for a license Monday morning."

"Who do you plan to marry?" she asked in identical tones. "If you want to sacrifice yourself, Kyle Harris, you're going to have to get some other pregnant woman, because there won't be any wedding Monday—at least not one that includes me."

"Okay, okay," Kyle admitted. "I blew it. I seem to

do that on a regular basis with you. I want us to be married, Carrie. It's important to me that this child have my name."

This was an improvement over his last statement; she was willing to concede that much. "I need time to think," she said. "I'm going home."

"You can't," Kyle said automatically.

"Please, I'll be fine." She needed to be around things that were familiar. Kyle meant well, but he simply didn't understand.

"Then I'm coming with you."

She didn't have the strength to argue with him. "If you insist," she said listlessly. All at once she had all the strength of a rag doll.

She reached for her purse and headed for the front door but stopped cold when she opened it.

"Kyle . . . Kyle!" she cried. Abruptly, she whirled around and plowed into his chest and grabbed hold of his shirt with both fists. "He was here. He was here!" she said in near hysterics.

"Who are you talking about?"

"Sanders!" she cried, her inertia swept away on the winds of panic.

"How do you know?"

"Look," she cried, twisting away and pointing toward the porch. "He brought back our luggage!"

13

"Carrie, is that you?"

"Sh-h," Carrie whispered into the telephone receiver. "I don't want to wake Kyle." Unable to sleep, Carrie had phoned her sister. Not until she'd dialed the number did she realize that it was three in the morning and her sister was undoubtedly asleep.

"Where are you?" Cathie asked on the tail end of a lengthy yawn.

"My house. I needed to talk."

"Kyle's sleeping over?"

"It's not like it sounds. He's on the couch."

"You had a fight."

"Not exactly. Listen, I didn't call to discuss Kyle, at least not directly. I need to talk, and I couldn't think of anyone else I trust."

"You're pregnant."

"How'd you guess?" Actually Carrie had given her sister plenty of advance warning. Now that her suspicions had been confirmed she felt the need to confide in someone. Kyle had certainly been no help. The man had a one-track mind. All he could think about was sacrificing himself on the altar of honor, despite how that made her feel.

"How'd I guess?" Cathie repeated with a small laugh. "Well, let's just say the last conversation we had sounded promising. You took the home pregnancy test the way I suggested, and it was positive. Am I right?"

"Yeah." A baby wasn't the end of the world, but the idea of being a mother took some getting used to. Not knowing her condition had been far more comfortable than knowing, Carrie decided.

"What's Kyle have to say about all this?"

This was the reason Carrie had phoned her sister in the middle of the night. "He thinks we should get married."

Her words were followed by a soft, brief silence. "You make it sound like he's insulting you."

"He is," she said, louder than she intended. Her words seemed to bounce off the walls of her tiny bedroom. "He never once said he loved me or that he was pleased about us having a baby or anything else that indicated marrying me was what he truly wanted."

"Give him time," Cathie suggested. "He's dealing with shock the same way you are. He just needs a few days for his head to clear. Instead of complaining, you should be grateful."

"I know, but I can't seriously see myself married to Kyle. He's wonderful, or he can be, but I can't help feeling we're not right for each other."

"It seems to me you're simply confused. Sounds like you're in love for the first time in your life and it's stressing you out. You're looking for excuses not to be."

Carrie mulled over what her sister said and then laughed softly. "When did you get so smart?"

"I don't know, but then I've never been in love."

"How can you be so sure I love him?" Her sister spoke with complete confidence, whereas Carrie felt lost in a maze of feelings and doubts. She and Kyle got along perfectly in bed together. Unfortunately, they lived a whole other life outside of the bedroom.

"I knew how you felt about Kyle from the first," Cathie said smoothly, assuredly. "You turned up on my porch step wearing a nun's skirt, and I knew immediately something had changed. It took me a while to realize what. You'd fallen in love.

"Kyle wore that same confused, lost look when he arrived looking for you. Now, are you going to get married or not?"

Carrie hesitated. "I'm not sure."

"Don't let anyone pressure you. Be sure before you make up your mind," Cathie advised.

"I will," Carrie promised.

"I can hardly wait to be an aunt. Mom's going to go ballistic when she finds out."

"Mom," Carrie repeated wistfully. She wished there were some way of hiding this news from her parents, particularly her father, but that was out of the question. He'd need to know sooner or later. Her preference was later. Much later. Like four or five years later.

"You and Kyle are fighting?" Cathie asked next, cautiously, almost as if she was afraid she was prying.

Carrie wasn't entirely sure how to answer. No man had ever irritated her the way Kyle did, yet when they were apart she felt empty and alone. No man had ever said to her the terrible things he had, and yet when he took her in his arms it felt as if it was the most natural place in the world for her to be.

Some days she was convinced she never wanted to see him again, and the moment they were apart she started counting the minutes until they could be together again.

It made no sense. Nothing had made sense from the time they'd started out for the broadcasters' convention in Dallas. Which brought up another slate of worries, one that involved Max Sanders and the

Secret Service and someone named Nelson, whom she'd never even heard of before.

Only these weren't troubles Carrie intended on burdening her sister with. Not tonight. Her plate was full as it was.

"You'll phone me if you need anything?" Cathie asked.

"Probably." Until now Carrie had enjoyed the role of big sister, giving her younger sibling advice, listening to Cathie's troubles, and doling out wisdom as if she were the Dalai Lama. For the first time in their lives, their situations were reversed. It felt good to have a sister, someone she could confide in. Someone who willingly offered her a shoulder. "Thanks, Cathie," she said, her gratitude leaking into the words.

"No problem, sis, that's what I'm here for, to guide your love life and dish out advice. Now get some sleep, you're going to need it."

Carrie yawned at the suggestion to return to bed. Lately sleeping was about all she'd been doing. She couldn't seem to stay awake past nine o'clock.

"I'll give you a call early next week," Cathie promised.

"Thanks again," Carrie said and pushed a button to disconnect the line. Setting the cordless phone on her bed stand, she scooted under the covers and closed her eyes.

* * *

Kyle woke as the first bright streaks of dawn slid into Carrie's living room. He rotated one shoulder and grimaced when his neck muscles protested. Sitting upright proved to be something of a task as he discovered muscles he'd long since forgotten.

Like a fool, when Carrie had refused to stay at his place, he'd insisted on being a gentleman and sleeping on her couch. For the love of heaven, he hadn't been serious. Nothing could have shocked him more than when Carrie had brought him a lumpy pillow and a thin blanket. He wanted to tell her it was a little like closing the barn door after the horse had escaped, but he bit his tongue. Now he wished he'd taken the time and effort to sweet-talk himself into her bed.

This business with the pregnancy had confused him. Her too, he realized. He'd have thought she'd be grateful he was willing for them to marry. Not so. Not Carrie.

Maybe Carrie needed to know that he cared for her. Nothing more should be necessary to convince her of the wisdom of marrying him.

He wandered into the kitchen and sorted through no less than ten boxes of herbal tea before he found a canister of coffee. He'd suggested she try herbal tea because it didn't contain caffeine, and he was pleased to note she'd taken his advice. Ten times over.

He brewed himself a cup of decaffeinated coffee and walked into the bedroom where Carrie was sleeping. She was lying on her back with her arms raised on either side of her head. She resembled an angel with her hair, as rich and thick as chocolate, spilled out over the pillow.

She must have sensed his presence because she opened her eyes and blinked when she saw him.

"Morning," he said, leaning against the doorway, cradling the coffee mug in both hands. "Did you sleep well?"

She rubbed a hand across her eyes and leveled herself onto one elbow. "What time is it?"

"Morning." He hadn't bothered to look. "Eight, I'd guess."

She pulled the sheet up and over her breasts, a mistake as far as he was concerned because it brought attention to the very part of her anatomy she was trying to conceal.

"Did you sleep well?"

"No." He wasn't going to lie. "I'd have slept a whole lot better with you."

"I see." It amazed him that she could blush so easily. Kyle would never have suspected it of her.

"Would you like some tea?"

"Please."

He moved back into the kitchen and poured her a mug. She was sitting up in bed when he returned, and smiled her appreciation when he handed her the tea. He gave her the opportunity to take the first sip, then removed the mug from her hands and sat on the edge of the mattress so that their gazes were level. "You're beautiful in the morning."

She opened her mouth, and he stopped her by pressing his finger over her lips. He didn't want her to contradict him. Yes, her hair was mussed and she wasn't wearing makeup, but then she never did wear much. She was beautiful because that was the way he felt about her, and never more so than now, nurturing his child in her womb. Fear struck him then: the fear of losing her, of living his life without her. He couldn't have borne that, not now.

Gently he brushed the hair from her temple, then leaned forward and kissed her. Tenderly. Without passion. Without urgency. Just so she'd know how deeply he cared.

When he eased away from her, he was shocked to find her eyes glistening with tears. She sniffled and ran the back of her hand beneath her nose.

"Tears?"

She nodded. Making a weak motion with her hand, she whispered, "I'm not generally much of a crier. My emotions seem closer to the surface all of a sudden."

Kyle gathered her hands in his own and kissed her knuckles. "We need to talk about the future."

"Do we have to?"

"Yes. I want to marry you, Carrie, and provide the family our baby deserves." Kyle didn't want to pressure her, but at the same time he felt they needed to take action and—for his peace of mind—the sooner the better.

"Let me think about it, all right? I need time."

Kyle resisted gritting his teeth. Carrie often left him feeling powerless and vulnerable. It was what disturbed him most about their relationship. The upper hand seemed to be hers. He'd swallowed his pride so often it had almost become palatable.

"Give me a few weeks to sort everything out," she repeated. "It's all still so new. I don't know what's best, what we should do."

Kyle sighed. "Would you think I was trying to sway you one way or the other if I told you I wanted to kiss you again?"

Her long lashes brushed her cheek as she shook her head. He bent forward and kissed her slowly, thoroughly. He managed to control it, but just barely.

Breaking away from her, he noticed how silky her hair looked as it tumbled about her face. More than anything he wanted to take her in his arms and make love to her.

"I need to make love to you," he whispered. "I've dreamed about it ever since Dallas."

"Oh, Kyle, please don't talk like that." Her voice heaved with emotion. She made it sound as if he were mocking her.

"Talk like what?"

"Like I'm beautiful and desirable and I drive you wild with passion."

"It's like you own me," she whispered, fighting him as hard as she was fighting herself. "I tell myself I won't let matters develop this far, and the next thing I know we're in bed together. My head's clouded enough without complicating everything with love-making."

Kyle was stunned. "You're serious, then. You honestly don't want me to touch you?"

"Just for a little while, until my head's clear."

His own head was lost in a thick fog of disbelief. The only way he could comply with her request was to move off the bed.

"Where exactly does this leave us?"

"I'm not sure I understand the question."

"I need to know what you're looking for in our relationship," he demanded in steely tones. "Because I'm telling you we can't live like brother and sister, and that seems to be what you want."

"That's just it," Carrie said, reaching for her coffee and holding on to the mug with both hands. "I don't know what I want."

"So you expect me to hang around with my tongue hanging out of my mouth while you take your own sweet time deciding."

This whole business was becoming more and more unacceptable. Who would have ever thought he'd have such a difficult time persuading Carrie to marry him? Especially now.

"You've turned my proposal into an insult, you've

trampled all over my pride," he told her. "I'm beginning to think the only thing that would satisfy you is if I turned my back on you and walked away."

"I'm not trying to be difficult."

"For not trying, you're doing a bang-up job."

"Look at it from my point of view," she pleaded. Setting the coffee aside, she knelt on top of the bed, her hands clenched at her sides. "For most of my life, other people have made my decisions for me. My father did his best to steer me into a nursing career because he felt he knew what was best for me. He chose the college I attended, the boys I dated, the clothes I wore. My parents always seemed to know what was best for me. For once in my life I want to make decisions myself."

"I'm not your father."

"But you certainly seem to have a strong opinion about what I should do."

"You're pregnant with my child. We should be married."

"There," she said, pointing an accusing finger at him. "You just proved my point far better than any argument you might have offered. Why is it so all-fired important that we marry right now?"

He glared at her, not fully understanding his insistence himself. "Because it is."

"I'm fully capable of raising a child on my own."

"Oh, great," he said sarcastically, tossing his arms into the air. "It's just my luck to fall head over heels in love with another Gilmore Girl. A baby needs a father just as much as a mother. I want to be there for my child, the way my father never was for me."

"You can be," she argued. "Nothing says you can't play a major role in our child's life."

"Right. What are you willing to offer me? Weekend visitation rights?"

"Of course not. I was thinking we might consider living together for a while. . . ."

Kyle froze, the very suggestion irking him.

"No, Carrie, I'm not willing to live with you. As far as I'm concerned, it's a situation in which we both end up losers. If you don't trust me enough to marry me, we have no business playing at being man and wife."

"You need to understand where I'm coming from," she argued.

"You need to understand a few things about me as well," he said, his voice raised and hard. "I never knew my father. He walked out when my mother was pregnant with me. You're worried about a man dominating your life. I would have welcomed a father with both arms.

"I want our child to have my name, not yours. I want to give our son or daughter the family I never had, to grow up feeling loved and secure. All you can think about are your rights. What about mine? What about our child's?"

They stared at each other for several moments, each of them needing to absorb the other's words.

"I'm not saying no to marriage," Carrie murmured, "just that I need time."

"You've got it," Kyle said flatly. "One week." With that he left the room, grabbed his shoes, and stalked out of the house. He moved quickly, needing to escape, so angry he could feel it on the soles of his feet.

He was at his rental car when Carrie threw open the front door. "I refuse to be put under time restrictions!" she called.

He didn't dignify her words with a reply.

Carrie had rarely spent a more uncomfortable week. Kyle was polite, cordial, and cool. Not once did he pressure her, about marriage or anything else. It was as if they had no life outside the radio station. He was more polite than friendly, always congenial. Yet she felt as if they were separated by a barbed-wire fence. She was ill one morning, barely making it to the ladies' room in time. Kyle was conveniently in the hallway outside the transmitter room when she came back out, but after mentally assessing her condition and deciding she was all right, he returned to the newsroom without a word.

In the evenings Kyle insisted upon coming home with her and checking out her house before he left. Although she didn't see him again until the following morning, she had the distinct impression that he stopped by several times each night. For instance, he knew when she'd gone for a walk and when she returned and what time she'd gone to bed.

As far as she was concerned, this whole business with Sanders had been blown out of proportion. She'd seen neither hide nor hair of the counterfeiter, and she didn't think Kyle had either. But she didn't tell Kyle not to come.

Friday morning, Carrie arrived for work and found Kyle already at the news desk. He looked up expectantly when she came into the studio, as if he was waiting for something. It came to her then that his one-week deadline had passed.

"My week's up?" she asked, playing it cool. She sat on the corner of his desk and dangled one leg.

"Have you decided what you want?" he asked calmly.

He wore the smug, superior look that used to drive her nuts. If he believed she would marry a man who planned to dominate and control her, he was destined for disappointment.

"I've done a good deal of thinking," she murmured. Now wasn't the time to allow pride to stand in her way. "I've taken into account what you've told me about your family, and I hope you've listened to what I've told you about mine."

"I've listened." His back was ramrod straight, his eyes hard and unyielding, as if he were braced for bad news.

"You want to give our baby your name? What if I told you there were ways we could do that without rushing into marriage?"

"Then I'd say you've made your decision." She might have been wrong but it seemed to her that his eyes softened, and when he looked at her he didn't seem nearly as stern or unforgiving.

She hopped down off his desk. "I've missed you."

His eyes held hers and the beginnings of a smile touched his mouth, however briefly. "I've missed you too. You've become an important part of my life."

"Your car's out of the shop." She'd noticed his BMW in the parking lot that morning.

"Finally."

"Any problems?" It had been in the back of her mind from the moment she'd seen Sanders that he was waiting for Kyle's vehicle.

"No," he told her, walking over to the news wire as though checking scores for the latest Wimbledon matches.

"You went over the car yourself, didn't you." She would have done so too. From the way his gaze shifted she had her answer. "You found something."

"Yes," he admitted softly, as though afraid someone might overhear their conversation.

"What?" She sat in the chair opposite his and rolled forward.

"This." He removed a magnetic key holder from his

pocket and held it in the palm of his hands. "Sanders didn't hide the plates with me, he hid the key."

"What's it do?"

"Hell if I know. Probably a safety deposit box, but only God knows where."

"You've told Richards?"

"Not yet."

Her heart was pumping at record speed with dread and fear. Kyle was holding a lighted stick of dynamite.

"Why not?" she cried, vaulting to her feet. Kyle's life wouldn't be worth a plugged nickel if Sanders or that other bozo—Nelson somebody—got hold of him with that key.

"The significance of it didn't hit me at first. I have one of these key boxes myself. It wasn't until this morning after I'd arrived at work that I realized it wasn't where I'd put it. I checked and, sure enough, there were two."

"You didn't realize there were two keys until just now?" she cried.

"I'll contact Richards this morning. Trust me, I don't have any desire to end up at the bottom of the Mississippi River wearing cement shoes."

"Let's put it someplace safe," she suggested. "In Clyde's office. He'd never know, and not knowing isn't going to hurt him."

"We can't do that to Clyde."

"Sure we can."

"If you're so worried about it, I'll lock it in my desk."

"Just get rid of it," she pleaded. "Please."

"All right, all right. There's no need to get so upset."

"No need? You could be killed!"

Every minute of her broadcast Carrie was aware of the key in Kyle's possession. It was like a time bomb ticking away in the other room. As luck would have it, the day was filled with newsworthy events, and she didn't think Kyle had an extra minute to himself.

When she'd finished with the morning program, she was sure Kyle hadn't contacted Richards and was about to volunteer to do it herself when she heard a commotion in the reception area in front of the station.

"What's that all about?" Kyle asked, sticking his head out of the newsroom.

"I don't know." Carrie stood in her office doorway. Then it hit her. The voice she heard was all too familiar. It belonged to her father.

Just then he broke past the receptionist and strode down the hallway toward Carrie.

"Carrie, baby," he boomed, studying her carefully. "Is it true?"

"What, Daddy?"

"Are you pregnant?"

"Uh . . ."

"Answer me."

"Yes," she whispered.

Her father leveled his gaze at the growing crowd of onlookers. "Now all I need to know is which one of these young men will own up to being the father of my little girl's baby."

14

"*That would be me*," Kyle said, stepping forward without the least hesitation.

Michael Jamison tried to stare him down. "Do you plan on making an honest woman out of my little girl?"

"Daddy!" Carrie cried, mortified to the very marrow of her bones. She could feel color reddening her face and avoided making eye contact with anyone.

"What's going on here?" Clyde asked, cutting through the milling crowd. He stopped dead in his tracks when he saw Michael Jamison glaring at Kyle as if he meant to tear him limb from limb.

"Either this young man agrees to marry my Carrie, or by heaven he'll face the consequences," Carrie's father muttered.

"Daddy, leave the station right this minute!" Carrie demanded, stepping in front of Kyle. Outraged, she was ready to do battle, if it came to that.

"You going to hide behind a woman, son?"

"Not on your life," Kyle said, firmly placing Carrie behind him.

"It seems the two of us have some talking to do."

"No problem," Kyle answered.

"Mr. Jamison—" Clyde started to say, but he wasn't allowed to finish.

"It'd be best if we stepped outside," Kyle said matter-of-factly.

"Kyle!" Carrie clawed her way in front of him. "My dad outweighs you by fifty pounds."

"I admit to being the father of your child," Kyle said readily. "And as of this morning we aren't getting married, so if your father cares to discuss the situation with me, he'd best do it now."

Exasperated, Carrie threw her hands in the air. "This is the most outlandish, stupid thing you've ever done."

"Me?" Kyle asked calmly.

"No," Carrie cried, "I'm talking to my father! Can't we please sit down and discuss this calmly?"

"You're going to have a baby with a ring on your finger. Let me tell you, Carrie, that's pretty damn emotional. We'll discuss it here and now, just the way I want. Your young man and I can settle our differences behind my pickup, man to man."

"Michael Jamison, you're making a damn fool out of yourself."

"Mom!" Carrie was never more relieved in her life to see her mother. The two women hugged briefly.

"Us two men have some talking to do."

"Then for the love of heaven, do so," Patsy Jamison cried. "I swear, Michael, you're enough to test the very saints."

Carrie's father looked downright sheepish. "I just couldn't bear the thought of our little Carrie being an unwed mother."

"Perhaps you and Kyle would like to talk this over with your parents privately," Clyde suggested, wiping his forehead with his handkerchief. "I believe we could all do with a bit less excitement." And Clyde promptly dispersed the crowd.

"Mom, Dad," she said, ushering her parents into her office. Kyle followed, rolling in another chair.

Carrie checked her watch and was grateful to note that Kyle wasn't due back to report the news for another twenty minutes. With luck that would be time enough to resolve this mess.

Carrie wasn't exactly sure whether or where to start. The first burning question was how her parents had learned of her pregnancy. She couldn't believe her sister would break her confidence.

"Mr. and Mrs. Jamison," Kyle said, taking control of the situation. He sat Carrie down and stood behind her, his hands gently cupping her shoulders. "First of all, you should know I care for your daughter."

"You have a name?"

"Kyle Harris."

"Kyle Harris." Her father repeated it as if he needed to test the name on his tongue to gauge Kyle's character. He repeated it a second and a third time until he was satisfied, then directed his attention toward Carrie.

"Then all I want to know is when's the wedding?"

Carrie straightened and opened her mouth to defy her father, who had humiliated her beyond reason. But Kyle tightened the grip on her shoulders and spoke before she had the opportunity. "I believe that's between your daughter and me."

Her father's face tightened.

"I can understand your feelings," Kyle interjected smoothly. "But we're both over twenty-one and perfectly capable of making our own decisions."

"He's right, dear," Patsy Jamison agreed, with a nod of her head.

"Did Cathie tell you?" This was the most pressing question on Carrie's mind.

"Not directly," her mother responded. "I phoned her a couple of days ago and she seemed so pleased about something, and when I pressed her she told me a very good friend of hers was having a baby."

"You guessed from that little bit of information that it was me?"

"Oh, no," Patsy said hurriedly. "I got to talking about this new crochet pattern I found for a baby blanket and how I'd buy yarn and make one up for her friend. Cathie changed the subject. That seemed odd to me, but I didn't let on.

"Then, later in the conversation, I asked her how the visit had gone with the two of you while you were in Dallas, and Cathie told me you'd left abruptly because of problems with a newscaster."

"Is that you, young fella?" Michael wanted to know.

"Yes, sir."

"That was when Cathie mentioned that you two were involved, and I immediately started asking about the possibility of a wedding and how we should start making plans right away if the two of you were truly serious.

"The country club is booked all the way into next April, and if there's going to be a wedding I want the reception there. I have no intention of pressuring either of you. I just feel it's important for me to know exactly how serious you are." She paused and drew in a deep breath before continuing. "That was when Cathie said she felt you and your young man were *very* serious. She even hinted that I shouldn't be disappointed if you decided to get married real soon."

Carrie realized her sister had gotten caught in her own trap.

"Something in your sister's voice clued me in to the fact that when she was talking about her pregnant friend she was really talking about you," Patsy concluded.

Her father wiped a hand across his weary face. "When your mother got upset, I figured we'd better drive up and ask you face-to-face if you were pregnant or not."

"I had no idea your father was going to rush in here and behave like an idiot while I was in the ladies' room," Patsy said apologetically, tossing a pointed look at her husband.

"I know my daughter," Michael insisted. "That girl's as stubborn as a mule. The two of us have been butting heads for more years than I can count."

"Oh, Michael, stop. I'm going to be a grandmother. Just think of it!" She dabbed at the corners of her eyes. "We're about to become grandparents. I can hardly wait."

"You gonna marry my little girl or not?" her father demanded of Kyle.

"That's up to Carrie."

"She'll marry you," Michael said with complete confidence. "I'll make sure of that."

"Listen, Daddy, I'm fully capable of making up my own mind."

"Seems to me you made it up the first time you went to bed with this young man."

"Mr. Jamison," Kyle said in a strong, even voice, "Carrie and I respect your opinion, but whether or not we marry is based on several factors, none of which involve you."

After having stood up to her father alone most of her life, it was a relief to Carrie to have someone on her side. Kyle surprised her. She would have thought this was a golden opportunity for him to pressure her into getting married, but he hadn't. She loved him so much in that minute it was all she could do not to hurl her arms around his neck and thank him.

Instead she looked calmly at her parents and said, "Mom and Dad, I appreciate your concern and I promise you that Kyle and I will let you know what we plan to do as soon as we've made that decision ourselves."

"Seems to me you're the one causing the problem," her father said. "Kyle looks like a fine young man. If you're willing to sleep with him, then by all that's right you should be willing to marry him."

"That's our business, Daddy."

"It might be best to leave them be," Patsy said, looking to her husband of twenty-nine years.

"Young people these days don't respect their elders

the way they once did," Michael grumbled. "Where'd we go wrong with Carrie? She was such a sweet baby. She never caused us a lick of trouble until she turned thirteen."

"Yes, dear."

"My only hope is that Carrie will give birth to a daughter. Then maybe someday she'll know what it's like to have your guts ripped out by learning your baby girl's about to have a baby of her own without a husband. Trust me, you love your children so much you're willing to do anything to make sure they're happy."

"I'm happy, Daddy," Carrie felt obliged to tell her father. "Really happy."

"Are you pleased to be having a baby out of wedlock?"

"I'm excited about this child," she said honestly. She didn't feel now was the time to admit how mixed her feelings had been in the beginning or how she'd struggled with her situation.

"I think we should go back home, Michael," Patsy suggested softly. "We've done enough damage here."

"I'm not leaving until my little girl's future is settled."

"To your satisfaction," Carrie inserted. It was the same argument: different chapter, identical verse. Her father felt he knew what was best for her and was intent on forcing her to comply with his vision for her future. Carrie had been rebelling against his domineering ways since she was a teenager. She'd believed that, as an adult, she'd escaped, but apparently not.

"You're going to have a baby," Michael blared, as if she would see the light if he said it loudly enough. "A baby needs a father."

Carrie half expected Kyle to leap in now and side with her dad. Kyle had been giving her virtually the same argument.

"Carrie knows what she's doing," Kyle said on her behalf.

"How long have you known my daughter?" her father wanted to know.

"Long enough," Kyle answered calmly. He looked at his watch and then pointedly opened the door. "One of us will be in touch with you soon."

"I could grow to like this young man," Michael said to his wife, but Carrie had the distinct impression he was announcing this for her benefit as well.

What father wouldn't like Kyle? she wondered. He'd make the ideal husband. Ideal son-in-law. He was intelligent, dedicated, generous. Perfect husband material even if she wasn't carrying his child.

"I believe an apology to the manager might smooth the waters," Patsy said on her way out of Carrie's office. "We really must talk about the way you handle these matters, dear. Rushing in here the way you did! Why, we're lucky someone didn't phone for a SWAT team."

"Don't be ridiculous. I'm harmless."

"Michael, really."

Without further comment, Kyle bid them both a safe trip home and returned to the newsroom for his on-the-hour broadcast. Carrie admired his restraint. She escorted her parents down a narrow hallway past the transmitter room and the control room. Following Kyle's example, she didn't berate her father, although heaven knew he deserved it.

"I'd like to speak to you when you're finished," Clyde said, sticking his head out of his office as she passed by.

Her father stepped forward and offered Clyde his hand. "The wife says I made a jerk of myself and owe you an apology."

"My husband tends to get carried away when it comes to his daughter's welfare," Patsy Jamison added.

Clyde shook her father's hand and made some remark that Carrie couldn't quite make out, but the fact he'd asked to speak to her didn't bode well. He had every right to be upset, although she had no control over her father's behavior.

After she'd returned from seeing her parents out, Carrie returned to Clyde's office and knocked briskly against his solid wood door. She might as well get this over with as quickly as possible.

"You wanted to see me?" she asked, after he called for her to come inside.

"Yes," he said, reaching for a cigar.

So it was going to be one of *those* talks. The only time Carrie ever saw an unlit cigar in Clyde's mouth was when he faced an unpleasant task—like firing someone.

He motioned toward the chair on the other side of the desk. Its straight back reminded her of an electric chair she'd once seen in an article about capital punishment. She sat on the edge of the cushion, ready to spring upward the instant she was dismissed.

"I've already fired you once this year," he said, his voice gravelly and deep.

"Are you going to do it a second time?" Carrie asked, thinking it would be better to face the idea head on. She wasn't sure what she'd do, especially now. There were other jobs, other radio stations, other means of supporting herself and her child, if it came to that. Losing the morning slot at KUTE wouldn't be the end of the world, but it would surely feel like it.

"Your job's secure for now," Clyde surprised her by saying.

Carrie was so relieved her shoulders involuntarily slumped forward.

"I'm sorry about what happened with my parents." She wanted to clear the air about the scene as much as possible. Generally her father didn't behave like a bull moose with strangers.

"I'm not the least bit sorry your parents stopped

by," Clyde said smoothly, rolling the cigar to the corner of his mouth. "It explains a good deal, especially your . . . condition."

"It does?" After frequent bouts of morning sickness, she didn't think the news of her pregnancy came as a surprise to anyone on the station staff. True, she wasn't thrilled to have her father announce it the way he had, but that couldn't be helped.

"I thought everything was going pretty well between you and Kyle. Not *that* well, mind you, but there's been a definite improvement."

"I'm in love with Kyle." Funny, she had no problem opening her heart to her employer, but she hadn't once told her parents how she felt. It made a weird sort of sense. If either her mother or father knew how she felt, they'd use it against her. Clyde wouldn't.

"I believe Kyle feels the same way about you," Clyde said. "That's why it's difficult to explain this." He handed her a sheet of paper. Carrie read the single-spaced letter twice, unable to believe what was before her very eyes.

"This is Kyle's two-week notice," she said, in a voice that was reed thin. She felt as if she'd had the wind knocked out of her and was unable to get her breath back.

"So this is as much of a surprise to you as it is to me?"

"Yes. I had no idea," she said when she could. "Did he tell you where he's headed?"

"No. I got the impression he didn't know himself. My feeling is that it isn't anywhere near here."

"I see."

"You don't know what this is all about, then?"

She shook her head. "I don't have a clue."

Kyle was turning his back and walking out on her. After all the times he'd said he cared for her and wanted to marry her and give their baby his name.

Now she knew the truth.

Despite his words to the contrary, Kyle was doing exactly what his father had done to his mother: walking out.

Then again, she might be leaping to conclusions. She'd been guilty of that in the past. "I'll talk to him," she announced, knowing without Clyde's having to say it that this was what he wanted her to do.

"KUTE doesn't want to lose Kyle."

"You were willing enough to let us both go not so long ago," she reminded him.

"Naw," Clyde said with a cocky grin. "That was just a ploy to smooth the waters between you two—and it worked. Far better than anyone ever imagined, I might add. What you young people failed to recognize is that there's often a thin line between love and hate."

"In other words, you set us up."

"Something like that. I figured you'd end up either passionately in love or murdering each other. My best guess was that you'd fall in love, and I was right."

So he'd thrown them together and then stood back to watch the fireworks, like a display on the Fourth of July.

"Talk to him, Carrie. See if you can find out what's bugging him. If anyone can convince Kyle to stay on at the station, it's you."

Carrie wasn't convinced this was true. She had every reason to believe he'd given notice in an effort to get away from her. What hurt her so terribly was that he'd gone behind her back, leaving her to learn what he'd done from Clyde.

She left Clyde's office, and moved down the hallway past the control room to the enclosed cubicle that served as the newsroom. Kyle was reading the news wire. He took stories that came from the Associated Press and rewrote them according to the amount of interest there would be for each specific story in their area.

"You busy?" she asked.

"Not particularly," he said absently.

Carrie stepped inside and closed the door. When it clicked into place, Kyle glanced up, seemingly surprised. She offered him a shaky smile that cost her a good deal, in light of what she'd just learned.

"I'm sorry about the scene with my parents."

"No problem." He turned back to the news wire. "I see what you mean about your father."

"He didn't intend to come off like such a jerk. He's worried about me, is all."

"So he said."

"You did everything right. He thinks you're the best thing that's ever happened to me. You're great, exactly the type of son-in-law he's wished for all these years. He thinks you're just the kind of man I need to whip me into shape." She made a fist and punched the air with it. "By golly, you've already proved yourself. One look at you, and Daddy knew you'd keep me barefoot and pregnant for years to come."

Kyle glanced her way as if he wasn't sure he should be amused or angry. "I sincerely doubt that."

"But you are," she said sarcastically, then regretted the childish display of emotion. "I just finished talking to Clyde."

She had his full attention now. The news wire might be typing out the late-breaking story of World War III and he wouldn't notice. His eyes all but drilled holes into her.

"He showed me your letter," she said.

His attention returned to the news wire. "So you know?"

"Yeah, I know. When did you plan to break the news? Or did you intend to tell me at all?"

"I doubt that I could have kept it a secret."

"Probably not," she agreed with a certain lack of graciousness. "When did you decide to leave the station?" Despite his proposal, she guessed it had happened when he'd had time to consider the consequences of their one fateful night.

He didn't have any reason to feel responsible. She'd absolved him from that in the beginning. As he'd so eloquently put it, she'd been the one to come to his room.

She guessed he was testing her now to see if she was serious or not. She'd meant every word earlier, when she'd said it. Now it felt wrong. She bit back the words that would force him to face up to his obligation to her and their baby.

"I made my decision this morning," Kyle answered her.

"Before or after meeting my father?" she asked with a shaky laugh.

The hint of a smile touched his lips. "Before."

"Do . . . you have another job waiting for you?"

"Not yet."

"I hear KAKY radio has need of a newsman." She knew nothing of the sort but was looking for his reaction.

"Thanks."

"Will you apply?" she pressed.

"Probably not."

"Why? You'd be a shoo-in, especially with a letter of recommendation from Clyde."

Kyle walked around her and returned to his desk. "I was planning to look for work out of state. If you must know, I've been considering heading for the South Pacific. I've always had a yen to visit Australia and New Zealand."

"Oh." Carrie felt as if a giant football player had tackled her. It sounded as if Kyle wanted to be as far away from her as he could get.

"In other words, you're walking out on me," she said, struggling not to come off as accusatory.

"Not really."

"Not really," she echoed, with a soft hysterical laugh. "It seems to me you're following in your father's footsteps. From what you told me, he walked out on your mother. Now you're doing the same thing to me."

"No, Carrie, I'm not." Just the way he spoke told her how angry he was. "I'm giving you exactly what you asked for. Space and time."

"Fifteen thousand miles is a bit more space than I need."

"I was planning to visit once the baby's born." He made a few notations on an article he'd pulled off the wire.

"Isn't this decision rather sudden?" She thought about their conversation that morning. He'd seemed more relaxed, and now she understood the reason. He was abandoning her, something she would have sworn he'd never do. She noticed that he hadn't mentioned his plans to her father. Not that she particularly blamed him.

"I must say you put on a wonderful performance for my parents. I guess I should thank you for that."

He tossed her a surly look. "Did it ever occur to

you to inquire why I'm uprooting my life and moving myself bodily as far as I can from you and our child?"

"No," she said in a tight, small voice.

"Because I've lost the ability to think clearly any longer."

His reason hit Carrie hard. "I don't want you to leave Kansas City. I need you . . . more now than ever." Her pride came crashing at her feet. Her voice trembled, but she managed to sound confident and secure by the time she finished.

"You want to make a lapdog out of me."

"That's not true."

"I'm not willing to follow you around while you decide if you'll deign to marry me or not. I'm a man, Carrie, and although I don't have much pride anymore when it comes to you and our baby, I have enough to protect what little ego I have left."

"But—"

"You've already given me a valid list of reasons why you won't marry me," he said, cutting her off. "I respect those reasons. I respect your freedom of choice. That's all fine and dandy, but I have needs too. It all boils down to one thing."

"What's that?" she asked in an incredibly fragile voice.

"I couldn't bear to watch my child grow in your womb week by week and feel helpless. It's bad enough having you push me out of your life this way."

"I'm not pushing you out of my life," she insisted, ready to become involved in a lengthy battle of words, but apparently he didn't want that because he ignored her comment.

"I'm respecting your wishes. All I ask is that you respect mine."

"But—" She bit her tongue to keep from saying anything more.

"I'm trying the best I can to do what's right for you, for me, and for our baby. If you change your mind about marrying me, let me know."

"So that's what this is all about," she said incredulously. It was all beginning to make sense. Kyle was blackmailing her into caving in to his wishes. Since he hadn't been able to convince her to marry him, this must be Plan B.

It was as she'd always suspected. Kyle was just like her father, only far more subtle.

"I'm going to miss you" she said, as if his leaving were of little concern to her. "I hope you'll keep in touch."

"I will."

"A postcard now and again from the outback would certainly be interesting."

Kyle walked over to the news desk and Carrie slipped out of the office. She was shaky and uncertain. Returning to her own office, she sat in the chair and pressed her forehead against the heel of her hands.

"How'd it go?" Clyde asked, sticking his head in the door.

She didn't look up. "Not good. He's thinking about traveling to the South Pacific."

"That's a bit drastic, isn't it?"

Carrie smiled sadly. "My thoughts exactly."

"Did he give you any indication why?"

"Yes," she whispered, turning to face her employer. "He says it's because he can't think clearly any longer."

15

The phone was ringing when Kyle walked into the house that night. He stared at it for four rings before answering. "Hello."

"Kyle, something's wrong. My crystals have been hot all day. Tell me what's happening with you so I can help."

He should have known it would be his mother. She had a knack for sensing when he was at a low point and then going all motherly on him. He'd practically raised Lillian, and to have her suddenly decide to be the parent was seldom any comfort.

"Tell me," Lillian insisted.

"Have you ever considered that your crystals could be wrong?" Kyle asked, not wanting to get into a long-drawn-out discussion. Not tonight. He had far more important matters on his mind.

"I can always tell when something isn't right. My crystals haven't led me wrong yet."

"If you must know, I quit my job today." It would be simpler just to admit it and be done with it.

"You quit your job? But why? Kyle, you're beginning to make a name for yourself at KUTE. You and Carrie are the two most popular morning personalities in Kansas City."

"Mother, if you don't mind, I have to get off the phone."

"You'll call me?" She used the low voice that let him know he'd hurt her feelings.

"Of course, I'll phone you soon," he promised. He glanced at his watch to gauge how much time he had before he had to meet Richards. "Don't worry about a thing."

"Don't forget to call me."

"I won't." By this time he would have willingly agreed to just about anything. "I've really got to go now."

"Okay, okay," Lillian agreed reluctantly. "I want you to know you can come to me for anything. You know that, don't you?"

"Of course."

Kyle replaced the receiver with a sigh of relief.

Once more he checked his watch. His rendezvous with the Secret Service agent was scheduled for a movie theater. The location had been Richards's choice, not his. Kyle had agreed, although he didn't understand why they couldn't meet at his house the way they had before.

The sooner he got rid of the key, the better he'd feel. He wasn't much for these cops-and-robbers games, especially now when his personal life was a mess. Although Carrie and he had been warned about being in danger, Kyle hadn't sensed that it was anything immediate. Perhaps he should be more concerned, but he hadn't seen any real evidence of trouble. At any rate, it would soon be over, and frankly he was just as glad.

Kyle reached for the telephone and punched out Carrie's number. She answered on the third ring.

"Hello." It sounded as if she had a bad cold.

"It's Kyle," he said stiffly. "Would you like to go to the movies with me?"

His request was followed by an intense silence. "You're asking me to the movies?" she asked, as if she wasn't convinced she'd heard him correctly.

"Yes." His first inclination had been to explain what they'd be doing at the theater and state that it was her duty to see this fiasco through. He'd really invited her as an excuse to be with her. Such times would be precious few in less than two weeks.

"You handed in your notice this morning," Carrie

said in a clear, crisp voice, as if she were a professional reporting the news. "You came right out and told me you're walking out on me and the baby, and now you're asking me to go to the movies?" The last few words came out high and mildly hysterical.

"Basically, you're right. I'm meeting Richards there to give him the key I found. Do you want to come or not?" He took exception to the way she suggested he was abandoning her and the baby but let it pass.

"I'll come."

"Fine. I'll pick you up in fifteen minutes."

She was ready when he arrived, and he was struck by how radiantly beautiful she looked in her pale blue cotton dress. An oversized bag was draped over her shoulder. She wore her hair down and tied at the neck with a silk scarf.

He tore his gaze away because he couldn't look at her and remain unaffected. It had been that way from the moment the pregnancy was confirmed. Even before. He couldn't look at her without having to fight down the desire to hold her and make love to her.

They drove in silence to the theater complex, which was adjacent to a nearby shopping mall.

"Richards suggested we meet him here?" she asked after they'd parked and were in line for tickets.

"Yes. I was surprised too, but he must know what he's doing," Kyle said. The stupid key felt as if it were burning a hole in his pocket.

"I'll be glad when this whole thing is over."

Kyle shared her feelings. The movie was some ridiculous good-guys and bad-guys thriller he never would have paid to see otherwise. Apparently Richards had an ironic sense of humor.

"Do you want popcorn?" Kyle asked as they passed the snack bar.

"I brought my own," Carrie whispered, looking from side to side to be sure no one overheard her. "Drinks too."

Kyle couldn't believe what he was hearing. "You can't do that," he said, cupping her elbow and directing her to a corner of the lobby where they could speak privately. "Didn't you read the sign on your way in the door? It says no one is allowed to bring food into the theater."

"Sure, they want you to spend three bucks for a soda and twice that for a bag of popcorn. It's highway robbery. I refuse to pay such outlandish prices."

"Then don't eat." Kyle was fast losing his patience.

"I like popcorn with my movie."

"Carrie, they could kick you out of the theater."

"Let them," she said with a defiant tilt of her chin. "Don't worry, I promise not to implicate you." She regarded him in a way that suggested she'd gladly stand before a firing squad before she so much as hinted he was involved in her hideous crime.

"Fine," he muttered, but it wasn't. Perhaps he should count his blessings that Carrie had refused to marry him. Heaven knew she could find the most unique ways of irritating him.

A teenager with a bronze tan that Kyle suspected came from a tanning booth took their tickets and directed them to the appropriate theater.

"I suppose you're one of those people who like to sit way in the back," Carrie said as they entered the theater, which was fast filling up.

"Generally I do sit in the back." It went without saying that little Carrie would prefer a front-row seat. "This evening we don't have any choice. Richards told me exactly where to meet him."

"What if someone is already seated there?" Carrie asked.

"No one is, so we don't need to worry about it. I'm to take the aisle seat." Kyle stepped aside at the third row and allowed her to go in first.

At least the seats in the first few rows were wider and more comfortable, Kyle noted gratefully.

"When's Richards planning to arrive?" she asked, knifing into his thoughts.

"I don't know."

"I was just thinking," Carrie said, in that easy-going way of hers that was indicative of anything but nonchalance. Kyle had been taken in far too often not to know how serious she was.

"Thinking about what?" he asked, making sure he sounded interested. A teenage couple claimed the two seats directly in front of them. They had both dyed their hair jet black and then let someone with a Weed Eater style it for them. The girl wore hoop earrings that were so big a seal could have leaped through them.

"I was thinking about doing some traveling myself," Carrie continued. "I've always wanted to visit the South Pacific. The baby and I could come visit you, and you could show us around."

"If that's what you want," he said, noncommittally.

"Would you like it if I came?" she asked, with the same nonchalance.

"I'd like it very much."

That seemed to appease her, but it did little to ease Kyle's mind. He wanted to take her by the shoulder and shake some sense into her. The words to suggest she marry him were on the tip of his tongue, but he'd vowed he wouldn't ask her again. When and if they married, the proposal had to come from her.

"Cough," she said under her breath.

"Excuse me?"

"Cough," she repeated, taking a soda can from the bottom of her purse.

He coughed once politely and she used that as a diversion to open her soda can. Unfortunately his faked malady did little to disguise the popping and fizzing sounds. Nervously, Kyle turned around to see how much attention they'd generated. He was relieved to notice that no one seemed to care.

After taking a deep swallow of soda, Carrie looked at him. "Want some popcorn?" She opened her purse, and he saw that the inside was stuffed full of popcorn, carefully packaged in a plastic bag.

"No, thanks," he said, worried Carrie was going to get them kicked out of the theater. He wished he had thought to ask her to wait until after meeting Richards.

"Suit yourself."

The minute the lights lowered, she began to munch happily on her snack. Kyle's stomach grumbled. He hadn't had dinner, and he hadn't realized how hungry he was. He hated to admit how good the popcorn looked and smelled.

Previews were being shown when he reached over. "Are you still willing to share?"

"Of course," she said, working a handful of kernels toward her mouth.

Kyle took his first sample, surprised how weak his principles were when it came to his stomach.

"Do you want a soda too?" she asked.

He might as well hang for a sheep as a lamb. "Sure."

She dug around in that bag of hers and came up with a root beer, his favorite. "Thanks," he said and when he went to open it, she coughed as if she were having some kind of seizure. Unfortunately his soda can wasn't any less noisy than hers had been. The sound seemed to reverberate around the theater like the gun off a warship.

When he'd finished, their eyes met in the dimly lit theater and she smiled. Kyle didn't know what it was about this woman's smile that affected him so profoundly. He felt the power of it go through him like an electric shock. He tried to think of what his life would be like without her. Pride had demanded that he make his trek to the South Pacific sound like a lifelong ambition, but in reality he would give it up in a heartbeat if Carrie agreed to marry him. Half a heartbeat.

But even without factoring in her pregnancy, Kyle wasn't sure he was keen on a long-term relationship. There was too much pain involved, especially when the other party might not return his feelings. There was nothing left to do but to cut his losses and remove himself from more potential misery.

"Excuse me." A flashlight was aimed at the purse that rested in Carrie's lap. The butter on the contraband glistened like diamonds under the glow. "Could I speak to both of you in the lobby?"

It was the same tanned teenager who'd taken their tickets earlier.

"What's this about?" Carrie asked in a loud whisper.

"Shh." The teenage girl with the hula hoops for earrings turned around and pressed her finger over her lips.

"Please, we prefer to talk to you in the lobby," the usher insisted.

"They're kicking us out of the theater," Kyle muttered under his breath, blaming her. He could feel the stares of those around him, including the teenage boy with the weird haircut. Kyle glared back, although he felt like a first-class fool.

"They won't actually kick us out, will they?" Carrie asked in a whisper as they followed the usher into the lobby.

"You'll need to discuss that with the manager," the usher explained.

Kyle reached for Carrie's hand. For all he knew this could have something to do with Richards, although if it did, he certainly intended on making his opinions known. There must be ways of obtaining the key without publicly humiliating them.

They were directed into the manager's office and told to sit down and wait.

"I knew this was going to get us into trouble," Kyle said uncharitably as he paced the small office.

The manager, a middle-aged, overweight man, appeared in the doorway and hesitated when he saw them. "This generally happens with kids," he said, frowning at Kyle as if to say he should know better. "This is the first time I've had to ask two adults to leave the premises."

"Exactly what have we done that's so terrible?" Carrie demanded, the picture of innocence.

"You smuggled soda and popcorn into our theater," the manager said, as if this was a well-rehearsed speech. "Our parent company has a strict policy against such behavior. It's posted throughout the theater complex, so don't try to say you didn't see the signs."

"But . . ." Her indignation died a fast death, Kyle noted, as the manager held up her soda can and removed the plastic bag of popcorn from her purse.

"You're welcome to come back to the theater with a written permission slip from your parents that states—"

"My parents? I beg your pardon," Kyle said.

"Sorry." The manager's smile was apologetic. "As I explained, this generally happens with youngsters. You're welcome to patronize our theater again as long as you understand that any food you consume must be purchased from our snack facilities."

"Now that you have the contraband we'd like to return to the movie," Kyle said sternly. He was an adult and refused to be treated like a juvenile.

"Then you shouldn't have smuggled in goodies." The manager's voice rang with righteousness. "If you care to watch the movie, you'll need to purchase another ticket."

Kyle was not appeased. "I'll see my attorney about this."

"You do what you feel is necessary," the manager said, without revealing the least bit of concern over a lawsuit. With that he escorted them to the front door and held it open. Once they were on the other side, he all but brushed his hands as if he were pleased to be rid of them.

Kyle was outraged at the way in which they'd been made to feel like criminals. The fact that they'd been forced off the premises and instructed to purchase a second set of tickets didn't sit any better.

"Come on," he said to Carrie, ushering her back to the box office.

"I'm sorry, Kyle," she said.

"Don't worry about it." Hell would be sponsoring ice skating competitions before he'd ever visit *this* theater again.

"Everything I do backfires," she murmured, her eyes avoiding his.

"It's no big deal," Kyle said.

"It isn't just the popcorn," Carrie continued, sounding close to tears. "It's everything. Look at what's happening with us."

Now was not the time for this. They needed to get back inside the theater. Richards was looking for them.

"Nothing's happening," Kyle said, glancing at his watch and wondering if they were going to miss the rendezvous with the Secret Service agent.

"That's my point," Carrie continued. "I've messed up our relationship so badly I'll probably never see you again. I don't know if I could bear that."

"Do you mind if we discuss this another time?" Kyle asked, impatiently studying the line. It could take them another five minutes or longer to get back inside the theater.

"It dawned on me how much I'm going to miss you and how much I need you, and all at once nothing else matters," Carrie continued, undaunted by his lack of enthusiasm. "I talked to Cathie when I got home from work this afternoon, and she helped me see that I was fighting the very thing I want most. For once in my life it's the same thing my father thinks is best too, and because of that I started to doubt myself. You see, Dad and I never agree. You and I don't either, but we can work around that."

Kyle froze, unable to trust what he was hearing. He gripped Carrie by the shoulders and studied her upturned face. "Are you telling me you're willing to marry me?"

Her eyes glistened with unshed tears as she nodded. "It isn't just because of the baby, either. I love you, Kyle. I honestly love you. I don't know when it happened or how, but the trip to Dallas was the best thing that's ever happened to me. The baby is a bonus."

Kyle was speechless.

"If you're still set on traveling to Australia, I'll go with you. Only I'd prefer the baby be born in the United States. Otherwise he or she can't be President."

"President of the United States?"

"Yes," she said, nodding eagerly. "In case you didn't know this. It's the law of the land. And with your intelligence and my knack with people, it seems natural to expect great things from our child."

Kyle brought his arms around Carrie and hugged her close. He would have much preferred to kiss her, but with the way matters were going he might be expelled from the theater for a public display of affection.

"You buying a movie ticket or not?" the man behind him in line asked.

"Yes. Sorry," Kyle said, reaching for his wallet. He'd taken out a twenty-dollar bill when the theater door flew open and a young girl, the one with the weird haircut, staggered out. She closed her eyes and took several deep breaths.

"Someone was just murdered in the theater," she cried and bent over as though she was going to be ill. Her boyfriend came out and stood beside her, holding her shoulders, but he didn't seem to be in any better shape than the girl. Both youngsters looked pale and badly shaken.

The manager stuck his head out the door and calmly instructed the pair to return to the theater. "The police said no one could leave until they'd been questioned."

Kyle exchanged meaningful looks with Carrie.

"What happened?" Carrie asked the girl and her boyfriend.

"These two guys were whispering behind us, and it seemed one was upset with the other, and then all at once there was this popping sound."

"A silencer, I guess." Her boyfriend spoke for the first time. "But it didn't really hide the noise."

"All at once this guy from the seat directly behind us fell into the aisle." The girl covered her face with her hands and trembled. "There was blood every-where."

"The seat directly behind you?" Carrie repeated, gripping Kyle's hand as if it were all that kept her from fainting right then and there.

"I think we'd better get back inside," the youth suggested to his girlfriend.

A siren could be heard screaming in the distance. Kyle stepped away from the cashier's window, his thoughts whirling at laser speed. That bullet might possibly have been intended for him. If it hadn't been for Carrie getting them kicked out of the the-ater, he might be the one who was shot. Or Carrie.

He put his arm around her and drew her away from the crowd.

"Did you hear what she said?" Carrie asked shak-ily. He heard and felt the panic in her voice, mainly because he was feeling much the same himself.

"I heard." Kyle pulled out his billfold and counted

his cash. He had less than fifty dollars with him. "How much money do you have on you?" he asked.

"On me?" She reached inside the large bag, sadly empty now except for her wallet. "Thirty dollars."

"How much can you get?"

"I don't know, why?"

"We're leaving town."

"Leaving town? We can't . . ."

He could almost see the list of protests working their way through her mind. "There's a cash machine here," he said in a low voice. "Take out as much money as you can. I'll do the same."

"I don't have much in my checking account," she admitted.

"How much?"

"About three bucks," she said with a sigh. "This has been an expensive month."

Kyle mentally calculated how much ready cash he had as well. Luckily he had access to his savings account, but that wouldn't last them long, especially if they were going to be on the run.

"I've got a credit card," Carrie volunteered, taking it out of her wallet.

"They'll trace us with that."

"Not this card. It belongs to my dad. He insisted I carry it for emergencies. On pure principle I've never charged anything on it."

Now seemed like the perfect opportunity. Kyle reached for her hand and noticed it was cold and clammy. His first duty was to protect Carrie. He needed to find someplace safe and fast.

Within a few minutes there was an ambulance, a fire truck, and no less than six police vehicles. Kyle and Carrie entered the mall from a side entrance, found the cash machine, and viewed what was happening from the anonymity of the milling crowd.

Kyle searched for a familiar face. He didn't see any until an unmarked car skidded to a stop and Charles Bates leaped out of the driver's seat and raced inside the theater.

"That's Bates," Carrie said excitedly, holding fast to Kyle's arm.

"I know."

"Aren't you going to talk to him?"

"No," Kyle said evenly. He didn't know if he'd been set up, but it looked suspicious. It had seemed odd to him that Richards wanted to meet him at a movie house, but he hadn't questioned it.

He'd brought Carrie along thinking she was safer with him than on her own. Little did he know. Little did he suspect.

One thing was certain. They weren't safe in Kansas City anymore.

He walked over to a pay phone.

"Who are you calling?" Carrie asked, sticking close to his side. She was terrified; Kyle didn't blame her. If the truth be known, he was badly shaken himself.

"I need to make a few arrangements," he explained.

"With whom?"

"My mother," he said, cupping his hand over the mouthpiece. "Someone needs to know where we're hiding. There's no one else I trust."

"But—"

"Don't worry, Carrie, I know what I'm doing. We're leaving town."

"Where are we headed?"

"My grandparents have a lake cabin in the woods. It's pretty rustic, but it's a great place to hole up until we can decide what to do." His best guess was that they had a week, possibly two, before being discovered. He needed to think, to analyze what had happened and why.

They made their way into the mall parking lot. Carrie was still pale, Kyle noted, but he wasn't in much better shape himself. He would have preferred to pack a suitcase, but he'd learned to travel light, compliments of Max Sanders. They'd make do with what they had. Once their cash reserve ran out, they'd use her father's credit card.

Max Sanders moved among the crowd, hoping to get a better view of what was taking place. He'd been in the theater when he heard the silencer. His first thought was that the two kids had been snuffed. Anger had burned through him as he worked his way across the back row of the theater.

But whoever was shot wasn't the kids. Good. He'd grown downright fond of those two and hated the idea of their being wasted.

Problem was, neither one seemed to understand they weren't playing with amateurs. The men who were after them were professionals.

Kyle Harris had found his key. Max had discovered it was missing from the undercarriage of the car and knew immediately that Harris had taken it.

Sanders had had to take a small side trip, something unavoidable to get Nelson off his track and stir up things with the Secret Service. He just wanted to make sure the citizens of these United States were getting their money's worth.

He'd followed Harris home from work, but before he'd looked for the key on the undercarriage of the BMW, Kyle had come out of the house. The newscaster had been whistling a hauntingly sad song that left him wondering what was plaguing the boy. He hoped it wasn't this business with the key but guessed that it probably was.

From the house Harris had picked up the woman and gone to a movie. The more he saw this couple together, the more apparent it was that the two were in love.

Sometimes Sanders forgot what it was like to be part of the real world where couples fell in love and married. He had never had a wife himself.

He'd been in and out of love a dozen times. But

there was just one special woman he couldn't forget. It had been years ago when he was young and stupid. He'd have married her, too, if that had been possible. There were times, when he saw young people in love the way Harris and his girl were, that he thought back to those days and wondered what might have happened if his life had taken a different turn.

Harris had the key in his possession, Sanders knew. What the newscaster didn't understand was that giving it to Richards or Bates would do little good. It was a key, all right, but they didn't have a clue as to what or where. Only he had that information.

The killing in the theater had shocked Sanders. His relief was great, once he realized it wasn't the two young people. He hung around long enough to discover that the dead man was Richards. Not that he was surprised.

Part of his assignment was to scout out the mole in the agency. He'd narrowed it down to three agents. Richards was one he'd long suspected of being on the take. He didn't need to be a genius to figure out who the assailant had been, either. Nelson was in town, which meant it was time for Sanders to take a short vacation from Kansas City. He just hoped Harris was smart enough to go into hiding too. There was nothing more he could do to help the couple; they were left to their own devices much the same as he was. He wished them well.

*   *   *

While Kyle put gas in his car, Carrie picked up a few items at the mini-store inside, including a map. Kyle paid the attendant, and they were on their way.

"How far away are we from your cabin?" Carrie asked.

"A couple of hours."

"What'd you tell Clyde?" she asked. He'd been on the phone quite a while with their employer.

"That we were getting married," Kyle said absently.

"What's wrong?" Carrie asked.

"The man who was killed was Richards."

Carrie swallowed tightly. "How'd you find out?"

"Clyde told me. It could have easily been us. So you see, now isn't exactly the best time to be thinking about a wedding."

Carrie laughed. She couldn't help herself. "Do you mean to tell me that after all this time you've changed your mind?"

16

"*But it just says* they sell fishing and hunting licenses," Carrie protested when Kyle parked outside a backwoods country store. They'd located the cabin and fallen exhausted into bed. First thing in the morning, Kyle had suggested they buy supplies.

"Places like this cater to a variety of needs," Kyle insisted. "My guess is the store clerk serves as a justice of the peace as well as postmaster, coroner, and just about everything else."

Kyle was right. They got a wedding license right then and there and decided to return a few days later for the actual ceremony.

In addition to purchasing a newspaper and the food they'd need for the next week, Carrie bought two stiff pairs of jeans and a handful of sleeveless cotton blouses. Kyle bought some clothes as well.

"It doesn't seem right to talk about our wedding with a man sitting on his front porch and whittling a dog out of a block of wood."

"Do you want to get married or not?" Kyle asked. He didn't seem to be in the best of moods this morning, withdrawn and uncommunicative. If anyone was having second thoughts about the wedding, it appeared to be Kyle.

"I want us to be married," she answered simply. It didn't seem fitting to buy a fishing license along with one for their marriage. But then, she told herself countless times, these were unusual circumstances.

As they drove down the long, narrow dirt road that led to the cabin, Carrie was able to view it for the first time in daylight. It was a bedraggled sight, against a backdrop of bright green trees and the crisp, clear waters of the lake. At the water's edge the long arms of a weeping willow swept spindly fingers against the glassy-smooth surface. The trees were mirrored there as well, in a setting of serenity and peace.

The cabin was a dreary shade of brown. Carrie doubted that it had ever been painted, but that didn't detract from its homespun appeal. The structure reminded her of a bygone era, sort of hillbilly style with one step leading up to the front porch. All they needed was a rocking chair to complete the picture.

The inside, however, had come as a pleasant surprise. It was apparent that Kyle had visited recently. The hardwood floor was swept and clean, and everything had been set neatly in place. There were some supplies, but most, he said, had come from his mother's health food store; there wasn't a single item Carrie would seriously consider eating. Kyle neither, judging by the dust they had accumulated.

In addition to a loft, the cabin had a lone bedroom, which was dominated by a brass bed, piled high with colorful patchwork quilts.

After they put away their supplies, Kyle said, "I've been doing some thinking." His tone told her she wasn't going to like what he had to say.

"Oh?"

"I've got to get rid of this blasted key. Otherwise we'll never be safe."

Carrie had thought of that herself. "Who do you intend to give the key to?"

Kyle rammed his fingers through his hair hard enough to cause her to wince. "The hell if I know."

"Can we trust Bates?"

"I doubt it."

"Do you think Richards set you up?" The thought of Kyle being the one shot brought a fear so great it made her tremble inside.

Kyle's lips tightened. "That's the problem. I don't

know who to trust anymore. I should have known something was wrong when Richards arranged the meeting in a movie theater. If I'd been running on all eight cylinders, I'd have asked him why, but I'd just met your parents for the first time, and—well, you know how that went."

Carrie didn't need to be reminded of the scene with her mother and father. "I doubt that I would have done any differently," she said, wanting to reassure him. Richards was a professional. If he'd asked her to meet him in a theater, she wouldn't have questioned it either.

"Who killed Richards?" Carrie wondered aloud.

"I don't know that either."

"Nelson?" Carrie suggested, remembering the name being bandied around as the bad guy in all this. The good guys and the bad guys weren't as clear as they had been.

"Your guess is as good as mine," Kyle said.

"Maybe we could contact the FBI," Carrie suggested. It made sense to her. If they couldn't trust one agency they could try another.

"The FBI doesn't know anything about this case. I could give them the key, but they wouldn't know what to do with it, and furthermore, none of the right people would learn that we'd gotten rid of it."

"You mean the bad guys, whoever they are, wouldn't learn we didn't have the key?"

"Right. I'd never have taken you to the movies if I'd known there was any danger." Kyle seemed to feel it was important she know that.

"I never suspected you would."

"You're safe here, for the time being," he said.

The cabin wasn't the Hilton, but it was livable. Personally Carrie wouldn't mind an igloo if she could be with Kyle.

"I've been going over our options, and it seems to me there's only one thing left to do." He hesitated as if he dreaded continuing. "I'm going to leave you here and contact Bates myself."

Carrie didn't hear anything more than the part about him deserting her. "No way," she said adamantly. "We're in this together, remember? I was there with you in the beginning, and I want to see this through."

"Carrie, no." Although his voice was strong and firm, she sensed a pleading quality. "You're pregnant, and I refuse to put you in further danger."

"But—"

He gripped her hands and knelt down in front of her. "It's the only way. Trust me, I'm not keen on leaving you, but I'll be back in a day, two at the most, and then we can be married."

"Kyle, no, please don't leave me. Where will you go? Who will you contact?" The words wobbled as if delicately balanced atop a precipice.

He closed his eyes and kissed her knuckles. "I

can't think of any other way to put an end to this craziness. One thing's for sure, I'm not placing you in a position of being hurt. Not again."

"But—"

"If there was any other way, believe me, I'd be the first one to hear you out, but there isn't. Now listen carefully." His serious, dark eyes held hers captive. "Do you know how to fire a gun?"

Swallowing became difficult. She shook her head. From the time she was a child, guns had terrified her. She'd never so much as held a handgun, never wanted to.

"Then I'll teach you."

"I can defend myself," she insisted. "Really, Kyle, you don't have anything to worry about. I know some karate."

"What?"

"You heard me. Remember that interview I did several months back with the guy who dressed up like a Ninja Turtle and lectured at grade schools?"

"Yeah, what about him?"

"We dated a couple of times, and Ronny—that was his name—gave me three lessons."

Kyle's mouth thinned with disapproval.

"There's no need to be jealous," she assured him, smiling. "You and I were at odds then, and he didn't mean a thing to me. As I recall we didn't so much as kiss. I couldn't get past the fact this was a grown man dressing up like a turtle. Although he was very nice."

"I'm not jealous," Kyle insisted, but Carrie knew otherwise and actually she was pleased.

"It's all right if you are," she told him. "I wouldn't want to hear about any of the women you used to date."

"I'm not jealous," he said a second time. "But it worries me that you believe you can hold off men with weapons because you've had three karate lessons from a Ninja Turtle."

"Try me," she said, leaping to her feet. She took the stance Ronny had taught her and raised her hands as if she intended to pulverize him with two well-placed chops. "You won't find it so easy to get past me," she said, bouncing around him. He had to catch her first, and after the first couple of tries, he gave up.

"Carrie, be serious, will you?"

"You think I'm not?" She did a little dance around him, kicking out her leg the way she'd seen Jackie Chan do in a movie. It looked simple enough when Jackie did it, and she was surprised when she saw Kyle's head lash back.

"I didn't hurt you, did I?" she cried, afraid she might have seriously injured him. She remembered Ronny telling her that the most powerful muscle in her body was in her thigh.

Kyle reached out and grabbed her around the waist, pinning her arms. Carrie let out a protesting cry, which Kyle ignored.

"What are you going to do now, O fighting Ninja woman?"

"Kyle, put me down!" She kicked out her feet and struggled, but not overly much. She felt far too good in his arms to put up much of a fuss.

Carrying her into the bedroom, Kyle fell onto the bed with her, collapsing so he took the brunt of the impact. Since it was a feather bed, there wasn't much of a jolt. Amused, he rolled over and pinned her hands with his own above her head.

"Now what have you got to say for yourself?" he asked as she squirmed beneath him.

All at once Carrie wondered why she was fighting him so hard. This was exactly where she longed to be, in his bed with his arms around her.

The laughter slowly drained out of her, and her chest heaved as she struggled to catch her breath. Having Kyle so close, within kissing distance, paralyzed her ability to reason clearly.

"What do I have to say for myself?" She repeated his question. "I don't know, but while I'm thinking about it, why don't you kiss me?"

The laughter was gone from his eyes as well, and the intensity of his look darkened them. He released her hands and leveled himself on his palms an inch or so above her. Fearing he was about to leave her, she wrapped her arms around his neck and eagerly anticipated his kiss.

Nothing happened.

Disappointed, Carrie opened her eyes.

"I don't dare kiss you," he said in a rough whisper.

Carrie swallowed her disappointment. "Why not?"

"Because I wouldn't be able to stop with a kiss. It's a battle every time I touch you not to make love to you."

"You have before," she reminded him, with a saucy grin she hoped he found seductive. He might have some compunction about kissing her, but she didn't share his reservation. Lifting her head from the mattress, she grazed her moist lips against his. He didn't so much as breathe, but Carrie knew him well enough to realize her kiss had the desired effect.

Encouraged, she kissed him again, this time using the warm tip of her tongue to outline the shape of his lips.

Kyle closed his eyes as if battling deep emotions. "The next time we make love we'll do so as husband and wife."

"Oh, Kyle," she whispered, loving him so much it seemed to spill out from every part of her. "I love you."

"I love you, too."

"You'd better not leave me standing at the altar," Carrie murmured, struggling to hold back her fears. She tightened her arms around him, knowing nothing she could say would turn him from this crazy plan of his. All she could do was sit back and wait— and slowly go mad with worry.

"Don't fret, I'll be back," he promised and kissed the tip of her nose. "Wild horses couldn't keep me away."

"But men with guns might try."

"They don't stand a chance."

Kyle didn't fool her. He was looking for ways to reassure her, but his words did little to ease her mind. He was leaving her and placing himself in grave danger.

"Just keep safe," she insisted, and then, because she was so afraid, she locked her eyes with his. "Kiss me once before you go."

He took her mouth, and she parted her lips in eager welcome. The familiar taste of him calmed her spirit in ways she couldn't define. In slow, sensual movements, he eased his lips over hers, molding her mouth, shaping it with his own, feeding her courage, lending her strength, giving generously of himself.

Without speaking a word, Kyle had convinced her he was completely hers. Vows weren't necessary. He'd already pledged his life to her. In that moment Carrie didn't doubt that he would put his life on the line to protect her and their unborn child.

Within the hour, Kyle was gone.

Until dusk, Carrie wandered around outside the cabin and walked along the shores of the lake. Being close to the water comforted her, soothed her, and she was badly in need of serenity. Kyle had insisted upon showing her where his mother kept a handgun. Although she insisted she'd never use it, Kyle seemed to rest easier knowing that it was there and that she had access to it if need be.

That night she slept fitfully, tossing and turning, disturbed by dreams of Kyle and monsters. She was awake before dawn, brewed a pot of tea on the temperamental wood stove, and sat on the porch to watch the sun rise.

Carrie managed to keep herself busy that day, but she didn't think she'd survive another night and day without Kyle. Her mind whirled with what she would do if he didn't come back. The trek into town, although it was a good ten miles, was walkable, but once she arrived she didn't know who she would contact or how she'd get back to Kansas City.

Carrie longed to talk to her sister. She missed her parents and, if the truth be known, she even missed Clyde, bless his black heart.

Everything felt strange and unfamiliar. She missed her home and the little things about modern-day life, and big things too. She would have given a week's wages for something that went flush in the night.

With no television and no radio, Carrie was completely shut off from news of the outside world. By the time it was dark, she was in bed, sleepless and tense.

A sound came from a distance, and she sat up and strained to hear.

It came again, a discordant noise that didn't fit with the familiar noises of the night. If Carrie were to guess at the source she would say it came from a car engine. Throwing back the covers, she nearly fell out of the bed in her eagerness to investigate.

Praying it was Kyle, her first inclination was to run out onto the front porch. But what if it was someone other than the man she loved? Carrie's heart collided with her chest at the thought. Perhaps someone else, Richards's killer, had learned of their whereabouts and had come, seeking the key.

In a panic, Carrie looked around for a hiding place. There wasn't one. The loft would be the first place anyone would look.

Kyle was right. When her life was on the line she didn't once seriously consider her three karate lessons. But she wouldn't use the handgun either. Call her a fool, but she hated the very thought of the weapon.

The sound grew close and Carrie braced her back against the rough cabin wall and inched her way toward the window. When she gathered the necessary courage, she turned and looked out.

It was a car, and it didn't belong to Kyle.

By this time Carrie's heart seemed to be pounding loud enough for telegraph messages in the African jungle. It felt as if it would explode inside her chest.

Not until the car had parked where the moon glowed on the side panel advertising HARRIS HEALTH FOODS did Carrie know it was Kyle's mother.

Weak with relief, she opened the front door and padded barefoot onto the porch.

"Hello," Lillian Harris called, standing next to her Ford Explorer.

"Hello. I'm Carrie Jamison."

Kyle's mother was nothing like Carrie had expected. The woman was tall and regal-looking with bright silver-colored hair that was styled short, almost boyishly. If it weren't for her hair, Carrie would have guessed her to be in her late thirties rather than the fifty she knew her to be.

"I'm looking for Kyle."

"He isn't here," Carrie explained, and held the door open for Lillian. "Come inside."

Fifteen minutes later, over brewed herbal tea, Carrie had finished telling Lillian the wild story of Billy Bob, alias Max Sanders, the key, Agent Richards's death, and why she was holed up in a cabin alone, frantically worried about Kyle.

"According to my runes, Kyle's in no real danger," Lillian said, as if this was authority enough to assure her of her son's well-being.

Carrie wasn't sure she should take comfort in that or not. For her part, she would have preferred a more modern technique, like a phone call or having him arrive at the cabin himself.

"I'm pleased to meet you at last," Lillian said. "I just wish it wasn't under these circumstances."

"I'm pleased to meet you too. Kyle's mentioned you often."

Lillian laughed at that, rocking in the wooden chair that sat next to the fireplace. "I'll just bet he has. I must say you're not what I expected."

"Me?" Carrie flattened her palm over her chest.

"I don't mean to sound unflattering, but I would never have guessed you'd be so tiny."

Carrie understood; she had expected something quite different with Lillian too. She'd thought the woman would wear love beads and sandals and have long hair. Lillian looked very much like what she was: a health food advocate who took her business seriously. Her hairstyle was chic, and instead of love beads she'd donned a necklace of three small crystals. As for the way she dressed, Carrie couldn't see that Kyle's mother's taste was that much different from her own—other than the crystals.

"It's been something of an experience to realize my son was falling in love for the first time in his life," Lillian went on to say. "I knew it would happen someday," she said wistfully. "It just took longer than normal. But then, what can I expect of a son who voted for George Bush?"

Carrie laughed.

"Perhaps now Kyle will understand the love that was so precious between his father and me."

Carrie didn't know if she should comment, and, if she did, what she should say. Kyle didn't think kindly of his father. The few times he'd mentioned Moon-runner, the statements had always been derogatory.

Lillian stared into her mug of tea. The dim light of the kerosene lamp illuminated the area about the stone fireplace. Carrie sat on the floor on a braided rug and sipped hot tea herself.

"Is he still intent on quitting his job?" Lillian asked.

"I don't think so."

"Good. You two are an excellent pair, on and off the air. I'd hate the thought of his giving up his career at KUTE at this point."

Now it was Carrie's turn to study her tea. "Did he tell you I'm pregnant?"

"Get out of here!" Lillian's smile lit up her face. "That's great!"

"We've decided to marry. The first thing we did when we arrived at the cabin was to drive into Jansenville for the marriage license. We saw Doc Henley, who's a justice of the peace." She didn't list the man's other titles.

"He's an ordained minister as well."

"He is?" Carrie felt better knowing that.

"I suppose Kyle told you about me and his father," Lillian said, her voice so low Carrie had to strain to hear her.

"Only a little."

"We met the summer I was nineteen. I was living in Haight-Ashbury at the time, convinced all the world needed was love. Naturally I opposed the war in Vietnam. I met Moonrunner at a protest rally where he and several of his friends burned their draft cards.

"I saw him, and the minute our eyes met I knew I'd never be the same again, and I was right. We sat up that first night and talked until dawn. I wish I could adequately explain the strength of our feelings for each other from that first moment. It was as if I'd waited all my life for this one person. He felt the same way about me."

"But he left you." Carrie regretted the outburst the moment the words left her lips.

"Kyle told you that, didn't he?"

"Yes," Carrie admitted reluctantly. "I'm sorry, I should never have repeated it."

"Moonrunner didn't leave me. Even now, after all these years, I refuse to believe that. He never knew I was pregnant with Ringo—I mean Kyle. If he had, I think he would have turned over heaven and earth to find me." Lillian smoothed a wrinkle from her skirt. "Perhaps what you're hearing is the wishful thinking of an old woman who'll never be able to forget the one true love of her life. There've been other men since, but I was only tempted to marry once, and that was years ago."

"You were opposed to violence?"

"Oh, yes. I still am, vehemently opposed."

"But you own a gun. Kyle gave it to me. He in-

sisted I have it for protection while he was away."
She glanced toward the kitchen cabinet where it was
stored.

"The gun belonged to his father. I hope to high
heaven you didn't attempt to fire it."

"No, I refused."

"Thank goodness. That thing hasn't been used in
over thirty years. Moonrunner gave it to me for the
same reason. He thought I might need it for protection."

"Against whom?" Carrie asked, curious to learn
what she could about Kyle's parents.

"The police. Moonrunner was into some *thing* he
could never talk about. He couldn't tell me for my
own protection, but I think I knew. You need to remember those were violent days. Our young men
were dying on foreign soil and we were losing the
very future of our country. People don't understand
now. I'm proud to have been involved in protest
marches. I firmly believe they shortened the war and
saved American lives."

"You were saying something about Kyle's father,"
Carrie said, not wanting to steer the woman away
from the topic that interested her most.

"Yes, Moonrunner. I suspected he was with a militant group that planned to bomb an ROTC building
on some campus."

"Did they?"

"I can't be sure. Several militant organizations

were bombing buildings in those days. One ROTC was hit, but it wasn't the one I suspected Moonrunner was planning to blow up. Of course, anytime one works with explosives there's terrible danger."

"Naturally." Carrie shuddered to think of young people putting their lives on the line in order to protest a war. If ever she needed proof that violence begets violence, she had it in Lillian's story.

"Several of us lost friends. One explosion . . ."

"Yes?" Carrie urged softly.

"It was an accident," Lillian said, her face tight with the painful memories. "Three college students were killed. I tried to find out about Moonrunner, but I never could. You see, I never knew his legal name. Moonrunner was all he ever told me. Again, that was for my protection."

"He knew yours?"

"No." She smiled regretfully. "I'd renounced it and my parents, both."

"I see."

"You probably don't, but remember I was young and very stupid. When I discovered I was pregnant with Kyle, I quickly reclaimed my name and came home to Kansas. I had wonderful parents."

"They helped you get on your feet?"

"Oh, yes, but it took some time. I had a difficult pregnancy and my morale was low. No matter how hard I tried to put Moonrunner out of my mind, I couldn't, even though I suspected he was dead."

Carrie closed her eyes and silently prayed for Kyle's safety.

"I'd like to think Kyle's father would get a charge out of our son. Who would have believed two hippies could have spawned a conservative Republican?"

"Give him time to come around," Carrie said with a wink.

"I swear I wasn't awake until I reached thirty, and by that time it was too late. Kyle's personality was already formed, and it resembled my father's far more than it did mine or Moonrunner's."

Carrie flattened her hand on her tummy, thinking of the baby growing there and wondering about the life their child would have.

"I nearly married when Kyle was ten—a natural yogurt salesman from Missouri. We got along real well and might have made a good life together, but when it came right down to it, I realized I was marrying Harold for all the wrong reasons. I liked him just fine. He was a good man, and he would have made Kyle a decent stepfather, but you know what was missing: that spark. It just wasn't the same as it was with me and Moonrunner.

"Sometimes I wonder what kind of life Kyle would have had if I'd married Harold. At the time Kyle thought it was a great idea. He was furious when I told him the wedding was off." She paused and laughed. "He ran away. Got a whole lot farther than I'd ever suspect. If we hadn't found him before he reached the Mississippi, my guess is we might never have seen him again."

She chuckled as if the memories amused her.

"You might find it amazing, but Kyle's a lot like me in ways you wouldn't suspect. He's the type of man who only loves once. When men like that make a commitment to a woman, it's for life."

Carrie felt strengthened by Lillian's words. "I'll do my best to be a good wife to him."

"You want some advice?" Lillian asked, leaning forward and bracing her forearms against her knees.

"Of course."

"This is probably the only time I'll give you any. I'm not good at this sort of thing, but I know my son through and through. I can tell you how to keep him content."

"Please do."

"Love my son with all your heart."

"I do," Carrie said firmly.

"And keep plenty of chicken recipes on hand. Kyle loves chicken."

17

Kyle needed to think, and he was having a hard time doing it. Every time he concentrated on the string of events that had led him to this point, Carrie's face came to mind, and that made it impossible to be rational.

All he wanted was to be done with this craziness and get back to her so they could be married. Rarely had there been a man more anxious for his honeymoon.

He wasn't sure he could trust Bates, but he had no option. The first thing he did when he arrived back in Kansas City was contact the agent and set up a convenient meeting place and time.

Then he waited near the rendezvous point for the Secret Service agent to arrive. He killed time in a men's store across the street from the Mexican restaurant they'd chosen, trying on winter coats. He'd been there long enough to examine a dozen or more overcoats and ward off a salesman twice, by the time he saw Bates arrive.

Bates was with another agent. Choosing to dine al fresco, the two men sat down at one of the white patio tables, whose multicolored umbrellas cheerfully endorsed a variety of beers. If Kyle hadn't known the men were government agents, he would have guessed as much almost immediately. They were clean-cut, businesslike, and they sat with their backs to the wall, a dead giveaway.

Amused, his gaze skirted past the only other patron sitting outside, an older woman sipping a heavily salted margarita. Kyle winced. The woman was ugly, dog ugly. It wasn't in Kyle's nature to be cruel, but he couldn't imagine sitting across the dinner table with someone who looked as if she'd spent the day sucking lemons. She wore a hat and gloves, as if this were an afternoon tea party instead of a Mexican restaurant.

Kyle moved away from the heavy winter coats and hesitated. Slowly his gaze returned to the woman and stopped. There was something vaguely familiar about her.

Then he knew.

Kyle felt as if someone had slugged him in the chest. Ms. Margarita wasn't any female. It was Max Sanders dressed as a woman.

Kyle had to give the felon credit; Sanders was a master of disguise. At first, even at second glance, Kyle would never have guessed. Bates and his new partner hadn't either, and they were supposed to be professionals.

One thing was certain: Kyle couldn't walk across the street and hand over the key. His heart sank. He felt as though he was never going to be rid of the stupid thing.

Having Sanders arrive on the scene presented a problem. Kyle wondered how he knew about the meeting. Had Bates told him? Kyle doubted that Sanders would go to the trouble of wearing a disguise if that were the case.

The only other possibility he could come up with was that Sanders had tapped his phone. Kyle wanted to groan at his own stupidity. Thinking Bates would put a tracer on the call, Kyle had phoned from his house, all the while patting himself on the back for being so clever. If Bates tracked the call, Kyle wanted it to appear that he'd been holed up inside his house all this while.

Kyle remained hidden from view behind a coat rack, debating his courses of action. He knew Bates was anxious to talk to him, mainly about what Kyle could tell him about Richards's death.

Sanders wanted him too, but Kyle wasn't foolish enough to believe it was friendly conversation the counterfeiter was after. Sanders wanted that blasted key.

Kyle had other considerations. He knew Carrie must be nearly frantic with worry by this time. Despite her promise, he didn't trust her to stay put. It would be just like Carrie to come looking for him and walk into a pack of trouble.

He had no choice. He had to get back to Carrie before she did something crazy.

Carrie sat outside the cabin with a box of tissues in her lap, staring at the wide dirt pathway that led through the scrub from the road. She'd been sitting there since early that morning. Waiting. Watching. Worrying. Kyle's mother seemed to believe he was in no immediate danger, but Carrie didn't have nearly as much confidence in a few runes.

Lillian had left early that morning, promising to return in a day or two. The house seemed quiet without Lillian's eager chatter. To her surprise, Carrie discovered that she liked the older woman immensely. Now she was sitting with a tissue box handy, in case she succumbed to a bout of self-pity.

A plume of dust rose from the top of the roadway. Carrie stood slowly, her heart in her throat, as she waited for the first sign of the vehicle. At this point she didn't care if it was friend or foe. All she sought was an end to this terrible waiting.

The familiar lines of Kyle's BMW came into view, and Carrie felt the moisture fill her eyes. Kyle parked the car and, sobbing, she raced to his side and hurled herself into his arms. He lifted her from the ground, holding her tightly against him, one arm about her waist, the other in her hair. His mouth found hers, and between laughter and tears and words that made no sense they kissed and clung to each other.

"You're late," she said when she could, between hungry, deep kisses. Her body had reacted automatically to his touch. The chill left her heart as the terrible fear she'd carried with her since he left slowly seeped away. It was far more than relief she felt in Kyle's arms. To her surprise she felt suddenly, inexplicably, dizzy with need. It startled her that she could be thinking such things now when all that mattered was that he was alive and had come back to her.

"I know. I'm sorry," Kyle said.

"What happened?" she asked, spreading wet kisses over his face, unable to get enough of him.

"Later. Let me kiss you."

And he did, again and again as if he'd never reach his fill. Slowly he lowered her feet toward the ground, his breathing heavy, as was hers.

"What happened?" she asked a second time, needing to know.

"Nothing serious. Don't worry."

"Tell me." She took him by the hand and led him inside the cabin, where it was cooler.

He sat in the rocker his mother had recently occupied and pulled her into his lap. He pressed a kiss to her temple. Carrie put her hand over his and kissed his palm.

"It dawned on me while I was driving toward Kansas City that I was handing over a key but I hadn't a clue as to what it opened."

"A cache of counterfeit plates," Carrie answered. "Richards told us that, remember?"

"Yes, but could we trust what he said?"

Carrie hadn't thought of that; she'd assumed whatever the agent said was gospel. "I don't know. But all we have—had," she corrected, "was the key."

"*Have*," he said, frowning. "I still have it. Max Sanders was at the rendezvous point as well as Bates. We may end up having this thing bronzed. I can't seem to get rid of it for love or money."

"Oh, Kyle." Their lives would never be the same as long as they possessed that stupid key.

"Only it doesn't lead to counterfeit plates."

Carrie's mind whirled with possibilities. Her first thought was that Kyle had found oodles of money instead—or diamonds, or some computer chip.

"First off, I examined the key more closely," Kyle said, answering her questions before she could ask them. "I had assumed it was to a safety deposit box, but I don't have one, never have. It just made sense that that was what it was. Then I noticed something etched in the bow. It looked as if it was a number, or had been at one time, only the paint had long since worn away."

"A locker key," Carrie said under her breath.

"Exactly."

"You found the locker? How? That's like finding a needle in a haystack."

"Simple. I tried to imagine what I'd do if someone were after me and I had something I needed to hide, so I started searching for lockers in small towns. I checked out the bus and rail stations in every town between Wheatland and Kansas City."

"No wonder you're late," Carrie said, awed by his patience and at the same time wanting to slap him silly for worrying her this way.

"You're right about it being a needle in a haystack," Kyle continued, "but I finally found the locker in a hick town where the bus station is the largest building in the county." He paused.

"What was inside?"

"Papers, memos, computer printouts. I sat down and read what I could, but I wasn't able to make much sense of it. Frankly, it looked like evidence."

"Evidence?"

"My guess is that Sanders is using it to blackmail Nelson."

"Of course." That made sense to Carrie. "Why didn't the Secret Service think of that?"

"Because they assumed the key was to a safety deposit box. That was what I told them."

"What are we going to do?"

"I don't know who to trust. I'm not sure what we should do."

"I know what we should do," she said, with a triumphant smile. "Get married." She checked her watch. "Does an hour give you enough time?"

He looked at her as if she'd just suggested they strip naked and jump off a cliff. "You want to go through with the wedding? Now?"

"Are you saying you've changed your mind?"

"No, it's just that I thought . . . wouldn't it be best to wait until this mess is settled?"

"Not as far as I'm concerned. I refuse to let you cheat me out of a wedding, Kyle Harris. Besides, your mother said—"

"When did you talk to my mother?"

"She drove out to see how we were doing. I like her, Kyle, and she gave me some advice."

"My mother? Lillian Harris gave you marital advice?"

"Yes. She said that in order to keep you content I had to love you, and in case you haven't noticed, fella, I'm downright eager to follow through with that part. It's the chicken recipes that threw me. I didn't tell her I'm not much of a cook."

"Chicken recipes?"

She giggled, kissed him, and climbed off his lap. "If you leave me standing at the altar you can bet my daddy's going to hear about it."

Kyle chuckled and headed toward the bedroom to change clothes.

The ceremony was short but beautiful. It took all of five minutes, Kyle calculated, to pledge his life, his love, his future to Carrie. And love her he did, beyond anything he ever thought possible.

She was radiant in her simple cotton summer dress with wildflowers woven in her hair, her face free of makeup, her eyes shining with love. He wondered if she'd always been this beautiful, or if he'd been blind all those months before Texas.

He wished this could have been the ceremony she deserved, with organ music and flowers and a big reception for guests eager to share in their happiness.

As it was, they stood alone in an empty church while Doc Henley had them repeat their vows, facing each other, holding hands. Afterward, he'd had two of his friends sign as witnesses and handed them the marriage certificate.

"You two have a good life together, and that's an

order," he said. He adjusted his hearing aid. "Darn thing always acts up when I've got something important going on."

"Thank you." Carrie was holding a small bouquet of flowers. She kissed Doc on the cheek, and his face turned as red as beefsteak tomatoes.

"I don't get to perform many weddings these days, but I make it a point of seeing that the ones I marry stay that way."

"We will, thanks," Kyle promised.

On the ride home, Kyle's heart was full with all the things he wanted to say to Carrie. "I wish I could have given you the classic wedding with a country club reception and your parents—"

"It was perfect in every way," she whispered.

Kyle parked under the shade of an oak tree outside the cabin. The setting sun was reflected in the still waters of the lake.

"Shall we have dinner?" he asked.

"Not yet," she surprised him by saying.

"You have other plans?"

"Oh, yes," she said with a lusty smile that caused his knees to go weak. She grabbed his tie and led him into the house toward the bedroom, not that Kyle needed any directing. He knew what he wanted: his wife.

"You may not have noticed," Carrie said, loosening his tie and slipping it from his neck. She hung it over the brass rail at the foot of the bed.

"Noticed what?" Kyle eased open the top button of her pale blue dress. He made certain that the weight of his hand brushed against her breasts as he reached for the second button. A third followed.

"Things," Carrie whispered, which made no sense to him. Not that it mattered, not right then. Eager now, he worked open the front of the dress.

They held each other afterward, kissing now and again, whispering and laughing. Kyle felt exhausted, deliriously happy, sleepy.

They must have slept, because the next thing Kyle knew Carrie was tugging at his chest hairs with her teeth.

"You fell asleep," she said, snuggling in his arms. "It seems a shame to waste our honeymoon night sleeping when we could be practicing ... other things."

He arched his eyebrows. "You have plans?"

"Indeed I do." Her dark eyes sparkled mischievously. Gently she pushed at his shoulder and rolled him onto his back.

Carrie woke the following morning feeling well loved, well satisfied, and well rested. Yawning, she rolled onto her back and stretched her arms high above her head. When she opened her eyes, she discovered Kyle sitting up and watching her.

"Good morning, husband," she said, sighing. It

didn't seem possible that they were man and wife, but it was true.

"Good morning, wife," Kyle returned, leaning down and kissing her. "Did you sleep well?"

She nodded. "What about you?"

"Like a rock." Brushing a strand of hair away from her face, his hand lingered there. His eyes seemed troubled, and she wondered why. Then he spoke, and she knew.

"We need to make some important decisions. Like going back to Kansas City."

"Not today, please." She didn't want to think about Max Sanders, that stupid key, or the Secret Service. Her attitude might be childish, but for over a month their lives had been disrupted by this insanity. She wanted some time for themselves. They needed it.

"But Carrie—"

She sat up and pressed her finger to his lips. "I want you to teach me to fish."

"Fish?" he said incredulously.

"Yup." She nestled against his chest. He tucked his arms under hers and flattened one hand against her tummy as if greeting their unborn child. "Your mother told me that at one time you were a world-class fisherman."

"That's a bit of an exaggeration."

"Your fishing pole's here. I checked. I think we deserve the luxury of a one-day honeymoon, don't you?"

"Does this include the night too?" he asked, and

she could tell from his tone of voice that he was tempted to do as she asked.

"Of course," she answered. "We need to fortify ourselves before facing the harsh realities of life. Just this one day," she coaxed, twisting her head around to gaze up at him. "I promise to make it worth your while."

He chuckled at that, and said something about her already fulfilling every fantasy he'd ever dreamed, and she loved him all the more.

Then he kissed her and whispered, his breath warm and moist against her skin. "I love you."

"I know," she said, wondering what had taken him so long to recognize the obvious. "I love you too."

"You realize we're risking our lives for the sake of a few fish, don't you?"

"Not really," she said with confidence. "Your mother claimed you were in no immediate danger."

"How does she know?" he asked, frowning, then shook his head. "Don't answer that. It's probably got something to do with those crystals of hers."

"Kyle, perhaps I'm crazy but I don't care. I'm tired of running. Tired of hiding. All I want is time alone with you. We can decide tomorrow what we're going to do with that stupid key. Frankly, if it was up to me I'd throw the damn thing in the lake."

Kyle smiled, and she knew she'd won. They would have this time—this day, and one last night—before they confronted the realities awaiting them.

Loaded down with fishing gear, Kyle led the way to the rickety dock that stretched six feet into the lake. He sorted through a variety of hooks and flies in his fishing box, choosing one and then another as if his choice were one of supreme importance.

"I'll get you set up first," he explained.

Carrie sat on the edge of the dock, leaning back and resting her weight on her palms. She dangled her bare feet in the water, softly splashing.

"You're scaring the fish away," he warned her. "If you want trout for dinner, you'd best stop warning them we're here. Fish are more intelligent than you think."

She sighed and lifted her feet out of the water, tucking her knees under her chin and wrapping her arms around them. "It's so beautiful here. I didn't appreciate it in the beginning. What you say about us being in danger just doesn't fit in with the tranquility I feel."

"It's been months since I spent any time at this old cabin."

"Your mother told me you love it here, and I understand why. I love it too. Hey, we've already found something we agree about."

"Speaking of my mother"—Kyle set aside his fishing pole and sat down next to her—"do you care to explain that statement about chicken recipes?"

Carrie laughed and pressed her forehead against her knees. "It's simple. She gave me an insider tip about dealing with you, and now I know how to keep you content, you can bet I'm going to use it, and often."

"I hope this has something to do with loving me."

"I do love you," she said firmly, "with all my heart."

He leaned forward and nibbled on her earlobe. "Have you ever made love on a dock?" he whispered.

Carrie jerked her head back with surprise. She would have sworn Kyle Harris had never made love outside a bed. The man was full of surprises. "Kyle?"

"Hmm."

"Aren't you afraid we'll get splinters?"

"I'm not worried about it."

"What about the fish? We might scare them away."

He paused as if he hadn't thought about that possibility. "To my way of thinking, the taste of trout is greatly overrated."

Kyle had never spent a time like this. Or loved like this. It had been against his better judgment when he agreed to put off returning to Kansas City. But Carrie was right; they needed this time together. No day had ever been more perfect.

It wasn't the lovemaking that was special, although heaven knew it had been incredible with them from the first: the closeness they shared, the way they laughed together, played together. They spoke of the future as if nothing could hold back their happiness. They talked about their child.

"Did you ever think about our baby as a person?"

she asked him at one point. Kyle was lying on his back in a meadow, his head nestled in Carrie's lap.

"Not really. But I've thought a good deal about what your father said about loving a child so much it feels like your guts are being ripped out."

Carrie smiled as she chewed on the end of a dandelion. "My father certainly has a delicate way of saying things, doesn't he?"

"I already love our child," Kyle said. His heart went tender every time he thought about the baby nestled in Carrie's womb.

"I do too."

He thought back to the years while he was growing up and realized he'd never fully appreciated his mother.

The sound of a car engine broke their tranquility. Kyle stiffened and sat upright. "Stay here," he instructed.

Naturally Carrie didn't. Luckily they had a clear view of the dirt road that led to the cabin. His relief was great when he recognized his mother's car. For one of the few times in his life, he was actually glad to see her. He would have Carrie ride back to Kansas City with her while he dealt with the Secret Service people.

Lillian climbed out of the car. Shading her eyes, she waved when she saw them coming down the hill.

Carrie hurried ahead of Kyle and embraced his

mother. "We're married!" she cried, her joy echoing around them like church bells.

Kyle tucked an arm around his wife's shoulders.

"I see you're back safe and sound," Lillian announced and gave him a motherly peck on the cheek. "And now I understand congratulations are in order."

"You're going to be a grandmother," he announced.

Lillian beamed. "So I hear. I imagine I'll make a better grandmother than I ever did a mother. It's like God's decided to give me a second chance to do something right."

"Come inside out of the sun," Carrie invited.

They were chattering away like a pair of magpies, Kyle thought, amused, when they stepped into the house. But their chatter died abruptly.

Max Sanders was sitting in the rocker in the middle of the cabin as if he'd been impatiently waiting for their return.

18

Kyle immediately placed himself between Sanders and the two women. But before he could speak, Lillian stepped around him and whispered, in a shocked, strangled voice, "Moonrunner?"

"Summerlove?"

Carrie and Kyle stared at each other in open-mouthed disbelief as Kyle's mother and Sanders hurried toward each other. Both were talking at the same time. Then they were in each other's arms.

All at once Kyle felt the need to sit down. He'd just found his father, the man he'd criticized and loathed all these years.

It was one thing to know Max had deserted his mother when she was pregnant; it was another to realize he was a felon wanted by more agencies than he could name.

"Kyle," Lillian said, wiping the moisture from her cheek as she turned to face her son, "this is your father."

"So I gathered," he said, with a decided lack of enthusiasm.

Max looked at Kyle as if seeing him for the first time. "I have a son?"

Lillian nodded. "I tried desperately to find you," she explained, emotion rocking her voice. "I did everything I could, but when I didn't hear from you after three months, I had no choice but to go home."

"I was in jail."

"Jail? But—"

"Mother," Kyle said, placing his hand on Lillian's shoulders and gently easing her away. "You should know this man is wanted by the Secret Service." He hated to disrupt their happy reunion, but Sanders could well be armed and dangerous.

"Moonrunner?"

"His name is Max," Kyle said. "Max Sanders."

"Max," she echoed. "My name is Lillian."

"Lillian," Max whispered. His gaze went from her to Kyle, and he seemed at a loss for words, which was just as well. Kyle welcomed the opportunity to figure a way to get his wife and mother away unscathed.

"Maybe it would be best if we all sat down and talked this out," Kyle suggested, but he didn't trust Sanders, no matter what his mother claimed.

They sat at the square wooden table. Max and Lillian stretched their arms across the top and held hands as if they couldn't bear to be apart ever again. They had eyes only for each other.

"You might want to explain why you abandoned my mother," Kyle said stiffly.

"I didn't know her by any name other than Summerlove," Max explained, without looking at Kyle, "and by the time I could get back to her, she was gone."

"I can't tell you how it warms my heart to know my father's a jailbird."

"Kyle," Carrie said softly, pressing her hand over his. Her eyes pleaded with him not to be sarcastic.

It was hard to refuse her anything, but Kyle had no warm feelings in his heart for this man who was said to have sired him.

"Has everyone gone daft?" he asked, unwilling to let Carrie's romantic soul taint his judgment. "We're dealing with a real live bad guy here. No one seems to realize we could be in grave danger. Frankly, I don't think it's a good idea to throw open our arms and welcome him into the family just yet."

Max grinned ear to ear. "He's my son, all right. He sounds just like me thirty years ago."

"Tell me everything," Lillian urged, ignoring Kyle's

outburst. "You were arrested for the bombings, weren't you? Why wasn't there anything in the news? I read the papers for weeks, searching for any bit of information I could find about you. It was as if you disappeared from the face of the earth."

"First," Max said, looking at Kyle, "you're in no danger, at least not from me. I'm working under-cover for the Secret Service."

"You don't honestly expect us to believe that?"

"But you said the locker was full of papers and other stuff that looked like evidence," Carrie was quick to remind him.

"You found the locker?" Any fatherly affection Max displayed was short-lived as he glared suspi-ciously at Kyle. "I hope to God you didn't take any-thing."

"You needn't worry, I put everything back, just the way I found it. I may have a fool for a father, but I'm not one myself."

"Kyle," Carrie said under her breath.

Sanders ignored the insult. "I'm curious how you knew where to find it. There must be a thousand lockers between here and Kansas City."

"Not quite a thousand." Kyle knew he sounded smug, but he didn't care. His mother and Carrie might be taken in by Sanders's smooth talk, but he wasn't nearly as gullible as the two women. Sanders had a long way to go to prove himself, as far as Kyle was concerned.

"Kyle told me he tried to reason it out, thinking what he'd do if he were in your shoes," Carrie volunteered.

Kyle silenced her with a heated look, wishing he'd never said anything.

"You even think alike," Lillian said. She sounded just the way she had when he was a boy and had done something clever.

"I figured you'd want whoever found the key to think the locker was one of countless hundreds lost in the big city. It made more sense to me that you'd choose an out-of-the-way location you could reach on short notice."

Max seemed impressed with his reasoning. "That's exactly what I thought."

"Like father, like son," Lillian put in cheerfully, a second time.

Max beamed toward Lillian and returned his attention to Kyle. "Then you know what's there?"

"I know."

Max's eyes firmly held his. "I've been working undercover on this case close to eighteen months," he said. "I had everything I needed when someone blew my cover. I barely managed to get away alive, and staying that way has been something of a chore since."

"You're running from Nelson," Carrie said with a touch of arrogance, as if she had everything figured out. Unfortunately, Kyle was in the dark.

"How much do you know about Nelson?" Sanders asked, his eyes narrowed.

"Enough," Kyle answered.

"He's the really, really bad guy," Carrie supplied. "He was the one who stole the counterfeiting plates from you."

"Stole the plates?" Sanders shook his head. "I don't know who told you that, but I wasn't interested in the counterfeit plates. The agency needs to link those plates to Nelson, not me. The plates are a large part of our case. If they're missing, I can guarantee you I didn't take them."

"But who blew your cover?" Lillian asked.

It irked Kyle how easily his mother and Carrie were taken in by all this.

"I'm not sure," Sanders said, "but I have my suspicions."

"Did you know Richards was killed?" Carrie made it sound as if the agent's demise was part of a soap opera plot she was currently following. "Personally, I figure Nelson was involved in that."

Sanders grinned. Kyle had the feeling it didn't happen often. "I don't doubt Nelson was responsible."

"But why would he kill Richards?"

Sanders hesitated, as if he wasn't sure he should explain.

"Go on," Carrie urged. "You can trust us, we're family. Besides, Kyle and I are already involved. We were supposed to have been in the theater but we—"

"Now just a minute," Kyle interrupted. He was as keen as Carrie to satisfy his curiosity, but he didn't want to hear anything that would place them in more danger than they already were. "There are some matters we're better off not knowing."

"Kyle's right," Sanders said. "It's best I don't tell you a lot of this."

Carrie tapped her finger against her lips. "Kyle and I think Richards might have been setting us up. We can't be certain of that, of course. All we know was that he asked Kyle to meet him in a movie theater and the next thing Richards ends up in the morgue."

"He was the one who told us you were a counterfeiter, but it wasn't plates I found in that locker," Kyle added, following Carrie's train of thought.

"Right," she said quickly. "And you were working undercover, and someone ratted on you." She propped her elbows on the table and slouched forward. "This is almost too easy. Richards was a bad apple."

"What about Bates?" Kyle wasn't sure he could trust Richards's partner either.

"I don't know for certain," Sanders admitted reluctantly.

"I don't either," Kyle said thoughtfully. "Who was that with him at the Mexican restaurant?"

"So you were there?"

"Yeah, I was killing time in the men's store across the street. When I saw you, I wasn't sure what to do, so I left. Who was with Bates?"

"That's Bowie. He's clean. At least I'd be real surprised if he wasn't."

"If you all know one another and you work for the same agency, why are you running from the Secret Service?" These were questions Kyle couldn't ignore.

"They don't know me personally," Sanders clarified. "They only know *about* me. For the last thirty years, most of my assignments have been undercover. The feds and I made a deal when I was arrested for the bombings," Sanders said, directing his words to Lillian. "I got off doing no time, if I helped identify other militants. I wasn't keen on turning traitor, but as I got deeper into the underground, I learned that several groups had their own agenda, and it had nothing to do with protesting the war in Vietnam."

"Are . . . are you married?" Lillian asked in a still, small voice, almost as if she were afraid to know.

"No," Sanders said, squeezing her hands. "I never could bring myself to put a wife and family through this kind of life." He hesitated and then asked, "What about you?"

"No . . . never," she whispered.

Kyle had never seen his mother blush, but she did so then.

"I couldn't forget you. Somehow I always believed we'd find each other again."

"There was this natural yogurt salesman several

years back," Carrie supplied, "but nothing ever came of that."

Kyle couldn't have been more surprised. "You know about Harold?"

Carrie grinned. "I told you your mother and I got to know each other, didn't I?"

Kyle scratched the side of his head. He'd never understand women. He wondered what else his mother had told her; no doubt she'd learned about the time he ran away from home. His mother had probably relayed every other embarrassing detail of his youth as well. All because Lillian thought they were cute.

"Let's get back to the matters at hand, shall we?" Kyle said impatiently. He hated to interrupt the reunion scene, but there were more pressing details to clarify. "First off, why were Richards and Bates after you if you're all on the same side?"

"That's a long story," Sanders said.

"I've got time."

"Actually, you don't. The sooner the three of you get out of here, the better. Nelson might have a tail on me."

"If you think I'm leaving you after all these years, you don't know me, Miles Sanders," Lillian said firmly.

"Max." Kyle corrected her. "My father's name is Max." It was then he realized he was acknowledging Sanders as his father. He would have liked to deny it, but he couldn't, not when the evidence sat across from him.

Carrie seemed to realize the same thing as well. "Remember when I said Sanders looked familiar?" she whispered.

"All I can remember is you claiming you'd seen him on *America's Most Wanted*," Kyle muttered.

"Okay, I admit he wasn't on any episode of my favorite crime show, but he did seem familiar. That's because there's a strong resemblance between you two."

"You know," Lillian said, her eyes sparkling with delight, "you're right. It's in the nose and the mouth. Why, now I see the two of you together, it's amazing how much you're alike."

Frankly Kyle thought he was a lot better-looking than Sanders and didn't take kindly to the idea of what his mother seemed to think was a striking resemblance.

"I'm serious about the possibility of my having been followed," Sanders said, breaking into the conversation.

Kyle was grateful. Having his mother and Carrie compare his facial features to Sanders's had become downright embarrassing.

"I did my best to cover my tracks, but I can't guarantee that Nelson and his men aren't on my tail."

"I'll take my chances," Lillian insisted.

Sanders ignored that and focused his attention on Kyle. "Give me the key, please."

Kyle had been waiting for this moment. Everything had been leading up to it. It was the reason Sanders was there; he wanted that key. Carrie and his mother were studying him, wondering what he was going to do. Kyle wished he knew himself.

"I'm not sure I can give it to you," he said, meeting Sanders's gaze straight on.

Despite his initial mistrust, Kyle wanted to believe the explanations Sanders had given. It helped that the little information he'd supplied was supported by what Kyle knew to be true.

"You still haven't answered all my questions," he added, stalling.

"I can't, and I won't until this is over." Sanders held out his palm. "I know this is difficult, you don't have a reason in the world to trust me, but I'm asking you to do so."

It impressed Kyle that Sanders didn't try to use the fact they were father and son to persuade him.

"Let's compromise," Kyle said after a moment.

"Compromise?"

Kyle could tell Sanders had little fondness for compromises. "Yeah," Kyle said, holding the older man's eyes. "I go with you. We'll see this thing through together."

"No." Carrie's reaction was immediate. "Kyle, are you nuts? You don't know anything about undercover work. You might do something stupid and get both of you killed."

"I'll risk it," he said, his gaze connected to Sanders, "if he's willing."

"This is the way you want it?"

"Yes," Kyle said without qualms.

"You know Nelson is after me," Sanders said starkly. "That man plays for keeps."

"I know." Kyle wasn't entirely sure why he felt it was so necessary to see the matter to the end. Perhaps he was more like his father than he was willing to admit. He actually found the promise of danger and intrigue exciting.

They could consider it a father-and-son bonding experience.

"You know what they're going to do, don't you?" Carrie said, watching the dust disappear from the driveway. "They're going to leave a trail a two-year-old could follow." Sanders had admitted that Nelson might already have tracked him to the vicinity. Now the men would make sure the trail didn't lead Nelson to the cabin. In order to do that, they had to make sure Nelson had another trail to follow: theirs.

"I don't think we need worry," Lillian said, fingering the crystals that hung from a gold chain around her neck, but her voice lacked confidence.

"One day of marriage, and my husband volunteers

for the front lines." Kyle had always possessed a knack for deflating her ego.

"Don't take it personally," Lillian murmured, but Carrie noted that Kyle's mother wasn't any more eager to move off the porch than she was. It was as though the longer they stood there, the more they were reassured that the strength of their love would bring the men safely back.

"I think I'll bake bread," Lillian announced all at once.

Bake bread! It was the hottest part of the afternoon, and Carrie had no interest in stoking up the antique stove.

"I'd better gather up the fishing equipment," she said.

"So Kyle did take you fishing?"

"Oh, yes," Carrie answered, but she didn't have the heart to tell her mother-in-law they hadn't so much as dipped a line in the water. Their intentions had been good, but there had been more entertaining ways to spend the morning.

Carrie walked out onto the dock. Her reflection was mirrored in the still water, and a warm breeze rustled the leaves.

Something moved, something larger than a branch.

She caught the action from the corner of her eye. Whirling around abruptly, she looked behind her.

There was nothing except elm trees and plenty of

scrub. Her imagination was working overtime, she decided. With a sense of urgency, she quickly gathered up the fishing gear.

Whistling, her gaze skirting the area, Carrie returned to the house. She couldn't shake the feeling that someone or something was watching her. Of course it could all be in her head, but the creepy feeling wouldn't go away.

Lillian was busy inside the cabin. Flour, shortening, and sugar were arranged on the table next to a large ceramic bowl. "Have you ever tasted oatmeal molasses bread?" she asked absently. She wore half glasses that were delicately balanced at the end of her nose.

"I can't say I have," Carrie said, putting Kyle's fishing gear away.

"You must think me a silly old woman to be fussing with bread at a time like this, but I bake when I need to calm my nerves. At one time I seriously considered opening up my own natural foods bakery, but I didn't because I loved it so much."

"If you enjoy baking that much, why not do it for money?"

Lillian reached for the flour bag. "I was afraid I'd grow to hate it." She set the bag down and stared into the distance. Carrie noted that her mother-in-law's hands were trembling. Lillian had been badly shaken by the encounter with Sanders.

"Why don't we sit down and have a cup of tea," Carrie suggested.

"That might be a good idea," Lillian said, walking over to the rocking chair. "I guess seeing Moon—Max again taxed me more than I realized." She eased her weight into the rocker. "I *did* hear him right, didn't I? He's never married."

"That's what he said," Carrie murmured, carrying a cup of hot tea over to Lillian.

"Can you imagine us finding each other after all these years? It's like a miracle."

"I think it must be," Carrie agreed, taking a seat on a bench across from Lillian.

"I don't think I realized how much I loved him," she continued in a whisper. "We knew each other for such a short while."

"But you had Max's son," Carrie said. "Raising Kyle, you couldn't help but remember Moonrunner and the love you shared."

"I can't believe he left me again."

"He'll be back," Carrie promised.

"You must think me very foolish."

"I don't," Carrie was quick to assure her. "How can I think you foolish to be in love when I'm in love myself? I'm not sure I told you this, Lillian, but I'm crazy about Kyle."

Her mother-in-law's smile was feeble. "I know. And he feels the same way about you. There's been a change in him since he's been with you. He's much more tolerant of others, less judgmental. I've worried about him, you see."

The feeling of being watched returned, and Carrie hopped up from the bench.

"Carrie, what is it?"

She didn't want to alarm Lillian and was unsure what she should say. Yet the feeling was growing stronger, and she was frightened.

"I think there might be someone outside," she said, in a squeaky, high-pitched voice.

Lillian set aside her tea.

"When I was on the dock, I thought I saw some-one."

"Saw or felt?" Lillian asked in a whisper.

Carrie closed her eyes in an effort to think. "Both."

"Then someone's here. I felt it myself."

"You did?"

"Not to worry," Lillian said, reaching for her wooden spoon. "We're perfectly capable of defend-ing ourselves."

"We are?" Carrie's voice was unnaturally high.

"Of course. All we need do is outsmart him."

Carrie was instantly relieved. "Then you have a plan?"

"Oh, no, I was going to improvise, unless you have a better way of luring him out of his hiding place."

"Not me."

"Then we'll wait."

Carrie didn't like the sound of this. She'd spent two miserable days anticipating Kyle's return, and now he was off again, to fates unknown. Now her woman's intuition told her there was someone outside the cabin. The likelihood of this person being foe, not friend, was strong.

Lillian was busy moving about the cabin with the familiarity of someone who knew every nook and cranny. She located a rope that looked as if it had once been used for a clothesline. Scooting a kitchen chair into the middle of the room, she paused and looked around once more.

"What's that for?" Carrie asked.

"First we'll tie him up and then we'll interrogate him."

"But—supposing there really is someone out there—he could be dangerous."

"You think we're not?" Lillian wiped out a cast-iron frying pan and flourished it.

"I've had some karate lessons," Carrie said tentatively.

"You see!" Lillian responded more positively than her son to this tidbit of information. "We're set, then. All we need to do is find a way to lure him inside the cabin."

"How do you propose to do that?"

Lillian rubbed her jaw in much the same way Carrie had seen Kyle do countless times. "We seem to have only one possibility."

"Which is?" Somehow Carrie had the feeling she wasn't going to like this.

"Tell him you know he's out there and invite him

inside to negotiate. If it's a man, which I strongly suspect, he's short on patience. He's probably hot and tired and bored. My guess is he'd do just about anything to put an end to waiting."

"What if there's more than one?"

"Did you see one or two?"

"One. I think. Lillian, this is too important to take a chance."

"My guess is there's only one, and even if he knows I'm in here with you, he'll think we're a pair of helpless females."

That was exactly the way Carrie viewed them. "You honestly think this'll work?"

"It's better than sitting here wondering, isn't it?"

Carrie wasn't sure.

"Now, walk out there on that porch and talk your pretty little heart out. All you got to do is lead him to Mama." Carrie wasn't sure what Lillian had in mind, but she speculated it had something to do with that frying pan.

Carrie was shaking so badly she had to stop and compose herself before stepping onto the porch. "Hello, out there," she called, surprised at how calm she sounded. "I saw you earlier by the lake. I know you're there."

Silence. Even the breeze seemed to still.

"It would help matters a good deal if we put an end to this nonsense and talked, don't you think? Naturally, you can stay out in the hot sun as long as you wish, but I just want you to know I'm ready to dicker when you are."

Having said that much, she turned around and walked back inside. She poured herself a tall cool glass of water, leaned against the doorjamb, and surveyed the area surrounding the cabin.

To her amazement a lanky man stepped out from behind an oak tree a dozen or more yards away. Carrie caught sight of a handgun under his belt.

Her smile wavered. "I'm pleased we can be reasonable about this," she called out. "It makes far more sense."

When she found the courage, she looked at his face and her heart seemed to stop dead right then and there. This man had the coldest, darkest eyes she'd ever seen. His gaze seemed to cut straight through her.

"Would you like a glass of water?" she called out as he neared the porch.

"Please."

Please. Manners, this cold-blooded killer actually had manners! Moving away from the door, she went toward the hand pump. Carrie swore her knees all but buckled from under her when he stepped over the threshold.

Lillian casually shifted away from the wall, and the minute their stalker was through the door she let him have it with the frying pan.

Carrie watched as his eyes rolled back in his head

and he staggered forward three steps. Thinking quickly, Carrie grabbed the chair and had it beneath him just as he started to fall. The full force of his weight came down hard on the seat of the wood chair.

Lillian took the rope and quickly ran circles around him so many times Carrie wondered if the man would be able to breathe.

"You know who this is, don't you?" Carrie said excitedly. Her voice trembled as badly as her hands. "This is Nelson. It has to be. No one else would have eyes that evil."

"You're wrong, my dear," said a hard voice from behind her.

Carrie and Lillian whirled around and came face to face with a second man. This one held a gun on them both. His eyes were blue and danced with wry amusement. It was his mouth that was evil, Carrie saw. It was smiling just then, cocky and confident.

Carrie raised her hands. Lillian did as well.

"I guess I should introduce myself," he said with a twist of his lips. "*I'm* Nelson."

19

"*Sit down, ladies,*" Nelson instructed, motioning with the gun toward the kitchen table.

The chair scraped against the wood floor as Carrie pulled it away and literally stumbled onto the seat. Lillian reacted far more calmly, walking with dignity toward the kitchen.

Carrie thought they'd been so clever, too. She should have known better. They weren't government agents trained in terrorist techniques. A health food store owner and a deejay didn't stand a chance against professional bad guys.

"I see we interrupted your dinner preparations,"

Nelson said, as though his lack of manners distressed him.

"I was about to bake bread," Lillian said conversationally, as if she often dealt with gun-wielding gangsters.

"In this heat?" Nelson wiped the moisture from his face. Walking over to the semiconscious man teetering on the edge of the chair, he slapped his associate across the face. "You all right?"

The man shook his head a couple of times as if to clear his head.

"Lawton?" Nelson snapped.

"I'm fine. Get me out of this, will you?"

"Give me a minute," Nelson said impatiently. "I thought you said these women weren't going to be a problem."

Lawton sneered at them. "I didn't expect to be hit over the head, either."

"I'm hungry," Nelson said, walking toward the kitchen.

Carrie looked to Lillian. "I think he expects us to fix him dinner."

"That's exactly what I want. Now get to it. I haven't had anything to eat all day."

Carrie hadn't given much thought to being held captive by gangsters before, but if she had, she never would have believed they'd want her to cook for them. She and Lillian were in danger now, but it would be ten times worse once they tasted her cooking.

"Go on," Nelson said, gesturing for them to get started. "I'm half starved."

"Are you sure you don't want to order out?"

"We got us a smartass, boss," Lawton muttered, investigating the back of his head with his hand. "Hey, I'm bleeding." He glared at Lillian and let loose with a string of curses, some of which Carrie had never heard. She doubted she'd find them listed in *Webster's* either.

Standing next to Lillian, Carrie tried to pretend she knew what she was doing. The men argued behind her. If she could get to the gun in the drawer, she might be able to hold off Nelson and his thug. Lillian seemed to read her thoughts because she caught Carrie's eye and gave a small negative shake of her head.

"What are we going to do?" Carrie whispered, not wanting to attract either man's attention, which was unlikely since they were involved in a heated conversation.

"I thought I'd whip up a couple of omelets," Lillian said, as if they hadn't a care in the world. She reached for the carton of eggs and a bowl.

"I wasn't talking about the dinner menu," Carrie said between gritted teeth. "I'm talking about Lawton and Nelson."

"Oh, them. Well, we don't have much choice, do we? We'll have to wait to be rescued."

"Don't you think we should at least try to escape?" Carrie whispered. "We have the . . . you know what."

"Don't even think about making a break for it," Nelson said unexpectedly. "I'd hate to have to shoot a lady." He motioned toward them with the gun. "But I have and I will again if need be," he added, in a voice that caused Carrie's blood to run cold.

"No problem," she said, raising her hands in a submissive gesture. It was just her luck to be captured by a man with an acute sense of hearing.

"Good. Keep it that way."

Nelson couldn't seem to stand in one place for long. He wandered restlessly about the cabin. While Lillian got the stove going and whipped up the omelets, Carrie cleared off the table and made herself look busy.

"What are you going to do with us?" she asked. Lillian might take all this in her stride, but Carrie herself was having something of a problem.

"I haven't figured that out yet," Nelson said. He found a toothpick in a drawer and began to clean his teeth with it. Lawton remained in the chair. Carrie guessed he was suffering with a well-deserved headache.

"I can give you a couple of ideas, boss."

Nelson's evil laugh echoed off the walls. "I bet you can."

"I'd like to string that skinny one from a tree."

For one crazy moment, Carrie hoped they were talking about her. Then she came to her senses.

"I think I'll let Fischer have the younger one. She looks like she's a live wire, and you know he likes his women with a little sass. He enjoys breaking 'em of their bad habits."

"He wouldn't like me," Carrie said confidently.

"If Fischer doesn't want her, I'll take her," Lawton volunteered. "She owes me big-time."

"What the hell," Nelson said, with a generous shrug of his shoulders, "you can both have her, and when you're through I'll give you the older one. A man can learn a few things from a mature woman."

Unperturbed by the sick turn of the conversation, Lillian piled a generous portion of eggs onto plates and set them on the table with thick slices of vine-ripened tomatoes.

"Better eat it while it's hot," she said, carrying the plates to the table.

Carrie felt sick to her stomach. She didn't need much of an imagination to figure out what Fischer and Lawton would do once they got their hands on her.

Both men downed their meal as if it were a contest to see which one could finish first. Lawton paused, and asked, his mouth full of food, "You hear something, boss?"

Carrie strained her ears but heard nothing. For a

moment she'd actually thought there was a chance someone had come to their rescue. Not that it was likely to happen. Lillian and she would need to see to that themselves.

"There's nothing out there except the wind."

"Yeah, you're right," Lawton agreed after a moment, but he didn't look appeased.

"I'm always right," Nelson said. "That's why I'm the boss."

"Sure thing, boss."

Carrie finished washing the cooking utensils while the two men ate. Lillian silently offered her a slice of tomato, but she refused with a soft shake of her head. She didn't know how her mother-in-law could think about food at a time like this. Lillian acted as if having a gun held on them was of little consequence. She made it seem like a game, but these men were criminals, capable of heinous acts.

The men cleaned their plates and seemed to be looking around for more. "You got any bread and butter?" Lawton asked.

Carrie carried the items to the table, keeping as much distance between the two men and herself as she could. Being close to them made her skin crawl.

"How about some coffee?" Lillian asked next, as if they were honored guests.

"Great," Nelson said, sounding almost appreciative.

Carrie delivered steaming mugs of coffee as well.

"I've got one killer of a headache," Lawton complained, glaring at Carrie. His look terrified her and she moved closer to Lillian.

"Aspirin?" Lillian offered. She opened her purse and brought out a small tin. Pressing against one corner, she took out two capsules and handed them to the larger of the two men.

Frankly, Carrie was beginning to think, Lillian was aiding and abetting the enemy. Only when her mother-in-law winked as she turned away did Carrie get a glimmer of hope. Lillian was up to something.

Twenty minutes later, Nelson was struggling to stay awake. His eyes drifted closed and his head sagged forward. Shaking his head, he forced himself awake. He stood, walked over to the sink, pumped water into his hand, and slapped his face.

"You okay, boss?"

"I'm a little tired is all."

"Go ahead and take a nap if you want. I've got these two covered. Besides, Fischer won't be here for another hour."

Nelson looked at his watch. "I just might do that." He disappeared into the bedroom, but not before warning Lawton to keep his eye on the women.

"Don't worry, boss, I ain't never trusted a woman yet."

"Keep it like that and you'll go far."

Within minutes Nelson was snoring loud enough to cause the drapes to sway.

Ten minutes later Lawton blinked twice, and then his eyes closed and he laid his head on the table, asleep himself.

With deliberate care, Lillian slipped the gun from his fingers and motioned for Carrie to tiptoe out of the cabin. Not that she needed Lillian's encouragement. Never had she been more anxious to get away from anyone.

The instant her feet hit dirt, Carrie took off in a sprint toward the main road. She'd gone only a few yards when she realized she should probably wait for Lillian. Turning, she looked back toward the cabin to be sure her mother-in-law was close behind her.

She didn't get the opportunity to see anything. The next thing Carrie knew she was grabbed around the waist. Before she could scream, a hand was slapped over her mouth. Squirming and kicking, she struggled with every bit of strength she possessed.

"Carrie, stop. It's me."

Kyle. It was Kyle! Sobbing, she twisted around and buried her face in his neck, holding onto him the way she would a rope dropped to her over the edge of a cliff.

"There's nothing to worry about now," he said. "The cabin's surrounded. Sanders and the others were about to go in for you when you both came running out."

"Someone named Fischer's coming," she said, breathless and panting for air.

"We got him."

"How'd you know Nelson was here?"

"Sanders was right. Nelson *was* on his tail, but the Secret Service had a tail on Nelson. As soon as we had cell phone coverage, Sanders called his contact and we learned that Nelson was at the cabin. Neither one of us gave a tinker's damn about that key. All that was important was getting back to you."

Carrie held her husband close.

He gazed down at her upturned face. "You're all right?"

"I am now." She'd be just fine for a very long time if Kyle stayed with her. She slipped her arms around his waist and hugged him close.

"I don't mind telling you, I was scared," Kyle whispered as he rubbed his chin over the top of her head. "I'll be glad to leave this cops-and-robbers stuff to those who know what they're doing."

Carrie laughed.

"What'd you two do?" The question came from Sanders, who was holding Lillian much the same way Kyle held Carrie.

"I fed them some of my sleeping tablets. Knocked 'em both out cold. Nelson ate his with his eggs, and the aspirin I gave Lawton was really sleeping pills."

"You carry sleeping pills in your purse?"

"I have for years," Lillian said. "Doesn't everyone?"

"No."

"I keep some in the cabin as well. There's nothing I hate worse than insomnia. Occasionally I take a pill to help me sleep, not often, but I make sure they're available when I need them. It's my security blanket."

Nelson and Lawton were paraded past them, their wrists handcuffed behind their backs. Both looked drowsily over at Carrie and Lillian as if they suspected this was all part of some weird dream.

"With the information I collected on Nelson, I don't expect him to see the light of day for the next forty years," Sanders told them.

"Can we go home now?" Carrie asked. "I want to take a bath and wash my hair."

"I have a few things in mind as well," Kyle said, keeping his voice low. "This is still our honeymoon, remember? It seems to me I've got several promises to collect on."

Carrie's gaze met her husband's, and they smiled almost shyly at each other.

Promises. Her whole life felt like a promise. There was the assurance of a child, one that had been created in love. Their child wouldn't be their only surprise, Carrie ventured a guess. Their married life was sure to be filled with many twists and turns. If she was looking for assurances she could think of only one. They'd face their differences.

They'd argue over the most ridiculous things.

Love and marriage weren't going to alter their opinionated ways. But when the dust settled, they'd make love. There would never be a dull moment, Carrie guessed.

And she was right.

Epilogue

"There's a letter from your mom and dad," Carrie said. Kyle walked out of the bedroom, holding their six-month-old daughter in his arms.

Carolyn Marie yawned sleepily as her mother reached for her and sat in the rocker. By the time she'd bared her breast, Carolyn was fussing, ready for her lunch. The baby latched onto the nipple and sucked greedily.

Carrie's heart ached with love for this child. She brushed a strand of fine blond hair from the cherub-like face and rocked gently. She was surprised when she looked up to find Kyle watching her.

"I remember the night Carolyn was born," Kyle said.

"Trust me, so do I," Carrie teased.

"The nurse put her on the scale, and she reached up and grabbed my finger and captured my heart. I don't think I'm ever going to get it back."

"Only now do I appreciate my parents' love."

"I want to be Carolyn's knight in shining armor, her hero."

"You're already mine."

His eyes met hers, and she was engulfed in the depth and strength of his love for her. "Carolyn's an angel on loan."

"I have the feeling we both may have second thoughts about that when she becomes a teenager."

Kyle chuckled, and then the laughter left his eyes. "I've been thinking," he said. He came farther into the room and sank into his leather recliner. His responsibilities were heavy, now that he produced the news of the ABC affiliate television station in Kansas City. He loved his job, but he worked long hard hours.

"Are you worried about the station?" Carrie asked.

"No. Everything's going well there."

"Then why do you look so troubled?"

"I'm not. I was just thinking about Mom and Max and the incredible set of circumstances that set everything in motion. All because you thought driving the interstate to Dallas would be boring."

"If anything, that should convince you to listen to me more often," she said, knowing there wasn't a prayer of that happening anytime soon.

"I still think of Richards every now and again," Kyle murmured absently.

"I wonder what went wrong for him to do the things he did," Carrie said, rocking their daughter as she nursed.

"The Secret Service people want to know the same thing."

"And why did Nelson kill him?"

"I don't think we'll ever have the answer to that. I suspect Richards told him he'd have the key, and when he didn't Nelson got impatient."

"Shooting him was a bit drastic, don't you think?" Carrie said.

"Perhaps it was what he intended all along. Max has a theory about that. Max thinks Richards gave Nelson a phony key, just to get him off his back, never suspecting Nelson intended to kill him," Kyle speculated. "He was buying time, and instead he sealed his own death warrant."

"It's sad, isn't it."

"Greed does that to a person."

"You should know," she said, glaring at her husband.

"Are you saying I'm greedy?"

"In a manner of speaking. Between the physical demands you make on me and the baby needing my time—oh, well, I might as well tell you. I think I'm pregnant again."

"What?" Kyle's legs shot out away from the chair as if he'd received an electrical shock. "But . . . I thought you said that since you were nursing . . ."

"Apparently I was wrong." She lowered her gaze, not knowing herself how she felt about having a second baby so soon after the first. If Kyle was upset, Carrie was afraid she'd burst into tears. Her emotions were all askew as it was.

"Carrie, sweetheart." He walked over to her, leaned over, and kissed her thoroughly until it was all Carrie could do to remember she had the baby in her arms.

"Are you sorry?" Kyle asked.

She shook her head. "Not if you aren't."

"I couldn't be more pleased," he said, a smile radiating from his eyes. "I'm just a little surprised is all."

"My dad's going to love you all the more," Carrie muttered. As it was, her parents thought Kyle walked on water. Presenting them with a second grandchild barely fifteen months after the first would only increase their admiration.

"I'll write and tell Mom and Max," Kyle said. "By the way, what did they say in their letter?"

"Just that they're happy. Who wouldn't be, living on a Caribbean island? Your mother's thinking of starting her own business."

"You know, I couldn't help wondering if their marriage was going to last," Kyle said, pulling out the ottoman and sitting down next to Carrie.

"Why not? They've been in love with each other for years."

"True, but sometimes reality falls decidedly short of the dream. I'm pleased for them both. For a while I was afraid Max was going to get bored, but I was wrong. He's got his hand in a dozen different projects."

Carrie knew Kyle wasn't pleased when she made father-son comparisons, but as a matter of course the two proved to be more and more alike with each passing month.

"He looked good when he was here for the trial, didn't he?"

"Wonderful," Carrie murmured. "I don't mind telling you I sleep better at night knowing Nelson and his group of hoods are behind bars."

"It's over, Carrie. We don't have anything to worry about now."

"Unless of course we take another road trip and the car happens to break down. In which case we can count on meeting a cast of unruly characters, spending time in jail, and arguing like cats and dogs."

"Why take a trip," Kyle asked, "when I've got all that right here in the comfort of my own home?"

"Kyle!"

He chuckled and leaned forward to kiss her once more. "I haven't drawn an easy breath from the moment I met you. The thing is, I wouldn't have it any other way."